World War 1990

World War 1990

Operation Arctic Storm

William Stroock

ISBN: 1505652995
ISBN 13: 9781505652994

INTRODUCTION

This novel is about the war that never happened, the Third World War, and it's the novel I have always wanted to write. Born in 1973, I was a child of the Cold War. The threat of nuclear war was always below the surface of daily life, a vague possibility a child might have wondered about when he went to bed, just as Roman children might have wondered about Hannibal or British children might have wondered about Napoleon.

About the time I turned 13, World War III was a subject I became interested in through the hobby of war-gaming. One spring I bought a copy of *NATO: The Next War in Europe*; a tabletop war game that simulated a battle between NATO and the Warsaw Pact in Germany. A few years later, I discovered *World War III* by Game Designers Workshop. This game positively dwarfed *NATO*, featuring three expansion kits enabling a war gamer to simulate the conflict from Norway's Nord Kapp to the Persian Gulf. It included thousands of game pieces; West German Bundeswehr, Soviet Spetznaz, American armored divisions, air assets, and on and on. It was truly massive and took up most of my mother's living room. I loved it. Another important game for me was 360 Games' *Harpoon*. This naval warfare simulation (still available, by the way) allowed players to fight for control of the North Atlantic and the all-important Greenland-Iceland-United Kingdom Gap.

There were a few important novels about World War III, and many readers no doubt are familiar with them. The first is Tom Clancy's *Red Storm Rising*. Over 700 pages long, this dyslexic 14 year old read it in one dreary, February winter break. I was hooked. In the 1980s one could also read General Sir John Hackett's *Third World War*. While Clancy's was a spellbinding novel, a techno-thriller the genre came to be called, Hackett wrote his tale of World War III from the perspective of historians a few years after the conflict. Of course, by the time I was discovering the possibility of the Third World War, the actual Cold War was thawing out, and then Saddam Hussein stupidly invaded Kuwait. I was 17 years old, and because I played tabletop war games and had read a few Tom Clancy novels, I knew more about what was happening than journalists with advanced degrees and decades of experience, but no understanding of military affairs whatsoever.

So in the summer of 1990, the United States military armed with the latest high tech weaponry, new doctrine, and a generation of leaders eager to use both in an epic battle of maneuver, was sent to the Middle East. In four days of war, the armed forces of the United States and her allies made mincemeat of the larger, battle tested Iraqi Army. Here were the high tech weapons built for Armageddon on the European battlefield; smart bombs, stealth fighters, M-1 tanks, cruise missiles used to deadly effect by remorseless killing technocrats like Dick Cheney and Colin Powell, and their battlefield commander 'Stormin' Norman' Schwarzkopf. The Iraqis never stood a chance. From there the best ever trained, motivated, equipped and led American military faded into history. A quarter century after the end of the Cold War the massive 28 Division United States Army and 600 ship U.S. Navy are gone, no longer necessary, really.

Writing this book was like coming home again. In their World War III novels, General Hackett and Tom Clancy made informed guesses which were generally right. Hackett's book, written in 1978 was a warning to NATO and the west, then reeling from communist advances in the 1960s and 1970s. Frankly, NATO would have lost a war fought in the 1970s. By the time Tom Clancy published *Red Storm Rising* in 1986 that calculus had changed. The Untied States was deploying the latest weapons, of which the nearly invincible M-1 tank was the most important, and training under the doctrine of maneuver warfare known as AirLand Battle 2000. Clancy understood the technological edge NATO had acquired. Also, he had intensely studied the Soviet Armed Forces and was not impressed. In *Red Storm Rising* Clancy portrays a Soviet Army that was cumbersome, top-heavy and slow to adapt. Its only advantage lay in numbers. Clancy, I think, was right about the Soviet Army.

Researching this book was both fun and interesting. In doing so I took two tracks. First, I read Cold War era books about the world militaries at the time. For the United States military I used the various non-fiction works of Tom Clancy, *Submarine*, *Armored Cav*, *Carrier*, and especially *Into The Storm*, which also gave me background on many of the personalities involved. Speaking of personality, Bob Woodward's *The Commanders* was a sensation at the time of its release in 1991 and indispensable to me. I am well aware of the weakness of Woodward's work and agree with most of his critics. It is all too easy for one to discern who Woodward's sources are as he rewards them in his books. However, many of the players in *The Commanders* came to the public eye again in the 2000s, and I think Woodward's sketches of these men stand the test of time. To anyone who was paying attention, George Bush the Elder came off as a wishy-washy wimp, an unfair characterization of a man who was shot down in the Pacific. Still, 1992 was my first presidential and I say without regret that I voted against him. Woodward shows a tough, decisive leader in charge of his government. I have tried to present a bit of the personality of the first President Bush, a man whose reputation has greatly improved in recent years; an assessment with which I agree.

As readers will see, I wanted *World War 1990* to have a strong British element. To get a feel for the British Army I used Antony Beevor's *Inside the British Army*, a detailed study of the BAOR and other forces. For the SAS I read Andy McNab's interesting tale of operations in the Gulf War, *Bravo-Two Zero*. Keeping with the Gulf War theme, General Sir Peter de la Billiere wrote an excellent account of his time in Desert Storm with Schwarzkopf in *Storm Command*. On the tactical level, Major General Patrick Cordingley gives a good account of his 7 Armoured Brigade, (the famed Desert Rats) with *In the Eye of the Storm*. Switching to the Royal Navy, I used Admiral Sandy Woodward's account of his command in the

Falklands *One Hundred Days*. Tom Clancy covers British submarine forces in *Submarine*. I also used Captain Richard Woodman's *Cold War Command*, his own account of serving aboard and skippering Royal Navy subs during the Cold War. To understand submarine warfare a little better, and the technical issues involved, I consulted *The Third Battle: Innovation in the U.S. Navy's Silent Cold War Struggle with Soviet Submarines* by Owen R. Cote, Jr.

For the opposing forces, I used a trio of old coffee table books that I bought around 1990 and never threw out. These are Salamander Books' *The World's Armies*, *The World's Navies*, and *The World's Air Forces*. They contain detailed sketches on the armed forces of the world at that time, all of them, with orders of battles where available. Another important book was *NATO-Warsaw Pact Force Mobilization*, edited by Jeffrey Simon. This was a massive academic work published by the National Defense University in 1988 and it goes into extraordinary detail about NATO and Soviet armed forces and the issues both faced. To understand the Soviet Union at the time I read Michael Dobb's excellent *Down with Big Brother*, which covers not only the rise of Gorbachev and the fall of the Soviet Union, but the unrest in Poland. Another useful book was David R. Marples *The Collapse of the Soviet Union 1985-1991*. Describing the inner workings of the Politburo is Pavel Ligachev's *Inside Gorbachev's Kremlin*. Ligachev's memoirs are just awful. They are a recitation of meetings, plenums, committee assignments and conferences. In spite of their awfulness, Ligachev's memoirs tell us much about the Politburo and the Soviet Union. *The Soviet High Command: 1967-1989* by Dale R. Herspring is an interesting book that describes the major personalities in the Soviet military, especially those responsible for the massive Brezhnev era arms buildup. William E. Odom's *The Collapse of the Soviet Military* describes the structure and doctrine of that nation's armed forces and everything that was wrong with them. In *A Cardboard Castle*, Vojtech Mastny and Malcolm Byrne do the same for the Warsaw Pact.

In most cases the ministers, generals and other high-ranking characters are real historical figures. In a few instances I made them up as needed to represent an idea or point of view. For readers who would like to follow the action, I have uploaded maps under the 'customer image' tab on the book's Amazon page.

Younger readers would do well to understand that in 1989 *nobody* saw the fall of the Berlin Wall coming. It was a surprise to everyone. On November 9th I simply turned on the nightly news and saw Tom Brokaw standing in front of the Berlin Wall. People were standing on the wall. Others were bashing great gaps into it. The clip may be found on YouTube.

Three years later, the entire Soviet Union was gone.

A note of thanks goes to; En2 Jesse Garza, and Ctt3 Jessica Judson, *USS San Antonio*, who patiently explained a lot of this navy stuff to a dumb civilian, Professor Lilly Borodkin who kindly reviewed the novel and helped me ensure the Soviets didn't come off as a lot of chain smoking, Vodka swilling cardboard Russians, Professor Voichita Nachescu, Mrs. Monika Boyle, and Mrs. Urszula Bazydlo-Chaberek, who happily talked to me about, respectively, Romania, Slovakia and Poland. Great thanks once more to my proofers, Lee and Sharon Moyer, and my editor supreme, the incomparable Stefanie Attia, subject of the Crown, who patiently explained to me that, 'Real Brits don't talk that way, you dumb Yank.'

William Stroock
Great Barrington, Massachusetts

PROLOGUE

Los Angeles
CNN-Los Angeles

Larry: Now, both of you gentlemen have written extensively about not only military affairs but about the possibility of conflict with the Soviet Union?

Tom: Yes.

Harold: Uh huh.

Larry: Tom, was there ever a moment when you thought the Soviets would overwhelm NATO and win the war?

Tom: Well, Larry, when they burst through the Fulda Gap, I thought they'd outflank NATO forces on the north German plain.

Larry: What about you, Harold?

Harold: When they won the battle for Bremen and made their push across the Weser.

Larry: So last week, you're telling me?

Harold: Yes.

Larry: Have we stopped them?

Tom: Too soon to say. Public information is limited of course, but the Soviets have paused after their offensive across the Weser River.

Larry: What could that mean?

Harold: They never paused before. If they took tremendous losses, they kept going. The Soviets don't care about human losses. This pause strongly suggests even the Soviet's supply of first-rate men and equipment has been exhausted.

Larry: What say you, Tom?

Tom: I agree.

Larry: So now what does NATO do?

Harold: Destroy that force on the west bank of the Weser...

The Pentagon

'General Powell,' began the Bloviating Hair Maniac from ABC News, 'we know there is massive activity in northern Germany. What can you tell us at this time?'

Powell replied in his usual soft-spoken manner, 'Well, I can't reveal much.' He tried to stroke the Maniac's ego a bit. 'But your sources are right. Something big is up. That's really all I can say.'

Bloviating Hair Maniac was undeterred. 'General, sources say a massive counterattack is underway. Can you confirm this?'

'I cannot reveal military details.'

'That sounds like you just confirmed my sources.'

'I have confirmed nothing. All I said was I can't reveal military maneuvers.'

'So there is a large maneuver in West Germany?'

'Please,' Powell responded. 'We will make an announcement at the appropriate time.'

'And when will that be, General?'

'When we've won.'

10 Downing Street

There was a knock on the door, it was subtle but urgent. After another such knock, the door cracked open, letting in light from the hallway.

'Prime Minister?' said the private secretary. 'Prime Minister?'

The prime minister sat up in bed. She never slept heavily these days. Wide-awake, she simply swung her legs out of bed and put them on the floor.

'Yes,' she said.

'Prime Minister, news from the General Officer Commanding, British Army of the Rhine.'

He waited a moment.

Thatcher cleared her throat. 'Will you get on with it, please?'

The private secretary cleared his throat.

From Commander, British Army of the Rhine:

As of 0130 hours, all Soviet/Warsaw Pact bridgeheads, west bank, Weser River have been destroyed. Combined British/West German counterattack highly successful. BAOR being reinforced by armored units, Royal Netherlands Army. To the south, American counterattack highly successful. As of midnight, had breached Soviet/Warsaw Pact line and driven at least twenty kilometers behind enemy forces. Soviet/Warsaw Pact forces in vicinity of Hanover reported to be in full retreat.

Be pleased to inform Her Majesty, that the Union Jack flies on the east bank of Weser River.

God save the Queen.

'Thank you,' the prime minister said. 'Make sure the Queen receives a copy of the message.'

'Yes, Prime Minister.'

'That will be all.'

The private secretary left.

Next to the prime minister, her husband stirred.

'What is it, Maggie?'

'I think I shall convene the War Cabinet.'

'Now Maggie,' Dennis said, 'the Queen herself reminded you that a wartime prime minister needs rest.'

'Yes.'

'Admonished you, in fact.'

'Yes.'

Dennis rolled over. After a moment he asked, 'What's so bloody important?'

'We've stopped them,' she said.

'Then we've won the war?'

'No', she said, 'Only the beginning.'

Outside Moscow

'What is wrong, Mikhail?' asked Raisa.

They walked for several seconds before he answered. 'The Politburo is filled with fools. Old fools.'

'Come now, Mikhail. You are tired.' Raisa placed her hand on her husband's arm. They continued walking along the trail leading away from the dacha.

'Yes, dear. I am tired.'

There was more silence. 'Why does this trouble you so much more than the rest?'

'I should not say.'

'You may tell me anything.'

'I know.'

A few more seconds of silence, 'Tonight, myself and a few others on the Politburo...'

'Shevardnadze?'

'Yes and a few others. We stopped the old men from making a very bad decision.'

'What decisions?'

There was more silence. 'They wanted to use nuclear weapons.'

Raisa said nothing.

'They think nuclear weapons will break the stalemate in Germany.'

'Would it?'

Mikhail shook his head. 'Fools. The war there is lost and they can't see it. They think they will scare NATO and the Americans.'

Gorbachev shook his head.

'We stopped the fools for now.'

'For now, Mikhail?'

'We make preparations for a nuclear attack.'

'A nuclear attack? Mikhail, they can't.'

'They can and are doing so.'

'What does the military say?'

Mikhail sighed, 'Minister Sokolov seems caught between the two sides. He had little to offer except equivocations. I do not think he knows what to do. In Germany General Ogarkhov is against it. When he was chief of staff, he always tried to deter the use of nuclear weapons. Always emphasized the conventional.'

They walked on in silence.

'For now, we make preparations only. Preparations for nuclear war.' Mikhail shook his head once more.

'What happens next?' asked Raisa

'Fools! The war will go on.'

PART I: THE CATALYST FOR CONTINUED WAR

CNN–Los Angeles

Larry: So what happens next?

Tom: That really all depends on the Soviet General Secretary.

Larry: Couldn't President Bush simply contact him and begin negotiations?

Tom: He could, I suppose. But if the general secretary wants more war, there will be more war.

Larry: Kremlin experts say…sorry, Tom, why are you laughing?

Tom: Oh, sorry Larry, Kremlin experts. Kremlinologists.

Larry: You find them funny?

Tom: Actually not really. I think they're very dangerous.

Larry: How so?

Tom: They're snake oil salesmen. They say they can interpret what's happening in the Kremlin. But nobody really knows.

Larry: Harold, would you agree?

Harold: Oh absolutely.

Tom: I mean, they never predicted, after Brezhnev's death, the new general secretary. They insisted it would be Chernenko or Andropov. Instead, both those members of the old guard were out maneuvered by the Young Turks. And when Grishin threw his support behind the young candidate it pushed the Brezhnev apparatchiks to the side.

Larry: Why would Grishin have done that?

Tom: It is believed he acted very tastelessly as Brezhnev grew older, trying to position himself as the general secretary's successor.

Harold: Yes, and there was also the issue of his actions when Brezhnev died. He practically jumped the throne. Brezhnev wasn't even cold when Grishin made his move.

Larry: And this alienated the Politburo.

Harold: Oh, absolutely!

Tom: So, having missed his chance, Grishin threw his support behind his rival and got the old timers pushed aside.

Larry: But the new man was no reformer.

Tom: Not at all. It seems he tried, but...

CHAPTER 1

The Kremlin

For the first time, the General Secretary wished he did not have the job. The gensek looked at the latest map updates.

Great gains, comrade, great gains, he said to himself. But it was irony.

Sure the Soviet Union had gobbled up half of West Germany and large chunks of Norway, intimidated the Greeks into neutrality and stuck by their Serbian friends in the Yugoslav Civil War. But to what end? The Soviet war machine was exhausted.

There was a knock on the door. A KGB aide, like so many around the Kremlin and Politburo, a holdover from the Brezhnev days, brought him two American Aspirin.

'Thank you, Pavel,' he said to the KGB man. 'Leave me.'

Without a word Pavel left. The gensec wondered how quickly he would have a report to the head of the KGB about the headache.

That bastard Kryuchkov will have more information on my habits than I have about the war.

When he received his daily briefings, the gensec had to read between the lies.

The octogenarians on the Politburo didn't, couldn't, wouldn't even question the reports; Brezhnev holdovers with puffed up chests full of medals. When he first took office, the gensec had tried to placate them in exchange for modest reforms. However, their appetite was insatiable. Always more steel for the navy, more cotton for military uniforms, more tractors for digging uranium, and more petrol for tanks.

Beneath it all, the Soviet people groaned.

How long did the octogenarians think the economy could be sustained, when the Soviet Union spent three times as much on the military as the Americans? Forever, they believed, until the socialist victory. So the gensec had outsmarted himself, he now knew. If the octogenarians insisted on a massive military to confront the capitalist threat, if he eliminated that threat, the massive military would no longer be needed, and so the gensec had cooked up a casus-belli and started World War III.

Two weeks. Two weeks to the Rhine, Defense Minister Sokolov had promised. In two weeks West Germany would be conquered, the Low Countries occupied, France cowed, and the United States defeated. The gensec thought of France again and laughed at that diplomatic failed effort. Now Sokolov seemed shattered almost. As if his faith in the Soviet military he had built was lost.

Yegor Ligachev took the two Aspirin and again wished he wasn't general secretary.

Moscow

Dirty ashtrays and discarded teacups littered the table over which Soviet officers shouted at one another. Some of the more disgruntled officers actually threw wads of paper at one another. There was shouting too, until the chairman pounded the table with the elbow of his prosthetic arm, earned after a tour in Afghanistan.

'Comrades! Comrades!' he shouted between thumps. 'There's a war on! Can we not act like adults?!'

Finally, one of the other officers quieted the room by shattering a teacup against the wall. 'Children! Listen to Comrade Colonel Nemov!'

The room quieted down, though Colonel Nemov heard grumbling toward the back of the far end of the table. He couldn't blame the officers for that. Nemov sipped his tea and winced. They had been drinking the damned awful stuff since the war began.

'Now, comrades, what are your objections to this report? Raise hands please!'

Colonel Danchev raised his hand. 'Comrade Colonel, have you read what I have here in my hand?'

'Why don't you read it for us?'

'I quote: "While we were to advance and gain ground along a broad front, follow-on forces were almost never quick enough to exploit our breakthrough. More often than not, by the time follow on forces arrived, NATO had brought in reinforcements of its own.'

Colonel Nemov spoke, 'We always knew our forces in the field would move slowly.'

'What about this?' Colonel Danchev held up another report. 'This is from a regimental commander. Quote: "We underestimated the tenacity of West German defenders. The German defense was fanatical. They contested every house, every hill. Many units fought on long after the tactical battle was won by my men. The West Germans fought on regardless of the situation, regardless of losses. Every time we believed we had finally cleared a town, there was always one more cellar, one more attic which held a West German reservist who was desperate to kill just one more Russian. Bringing in East Germans to talk surrender only enraged them.'"

Said Colonel Nemov, 'Comrade, we all knew officers who commanded units in Berlin in 1945. We understood well the tenacity of the German.'

'Speaking of 1945,' said Danchev, 'do you have any idea how many reports I have read, talking about old German men firing on advancing Russian troops? I read one report about how an elderly couple lured a few officers into their home and then blew themselves up!'

'Isolated,' someone said.

'Isolated?!' Danchev repeated incredulously. 'There must be hundreds of thousands of old Germans who remember 1945. This is their revenge.'

'I am not surprised,' said Nemov.

Replied Danchev, 'You know who was surprised? The Soviet soldier!' He flipped through a stack of reports until finding the one he was looking for. 'Listen to this, from a battalion commander in the 20th Guards Motor Rifle Division, "Time and again my men were stunned at the affluence they found in West German homes. They had been told that West Germany was dominated by small elite capitalist oppressors, only to find toothpaste and toilet paper in even the smallest, poorest apartments; items which are of course rationed in the Soviet Union."'

This time Nemov merely shrugged.

Danchev could feel his arguments gaining momentum, 'And speaking of morale!' He grabbed another report and flipped through it until he came to a page he had underlined, 'This is from a company commander with the 11th Guards Motorized Rifle Division.' Danchev held up a finger for dramatic flourish, 'Quote: "My company was beset with internal dissent. Disputes between whole squads that had simmered for months came to the forefront after the invasion. In one instance, C Platoon refused to provide fire support for B Platoon. In another instance, B platoon pulled its BMPs out of a West German village, leaving C Platoon to fend for itself. My heavy weapons platoon delivered fire support based on bribes from infantry platoon commanders."'

There were groans at the table.

Danchev picked up another report and held it aloft. 'It gets worse, comrades, oh yes. This report, from the 103rd Guards Airborne Division, no less says, "The NCOs in my battalion are completely undermined by senior enlisted personnel. Though expected to lead, the NCOs in my company lack the experience necessary to do so. Often times, senior enlisted personnel refuse to follow NCO orders and encourage other men to do the same."'

A new man spoke; Colonel Tulov. 'Our own shortcomings were not the only reason for the failure of the offensive.'

'What can you add, Colonel Tulov?' Nemov asked.

'I was at the front in week two, and saw the fighting around Frankfurt. Every time I thought we had achieved a breakthrough, in every instance when our armor punched through American defenses, it was set upon from the air, sometimes by those Apache helicopters of theirs.'

'Da, we know them well,' Danchev said.

'Sometimes by those even more horrible A-10 Warthogs.'

Nods around the table. 'The Devil's Cross,' someone said.

'Indeed,' Tulov said. 'American pilots flew low and slow. They were impossibly brave and very effective.'

'And those damn Abrams tanks!' someone added.

Danchev looked out to the table and saw Colonel Yuri Sverdlov standing.

'Would you please explain, Colonel Sverdlov?'

'Everyone here saw what the American Abrams can do. It is a monster. When 8th Guards Army was breaking out from Fulda gap, I watched as a single Abrams platoon occupying a rail embankment made minced meat of our lead battalion. Our shells bounced off their hulls. Their shells went right through ours. T-80 tanks, mind you, right through.'

'Ah, yes, said Danchev, 'those shells, what do they call them?'

'Sabot shells,' said Sverdlov.

'Yes, the Sabot shells.'

'They didn't even have to hit the ammo racks or fuel tanks.'

'Yes, I read the reports,' said Nemov, 'In one end out the other.'

'The crew with it.'

Someone at the table groaned.

Sverdlov said, 'Massed Abrams tanks supported by A-10s and those God-awful MLRS weapons were almost unmovable. They'd wait for the lead elements to pass then hit follow on forces. At Fulda Gap a suicidal counterattack by a company of Abrams, that's 14 tanks mind you, delayed the entire operational maneuver group by half a day.'

There was more back and forth and crosstalk as the colonels swapped stories about NATO missile and gun teams. One man spoke highly of the Belgian Folgor recoilless. Another spoke of British light infantry and their anti-tank missile teams. After a few minutes Danchev pounded his podium. 'Comrades, Comrades. We are not in the old soldier's home yet. Not yet. Back to business!'

After a few moments the officers quieted down.

Nemov scanned the room. 'So, comrades, I think we agree. NATO has stopped the Soviet invasion for several reasons. First, better training, leadership and equipment. Second, a last ditch stand on the Weser followed by a bold American counterattack against our southern flank. Third, overestimation of Soviet fighting capacities and underestimation of problems inherent in the Soviet military system. Da?'

The assembled colonels sipped tea, puffed cigarettes and nodded. 'Da…Da…' many said.

'Good' Nemov replied. 'Here is the report I have prepared for Stavka,' he said, referring to the Soviet general staff. 'I think we'll all sign our name to it.' He cleared his throat. 'Failure to live up to expectations of the Party coupled with an unwillingness to adhere to scientifically proven Marxist military doctrine allowed the imperialists to gain the upper hand and may have allowed them to….'

There was more nodding from the colonels.

Parliament

'I give way to the honorable gentlemen,' said the prime minister.

The leader of the opposition rose to the table. 'I would first like to express, as did the prime minister, my profound gratitude to Her Majesty's Armed Forces, and all NATO for their valiant effort on the Weser.'

A cheer went out from both benches.

'I ask the prime minister, now, what steps is she prepared to take to end the war?'

The Labour backbenchers nodded in agreement.

Thatcher stood up again, 'Surely Mr. Kinnock knows that wars are not ended. No, they are won!'

A great cheer went out from the Tories.

Kinnock stood again, 'Instead of slogans, I would like to know how the prime minister intends to bring about the end of the war, or does she wish the conflict to go on?'

As the Labour bench cheered Thatcher stepped to the podium and retorted, 'The honorable gentlemen knows all too well that the Soviets began this war. Perhaps he needs a history lesson? Shall I give him one?'

'I need no lessons on the background of this war.'

Thatcher held up a finger, 'But the leader of the opposition does I think.'

'Don't you wag your finger at me…' said Kinnock.

Behind him the Labour backbenchers howled in rage as the white wigged speaker pleaded, 'Order…order….' When the house quieted down, he pointed to Thatcher, 'The prime minister.'

'My right honorable friend, Mr. Kinnock, knows that when the Jaruzelski regime cracked down yet again on the Solidarity Movement in Poland, a union, mind you that the honorable gentlemen and his caucus did not see fit to support!' There were hisses from the Labour bench.

'Since when does Maggie mind union busting?!'A Labour MP from the coal ring shouted.

Thatcher continued. 'Mr. Kinnock knows that the Soviets used our verbal support, verbal support only, mind you, as a casus belli to gin up a war scare against the West.'

No one could quarrel with that.

'And then they accused MI-6 and CIA spies of sowing discontent in the capitals of the Warsaw Pact.'

The Tory backbenchers rapped their knuckles upon their seats, 'Here, here,' they said.

'And they ignored the assurance of both President Bush and I that we were not responsible for the growing discontent in their nations. Mr. Kinnock understands all too well that the plot (Thatcher used air quotes when she uttered the word 'plot'), the allegedly spontaneous demonstrations at the Berlin Wall was a sham; a hoax cooked up to give the East German Stasi an excuse to massacre its own people and then blame the West.'

Again, not even the staunchest Labour MP disagreed.

'From there the Soviets rushed to war, mobilizing their forces and demanding we withdraw from West Berlin, which they claimed was the epicenter of our massive, (they alleged) destabilization program. Well, the leaders of the West were all in agreement that we had to stand firm in the face of this intimidation. Even you sir, the right honorable Mr. Kinncok, agreed.'

A chorus of affirming 'here here' rose up from the Tory backbench.

'So no, I cannot end what I did not start.'

Another cheer.

'But I tell the right honorable gentleman this. I will not end this war. I shall win it!'

Helfwick, West Germany

The town hadn't been hit too badly during the war. An American air raid had destroyed two tanks as a Soviet armored column went through town and Helfwick's police station had been shot up by Soviet forces when they entered the town. But overall, for Helfwick the war had been quiet and the Soviet occupation benign. The townspeople, mostly middle-class professionals who worked in nearby Hanover had been cooperative. Too cooperative, really.

Which is why Loeb and his team were there. He took a piece of paper out of his jacket.

It was an American issue camo field jacket that he wore with blue jeans, heavy work boots a collared shirt beneath a sweater vest. His blonde hair was neatly cut and combed to compensate for a slightly receding hairline. He wore eyeglasses tinted yellow. It was an unmilitary uniform, which was fine since he wasn't *Bundeswehr*, but West German Intelligence.

'Ja, this is the house,' he said. 'Come with me.'

Loeb and two others walked into the backyard. The electricity had been out since before the Soviet occupation but they could see several candles in the kitchen window. Loeb led the trio up the back walk. Without ceremony, he kicked the door open and walked in, his companions behind him. They went right to the kitchen, where they found Mr. and Mrs. Schuler and two young women. Loeb held a shotgun aloft while his companions each pointed Uzis at the family. The father stood.

'Sit,' commanded Loeb. 'Sit, now Herr Schuler!'

Loeb leveled his shotgun at Mr. Schuler. He looked over at the two young women, teenage girls really. He started with the blonde, 'You are Rebecca?'

She nodded.

And then the red head. 'You are Troudl?'

She nodded.

'Herr Schuler. If either of you move from your seats I will kill both of your daughters. Is that understood?'

Mr. Schuler nodded, while Mrs. Schuler sobbed.

'Surely you know why we are here?'

Mr. Schuler nodded again.

'Not one word.'

Loeb grabbed Troudl by the hair and tossed her to the floor of the kitchen. 'Freda?'

One of Loeb's companions came forward.

'Up!' she commanded. 'Stand, now.'

Troudl did as she was told.

Freda grabbed Troudl by the shirt and tore it off.

'Remove your jeans.'

When Troudl hesitated Freda smacked her across the face.

Mrs. Schuler screamed.

Troudl took of her jeans and stood naked in the kitchen. Freda grabbed her by the hair and forced her to her knees.

'Scissors,' she said. When Mrs. Schuler did not move Freda repeated. 'I said scissors.'

Mrs. Schuler got up and took a pair of scissors out of one of the kitchen drawers. Freda took them and began roughly cutting Troudl's hair. Soon beautiful red locks lay in a heap around her knees. To finish the job, Freda took a pair of electric clippers out of her coat pocket and buzzed the young girl's head bald. They quickly did the same to Rebecca. The entire family cried.

Loeb took a red sharpie out of his coat pocket and grabbed Troudl by the face. Across her forehead he scrawled HORIZONTAL COLLABORATOR. He did the same to Rebecca.

'But they seemed nice,' Rebecca said between sobs. 'Yuri was nice..'

Loeb ignored the pleas, 'Anything else?' he asked Freda.

The other agents shook their heads.

'Let's go then.'

Without acknowledgement the trio went out the back door and into the night.

'Why are you crying?' Loeb asked.

Freda said, 'I am not crying.'

'Then what is that tear coming down your cheek for?'

Freda wiped the tear away. 'Maybe because I was once a smitten teenage girl.'

'But you were smitten with Americans.'

'British, actually,' Freda said.

'Ah.'

'Doesn't it bother you, that in three weeks all we have done is assault our fellow Germans?'

'That is the job, Freda.'

'You think those two teenage girls deserve to be humiliated?'

Loeb didn't answer.

St. John's Canada

The manager of the Delta St. John's Hotel was petrified. Sitting around his desk was a pair of Canadian security agents accompanied by an American Secret Service Agent and what the manager assumed to be, given their accents, British MI5 agents. They talked on the desk phone, which rang every few minutes. The manager's TV was turned to CNN, where one of the Secret Service agents watched for war updates. Outside were more agents.

They had blocked off the lobby and secured every exit out of the hotel. The manager heard French, not Quebecois French, but the Parisian version, and even, he thought, German. He had a strong suspicion as to why so many black suited security men with such diverse backgrounds were at the Delta St. John's Hotel. The mere thought terrified him. All those important leaders, here. What if the Soviets found out?

In the hotel's conference room, the leaders of the Free World gathered. At the head of the conference table, President Francois Mitterrand droned on about French interests in the war.

Sitting at the other end of the table President Bush was in awe of his French counterpart. *The nerve*, Bush thought, *the gall. What is the word the Jews use?* He wondered. *Chutzpah, yes that's it. The chutzpah.*

Mitterrand continued. Sitting next to Bush, the Canadian Prime Minister helpfully translated, 'France must...know that the sacrifice of her troops was not in vain. France must know that the peace will be just to France...'

President Bush wasn't really listening. *I know what you almost did*, he thought. *I know the game you played...*

Sitting on the other side of Prime Minister Mulroney, Thatcher spoke. 'This is all well and good, Mr. President, but we meet here to discuss our war strategy not the post war.'

An aide sitting next to Mitterrand translated. Thatcher continued to speak. 'The question before us, is how to win this war?'

Through his translator, Mitterrand said, 'We have already driven Warsaw Pact Forces out of Germany.'

'Excuse me,' interjected Chancellor Helmut Kohl, also via a translator. 'Much of the area around Hanover is still occupied.'

Kohl looked haggard but somehow invigorated. He had risen to the challenge of war. As evidenced by the fresh scar across his forehead, he had survived not one but two assassination attempts, the first on the opening night of the war by Soviet Spetznaz, the second by East German Stasi agents as he spoke at a rally in Hanover, just before NATO troops pulled out of the city. Kohl had insisted on being seen in public, arriving at impromptu rallies, giving speeches to the troops, to civilians through-out West Germany, and even marching west with refugees. The American press had already dubbed him the West German Churchill.

'There are tens of thousands of Soviet troops in West German terri-tory,' said Kohl. 'The war is not over. Not even close.'

'I agree with the Chancellor,' Thatcher said. 'All of West Germany must be freed.'

Kohl nodded. So did Mulroney.

'Also,' Thatcher added, 'We must destroy the Soviet's ability to wage war.'

'What do you mean, Maggie?' Bush asked.

'While it is true we have won the battle for West Germany, it is only the first phase of the war. We must secure a decisive victory.'

Mitterrand asked, 'What is decisive victory to you?'

'The destruction of the Warsaw Pact,' she said bluntly.

After he got the translation, Mitterrand laughed.

'You may think what I propose is ludicrous, President Mitterrand, but I am deadly serious. Without the dissolution of the Warsaw Pact, the Soviets will be free to remain in Eastern Europe. Our victory may only be tempo-rary and we will face the prospect of fighting this entire war again.'

'Do you think that's likely?' Bush asked.

'How many times, George,' Thatcher asked, 'have we in the west in-tervened in the Middle East to save the Arab's bacon, only for a new war between them and Israel to breakout?'

'Would a larger war have been better?' Mitterrand demanded.

'No, but a decisive war, yes.' Thatcher countered. 'One decisive war to settle the matter.' She looked at Kohl. 'Chancellor Kohl, your nation has suffered the most, not only from the war, but from Soviet occupation. Would you not like to guarantee it does not happen again?'

Kohl nodded. 'On this matter, the Prime Minister and I are in agreement.'

Bush managed to hold his surprise in check, though he looked over at Kohl.

The Chancellor spoke in somewhat animated German, 'I will not accept an outcome that leaves the Soviet threat intact. They have made millions of refugees and killed, by my government's estimation, one hundred thousand Germans.' He said. 'There is also the issue of East Germany.'

Ahhhh, so that's what he's getting at, Bush thought.

Thatcher nodded her head. 'I think the Chancellor and I are on the same page.'

'Ja,' Kohl said.

Bush could see where Thatcher with Kohl's backing was headed. 'I propose,' she began somewhat grandly, 'an invasion of Eastern Europe.'

After he got the translation, Mitterrand's jaw dropped. Mulroney remained silent.

Thatcher asked, 'George, what do you think?'

'Well....' Bush began. 'We had war plans for such a contingency, but that was all pre -war.'

'Any invasion will necessarily involve a massive American effort,' Thatcher pressed.

'Yes,' Bush said. 'Troops are pouring into Europe of course.'

Mitterrand spoke, 'Through French ports. An invasion would also require French help.'

'It would,' Thatcher said. 'We will need France. France will be integral.'

Mitterrand nodded.

Mulroney said, 'Are we seriously considering this?'

Bush thought for a moment. ' Secretary Baker is convinced that if we invaded Eastern Europe the Soviets would use nuclear weapons. Frankly, state is surprised they have not done so already.'

'Is your cabinet united on this, George?'

'Not at all, Prime Minister,' Bush said. 'But there is a lot of back and forth on the matter. No agreement yet.'

'So your cabinet is persuadable, then?'

Bush nodded.

'That's the risk, isn't it?' Mulroney said.

'Would the Soviets really launch nuclear strikes in Eastern Europe?' Kohl asked. 'In East Germany? In Czechoslovakia?'

'Or they could threaten Western Europe,' said Mulroney. He looked at Thatcher. 'Would the British people accept a possible nuclear strike to free the Poles? We already went to war once over them.'

Kohl became visibly angry. 'And East Germany should remain under the Soviet boot?'

Bush added, 'Brian makes a valid point. I do not know if the American people would support such an action. I do not think they would sacrifice New York for Warsaw.'

Thatcher gathered her thoughts, 'But we know the Warsaw Pact is hollow. After all, few Warsaw Pact troops were used in West Germany.'

'That is right,' said Kohl. 'The few Polish and Czech prisoners we have, expressed dissatisfaction with the Soviets and the war.'

'And don't forget the Solidarity Movement in Poland,' Thatcher added.

'Alright, Prime Minister,' Bush said. 'We know that that the Warsaw Pact is weak.'

'I'm so glad to hear you say that, George.'

'But what you are talking about represents a major commitment, and risk. Right now, the American people aren't willing to do it. I can't ask that of them. We've already lost 25,000 men.' Bush shook his head. 'An invasion of Eastern Europe? Not now. Not as things stand.'

'Besides,' offered Mulroney, whose troops were even then embarking on Canadian transports, 'Won't we need to destroy the Hanover Salient first?'

'Yes we will,' Thatcher said.

Bardufoss, Norway

'Chutes buried, sir,' reported Corporal Simon.

'Right,' said Sergeant Clarke. He looked to his Norwegian counter-part. 'Sergeant Gudmundson, lead the way.'

The Norwegian Special Forces member led the SAS team forward through the snow touched Norwegian wilderness. The three Brits and their Norwegian partner walked in ten-yard intervals clad in white winter camouflage each carrying a hundred-pound Bergen pack. They made footprints in the four inches of snow on the ground, but this did not concern the SAS men. They were under a thick canopy of evergreens and besides, the Soviets occupying Bardufoss Airbase didn't make many forays into the mountains above. The terrain was inhospitable and the locals decidedly hostile to the Russians.

For several hours they walked in near silence, talking on short breaks at the end of each hour. Near sunset they reached their target, a low rise overlooking Bardufoss. Clarke and Gudmundson dropped their Bergens and went to the top of the rise. As they went, Clarke rubbed his sore shoulders, and enjoyed the feeling of seemingly rocketing into the air with each step. At the crest, the two men crawled forward, taking cover beneath a low evergreen. The base came into view. The two men scanned the facility with their binoculars.

Captured from the Norwegians a few days into the war, Bordufoss was operational. A few dozen Soviet aircraft were parked on the tarmac or in the revetments. The town to the west was dark as the Norwegian night approached.

'Bastards blew up the power station, did they?' Clarke asked.

'They didn't,' Gudmundson said. 'We did. I set the charges myself.'

'What the bloody hell for?'

'Now the Soviets have to run the base on their own generators. Those require fuel. Planes, and more fuel are needed to fly it in.'

'Oy,' said Clarke. 'No such heroics this time, right?'

Gudmundson nodded. He surveyed the surrounding countryside. 'If we march over there,' (he pointed west to a clump of rocks maybe a kilometer away) 'those rocks will make an excellent hide and op point.'

'See the whole base and town from there, then?'

'Absolutely,' replied Gudmundson.

'Any reasons for the Soviets to go up there?'

'It is a tough climb. No one ever went up there when I was stationed here.'

'Alright, let's move out then.'

Portsmouth, United Kingdom.

Over the course of two days a dozen Royal Navy ships had come into Portsmouth for a quick refuel and rearming. Clyde and Faslane, on the North Sea would have been more convenient, but the brass at Northwood had not wanted to risk using those bases. The North Sea was still not entirely secure from Soviet submarines, and Soviet aircraft were flying across Norway with impunity. Despite the RAF's best efforts, Britain had been visited dozens of times by Soviet bombers. But the Channel was absolutely secure. The entrances were plugged up by RAF choppers and French subs, and the skies above patrolled by RAF Phantoms and French Mirages. So RN ships sallied into Portsmouth and then sallied back out again for the Irish sea.

Aboard *HMS Illustrious*, Admiral Mike Clapp watched as portside cranes hauled the carrier's anti-sub helicopters off the deck. For two weeks she had patrolled the GIUK Gap with an escort of frigates and destroyers. Day and night they had hammered Soviet subs as they attempted the passage into the Atlantic. Capp knew for certain they had sunk eight Soviet subs, and vectored countless British Nimrod and American Orion sorties against other contacts.

'Admiral,' said the OOD, 'Last of the helicopters is off.'

Clapp surveyed the deck. It was clear. 'Very well. Begin taking on the Harriers.'

Clapp tried to feel reassured as a crane loaded the first of fourteen Harrier Jump Jets onto *Illustrious*. He had seen them in action in the Falklands. British pilots had splashed dozens of aircraft and still they had lost five ships. And they had been up against Argentine Sky Hawks not Soviet Backfire and Bear bombers. Britain had rightly celebrated its triumph in the Falklands eight years before, but Clapp had been there, and knew that if it were not for some miss-set bomb fuses, the Argies would have sunk many more Royal Navy ships, and likely had stopped the amphibious invasion. Clapp thought of the Soviet Backfire Bombers and shuddered, as *Illustrious* made ready to lead another amphibious assault.

10 Downing Street

Still groggy after the long trip back from St. John's, Prime Minister Thatcher looked at the map while the secretary of state for defense went through the morning briefing. 'And so Prime Minister, the Task Force is assembling now in the Irish Sea…Prime Minister?'

Thatcher didn't look up from the map of West Germany.

'Something wrong, Prime Minister?'

'This bit on the map here, this Soviet salient.'

'Yes, Prime Minister. The Hanover Salient.'

'Why are we allowing the Soviets to maintain this hold in West Germany?'

Heseltine brushed his stringy blond hair out of his face and for the hundredth time, regretted coming back into the cabinet, 'We aren't, Prime Minister. Soviet forces are withdrawing.'

'Withdrawing?' she asked.

'The Soviets are being allowed to withdraw?'

'Yes, Prime Minister. SACEUR feels, and I agree that it would be for the best if Soviet troops inside the Hanover Salient were allowed to withdraw.'

'Well, how many are there?'

'The bulk of the 3rd Shock Army, m'am. About a hundred thousand troops.'

'One hundred thousand?'

'Yes, ma'am.'

'One hundred thousand Soviet troops are being permitted to withdraw,' stated Thatcher. 'What would I say to the nation?'

'Sorry, Prime Minister?'

'Stop this at once. The Hanover Salient is in our sector, is it not?'

'Yes Prime Minister. It is under NORTHAG's command.'

Thatcher consulted the map. 'This unit here…'

'Yes, ma'am. Our own 1 Armoured Division.'

'Tell them to close the salient. Send the order to NORTHAG at once.'

'Prime Minister, the Americans would object no doubt.'

'Nonsense,' replied Thatcher. 'That is our sector. Our troops. Send the order, Mr. Heseltine.'

'Yes, Prime Minister.'

Thatcher rose, 'Gentlemen, I am expected in Parliament. Excuse me.'

Once the prime minister left, Heseltine looked around at the assembled ministers and shook his head.

'What is she playing at?' John Major asked.

'She wants to outmuscle the Americans, I think,' said Heseltine. 'And she doesn't want those Soviet troops available to fight us in any future NATO offensive.'

'Future offensive?' Major asked.

'Oh, yes. The MOD staff is working on the problem now, and offensive into Eastern Europe.'

CHAPTER 2

UK 1 Armoured Division

General Smith liked his position. British 1 Armoured Division was deployed in a thick wood with good lines of sight forward and decent enough roads leading north, northwest for communications. On his right, in the town of Burghdorf, a Dutch infantry regiment protected his flank. One of his infantry battalions held the left and deployed east against Soviet troops there. Toward the division's front, one brigade occupied the line, while the other two deployed within the wood in a large camp running north. Deployed at the wood's northern edge, his artillery battalions hammered Soviet troops in the Hanover Salient, the guns producing an unrelenting thunder. The Soviets had gassed them earlier in the day, a nuisance more than a menace at this stage in the war.

This must have been what my grandfather saw in the Great War, he thought as shells screamed overhead.

Smith made his headquarters in one of the small lean-toos that dotted the forest. There he had a radio, a map and a few staff officers. A pair of MI-5 security personnel stood over him, a constant presence in addition to the regular HQ guard. Most of his headquarters staff dozed against trees outside, oblivious to the thunder above. Smith was shaken from a rampant bit of nostalgia about his grandfather by the division comm officer.

'Message from NORTHAG, sir.'

Smith took the piece of paper. He read it twice.

'Raise NORTHAG, will you, Colonel?'

'Sir.'

A moment later he was on the phone with General Inge, GOC commanding British Army of the Rhine, and C-in-C Northern Army Group.

'General,' Smith began, 'I am in receipt of your order. It was my impression that we were to leave an escape route for the Soviets.'

'We have new orders, General Smith. These come from the prime minister.'

'I see.'

'General, please read back the order you received.'

'Sir. On orders, One UK Armoured Division to develop attack south, STOP. Objective cut Highway A-2, STOP. Prevention Soviet egress east, highest priority. Attack to begin no later than zero zero, zero hours, present, STOP.'

'Do you understand your orders, General Smith?'

'I understand completely. But less than four hours remain until the appointed start time.'

'General Smith, I understand your predicament, but you are to overcome circumstances and attack. Can you do it?' He challenged.

'Yes, sir. absolutely.'

'Well done then,' Inge said enthusiastically. 'NORTHAG air control has been informed you have priority over all air assets.'

'Thank you, sir,' Smith said.

'I look forward to reports of your attack. NORTHAG out.'

Smith replaced the receiver on the radio. He summoned his headquarters staff.

'Well gentlemen. We have orders to attack. Where does this division stand?'

The chief of staff looked at a piece of paper and said, 'Seven Armoured Brigade reports 68 available tanks.'

'Sixty percent strength.'

'Yes, sir. Four Brigade reports 44 available.'

'Supply?'

The logistics officer replied, 'Route open, sir, but harried by Soviet helicopters.'

'So supplies will get through but not all of them?'

'I'm afraid so, sir.'

Smith thought for a moment. 'Very well. We shall advance as deployed. Four Armoured Brigade will provide covering fire. Seven Armoured Brigade will advance in column and deploy in line. They shall punch a hole open for 4 Brigade to exploit.' Smith looked at the chief of staff. 'Write up the order.'

'Sir.' The chief nodded to one of his nearby aides, who manned his type writer.

'Intelligence.'

'Yes, sir.'

'What do you know?'

'General, opposite our front is the Soviet 12th Guards Division. They are holding the A-2 route open as elements of the Soviet 3rd Shock Army pull back east.'

'What do prisoners say?'

'In the previous twenty-four hours we have captured seventeen prisoners. General, Ivan is talkative. He says he is tired. He says he is running low on supplies. One claimed to have "fragged" - to use the American term - his company zampolit three days ago.'

'Not the first we heard of such a thing,' Smith commented.

'No, sir.'

'Another expressed shock at the condition of the British barracks his unit overran earlier in the war.'

'How so?'

'He couldn't believe British Tommies had their own rooms, with radios and televisions even. Do British bourgeois fight in separate units? He asked.'

'Would you agree with the statement that Ivan is disillusioned?' asked Smith.

'Our reports support that finding, sir.'

Smith pursed his lips and then said, 'So the Soviets there might be ready to crack?'

'Could be,' the chief of staff said. 'But don't become over-confident. Remember the battle for Bremen,' he cautioned.

Smith winced. A week into the war NORTHAG thought the Soviets had been turned back outside of the important port city, only to see Ivan outflank him to the south and force a hasty withdrawal across the Weser.

He looked at the divisional CAC. 'Get me a list of available air assets.'

'Shall we call for an extensive preparation?'

Smith shook his head. 'No, that will just tip off Ivan.'

'Chemicals?'

'Cover the A-2.'

'And inform General… what's his name with the Dutch in Burgdorf…?'

'General Fortuyn, sir.'

'Yes, thank you. General Fortuyn.'

The division came to life. Weary veterans of three weeks of war pulled themselves together. Infantry drew ammunition, tank crews inventoried their load-outs. Soldiers grumbled throughout. The division Combat Air Controller assembled a flight of American A-10s and another of RAF Jaguars.

Smith was in the midst of preparations when he was summoned to the radio. 'Seven Armoured Brigade's GOC for you, sir.'

Smith took the receiver. 'What the bloody hell is this, Rupert?' demanded General Patrick Cordingley.

'Orders, Paddy.'

'I thought we were to keep the A-2 under observation only.'

'As did I general. Is there something you want other than pestering me about orders I have received from NORTHAG?'

Cordingley laughed.

'Then see to your brigade, Paddy.'

Though it was a bit rushed, the division jumped off at 2340 hours.

The barrage of chemical shells along the A-2 was the first indication Ivan had that the British were attacking. Local commanders were surprised, having convinced themselves eighteen hours earlier that if the British were going to hit the A-2 they would have done so already. When the British artillery switched from an area barrage to a rolling barrage, the Soviets knew for sure. The barrage rolled across two miles of churned over farm pastures before stopping on a belt of wood that engulfed the A-2.

Seven Armoured Brigade advanced along a two-battalion front, a line of almost 70 Challenger tanks followed by Warrior APCs. They crossed several ditches and tree lines, meeting no resistance save for an occasional Soviet artillery counter barrage. On the forward right flank, a mile into the advance lay the village of Arpke. It had been the scene of a fierce back and forth battle between the Soviets and a combined force of West German Bundeshwer and Royal Netherlands Armed Forces. The fight had reduced Arpke to a hollowed out shell. It was here that the British encountered serious resistance when Soviet troops within took out a pair of Warrior APCS with Sagger missiles. A fusillade of small arms fire poured out of Arpke, pinning down 7 Armoured Brigade's right flank.

Smith's CAC called in the first air strike, Jaguars that dropped napalm bombs that engulfed the edge of town in flames. On Smith's order, Cordingley deployed a battalion to cordon off the town while the rest of the brigade advanced. They deployed in a line just south of Arpke with the A-2 in their sights a mile away. Before the A-2 was the wood and on the left of that another village also reduced to rubble. Seven Armoured Brigade brought the wood under fire while divisional artillery shifted to the village, bouncing the rubble with a minute's long barrage.

'Breach is opened,' Cordingley reported.

'Very well,' Smith replied.

Smith ordered 4 Armoured Brigade to advance through the breach.

The CAC interrupted with a report of Soviet armor making its way west parallel to the A-2. Advancing in battle down a highway was suicide, a lesson the Soviets had learned the hard way.

'What strength?'

'Battalion at least.'

'Can the tanks be identified?'

'Recce thinks T-62s.'

'Very well,' Smith said. 'CAC, A-10 bombers released, hit the Soviets.'

'Yes, sir.'

'Communications, get a message to NORTHAG. Tell him, battle for the A-2 going well, request reinforcements.'

The White House

A week into World War III, the First Lady had asked the White House physician to prescribe sleeping pills for the president. The chief of staff intervened personally to prevent him from doing so. What if there was a crisis and the president couldn't be woken? Indeed, President Bush hadn't slept through the night since the war began. By the second week, even the slightest noise was enough to jolt him awake.

'Every time I hear so much as a creak' he explained to Barbara, 'I think it's the Secret Service coming to tell me we have to get aboard Air Force One immediately, because the Soviets have launched a nuclear attack.'

Even when the president did sleep, he didn't sleep well. Barbara had said that he mumbled a lot and it sounded like he was re-living being shot down in the Pacific.

Bush had at least dozed onboard Air Force One on the flight back from St. John, after a raucous teleconference with the Cabinet.

On this night, it was just past 0100 hours, Bush had reverted to thinking in military time, he was in his small private study in the White House Residence. On a legal pad the president had scrawled several names, and beneath them their arguments.

- Baker: Says goal of NATO is defense not offense, Western Europe successfully defended, end war while it can still be controlled.
- Cheney: Says only that US military exceptionally strong relative NATO, communist powers. Capable of further offense.
- Scowcroft: Fears upheaval of international order. Vehemently opposed further action.
- Sununu: Sees great political benefit from continuing war, historic legacy.

Bush shook his head.

The phone on his desk buzzed. It was the night secretary. 'Mr. President, I have the secretary of defense on the line.'

'Put him through…what is it, Dick?'

'Mr. President, an hour ago I was informed by SACEUR that British forces have attacked south and cut off the Soviets in the Hanover Salient.'

'You mean they attacked despite our plan?'

'Yes, Mr. President.'

'Who, gave the order?'

'It was Thatcher, sir. She circumvented SACEUR and gave the order directly to NORTHAG, which as you know is commanded by a British General.'

'So the Soviets in the salient are trapped?'

'Absolutely.'

'What is she doing?' the president asked.

'Frankly, Mr. President, I don't know.'

Bush rubbed his forehead. 'Does this affect Operation Arctic Storm? Has she issued any orders to the British Task Force?'

'No, Mr. President,' replied Cheney. 'Might I suggest a phone call to the prime minister?'

'Yes, Dick.'

The president hung up. 'First her performance at the St. John's meeting, now this. What the hell is she doing?'

UK 1 Armoured Division

Haze and stink drifted across Smith's headquarters. He sat on a simple folding chair looking at the piece of paper handed to him by his aide. It was a losses list. Twenty-three Challenger Tanks, 14 Warrior armoured fighting vehicles. One hundred and twenty-nine killed, three hundred and three wounded. Smith winced at the losses, though he knew the Soviets had suffered, far, far worse. In both directions the A-2 was choked with burning vehicles, many had even been abandoned, something Smith had not yet seen during the war.

Something has changed, Smith thought.

'General, NORTHAG on the line, sir.'

He took the secure receiver, 'Smith, here, sir.'

'General Smith,' Inge began, 'I would like your report please.'

'My staff is working on the written evaluation now, but I can give you a verbal assessment if you like.'

'Please, General.'

'The Soviets in the west, that is, those now trapped behind my division, launched a pair of attacks. The first was intense, lasting several hours, but we turned it back. A second attack was launched this morning, by a different formation. This effort seemed...' Smith searched for the word, 'lackadaisical. Frankly sir, their hearts weren't in it.'

'I see.'

'As soon as the American A-10s appeared over the battlefield the Soviets scattered. Our own Lynx choppers had the same effect upon them, sir.'

'What about Soviet forces approaching from the east?'

'We were struck by two divisions, sir. One advanced along the A-2 while the other advanced along their northern flank.'

'What kind of divisions?'

'Soviet Category B divisions, sir. Fresh.'

'How would you rate their performance?'

'Terrible, sir. One division simply stayed on the road.'

'Easy targets for the A-10s, then?'

'Yes, sir, also the Lynxes. I had two infantry battalions of 7 Armoured Brigade in the village Arpke. With air and artillery support, they easily turned back the other Soviet division.'

'Prisoners?'

'The old and the young, General.'

'What is your assessment of the current situation?'

'The A-2 is closed, General.'

'Do you see a way the Soviets can reopen it?'

Smith laughed wearily. 'Not unless you believe in miracles, sir.'

Henne, West Germany

Loeb looked at the map. 'That's it, right over there, across the street from that supermarket.'

'Ja,' Freda said.

The two walked up to the non-descript house as if they belonged there. Loeb walked up to the door and made a show of taking something out of his pocket, a key. He quickly punched through the window, reached inside and opened the door. He and Freda stepped in, closing the door behind them.

They looked around the ground floor but saw no one. 'Herr Breuer! Herr Breuer!'

There was rustling upstairs, and then footsteps.

'Hello?'

'Yes, would you please come downstairs? It is most urgent.'

Down the stairs came a man, 'How did you get in here?' he asked as he put a bathrobe on. 'Are you police?'

'You could say that, Herr Breuer.'

Breuer came to the bottom of the stairs. He was middle aged and thin with an unkempt beard.

'You are Herr Klaus Breuer, local delegate to the Green Party Congress?'

'What is this?'

'Answer, please.'

'Ja.'

'And you are a member of the Henne German-Soviet Friendship Committee?'

'Ja, I chair it in fact…'

Loeb took a knife out of his pocket and stuck it into Breuer's gut. He withdrew the knife and stabbed him again, and then again. By the time Breuer hit the floor he was dead. Loeb doubted if he ever knew what killed him or why he was killed. He gruesomely carved a hammer and sickle into the dead man's forehead and dropped the knife next to him.

'Did you have to do that?' Freda asked.

'Kill him?'

'No, carve up his forehead.'

'Yes.'

The Kremlin

The voting members of the Politburo had been gathered in the Walnut Room for only five minutes, but already a pall of cigarette smoke hung over the imported oak table. The old men in their expensive suits huffed and snorted and drank tea as they argued with one another and accomplished nothing. General Secretary Ligachev, himself approaching seventy, looked around the room and saw that one minister was actually slumped down in his chair asleep. Strands of stringy white hair fell down his face, his breath blowing them wispily. Ligachev shook his head in disgust. *These are not the men to lead the Soviet Union through the war,* he thought. Ligachev looked at the assembled ancients once more, and realized the minister of defense was missing.

'Where is Marshal Sokolov?' he asked.

The staff secretary shook his head. Ligachev scowled. The staff secretary snapped his fingers and nodded to a paige, who left the ornate room in search of the minister of defense.

'Let us begin, comrades,' Ligachev said.

The General Secretary gave a rambling statement about the conduct and progress in the war, punctuating his sentences with references to the coming victory in the Second Great Patriotic War and the daring exploits of the glorious socialist army marching across Europe, always driving on the Rhine but somehow never reaching it. When Ligachev was finished an eighty year old member spoke. He attributed recent setbacks, temporary though they may be, to anti-social elements within the army, many of whom were under arrest and even then confessing. Several times he made reference to the ancient medals on his chest, lined up in an absurd check-erboard of communist adulation. From member to member the Politburo spoke, each taking several minutes to hit on certain points about the Second Great Patriotic War. The first phase of the meeting required more than an hour. When the last speech had been made, by the Politburo's most junior man, the member from the Republic of Georgia, Ligachev took control of the meeting.

'Comrades!' Ligachev shouted. 'The Politburo must consider the op-tions on the table. If Comrade Sokolov were here now, he could present the military plans to you.'

'Military plans!' demanded Victor Grishin, head of the Moscow Communist Party and unofficial leader of the Brezhnev apparatchiks. 'What plan can there be if this latest report is true?'

'Is it true,' Ligachev said bluntly.

A great rumble came from the politburo's nonagenarian, the ninety-one year old Viktor Lysenko. He was an institution unto himself. Lysenko had served for so long, he made the Brezhnev holdovers look young and dynamic. The man was a holdover when Brezhnev took over. Lysenko rose slowly in his seat, his meaty arms pushing him to an almost standing position. 'At Moscow, not 40 kilometers from where we sit, we attacked the fascists again and again. I know I was there. I remember…'

Ligachev rolled his eyes. Since the war began, Comrade Lysenko had not gone a day without reminiscing about his role in the Great Patriotic War.

'We do not need your old stories!' shouted Grishin. Ligachev was grateful. 'Right now,' said the minister 'while you are on about your glorious war against the fascists, eight divisions are trapped inside West Germany.'

'Nine,' added General Kryuchkov.

'Nine divisions!' said Grishin. 'Nearly two whole armies! And he blovi-ates about the battle for Moscow!'

'Which is why we must counterattack!' Lysenko pounded the table, the act making his ancient knees wobbly and forcing his considerable visage back into his chair.

'With what divisions?!' shouted the minister.

'This is what they said in 1941,' replied Lysenko, 'And yet we attacked and triumphed!'

Ligachev rolled his eyes again. He knew for a fact that Lysenko was a political officer during the Great Patriotic War, and nothing more than that. Before the war, he had been a sycophant, Beria's dish rag.

Ligachev tried to take control of the meeting once more. 'Comrade, we are not here to reminisce about the Great Patriotic War. The question before us is what to do about the situation in West Germany?'

'Counterattack!' proclaimed Lysenko.

This time there was an audible groan from the assembled.

Finally, Kryuchkov said, 'What is the status of our forces?'

Ligachev spoke, 'Comrade, I cannot give you an exact status because Marshal Sokolov is not yet present. I can tell you that our category B Divisions are deployed on the East German border. Category C Divisions are advancing out of the Ukraine now. But they are low priority and will remain on the Poland-Ukraine Border area.'

'Why are they not being sent forward?!' demanded Lysenko.

Gorbachev said, 'As I am sure you saw from your political position during the war against the Fascists Comrade, our troops forward need to be supplied.

Ligachev smacked the table. 'Enough. What none of you are appreciating is that our forces are almost completely expelled from West Germany. Our position is tenuous in West Germany.'

'And eastern Europe,' added Shevardnadze.

'Preposterous!' bellowed Lysenko, 'Our socialist brethren…'

'Are seething,' Ligachev said. He looked to the head of the KGB. 'Marshal Kryuchkov.'

The hardliner leaned forward and in his most ominous voice said, 'Comrades, our socialist brothers in Eastern Europe are on the brink.' He began. 'In East Germany, several divisions which might otherwise have been on the offensive are needed to maintain security.'

'You doubt the loyalty of Honaker's government?'

'Of course not,' said Kryuchkov, 'Just the citizenry. Now, in Poland, 50,000 OZOM police and the entire Polish Army are maintaining order. Solidarity is banned and its leadership is in prison.'

'But Jaruzelski maintains order,' Grishin mocked.

'Those troops,' said Ligachev, 'would be better used fighting NATO.'

'Do you trust them?'

'Jaruzelski is maintaining order.'

'But only because he fears us.'

'Perhaps Jaruzelski needs to be summoned to Moscow again,' said Lysenko.

'I doubt he would leave Poland,' said Grishin.

'He most likely fears we would arrest him.' He cleared his throat. 'Now as to the Czechs, we have seen some agitation, in Prague and Bratislava, but the nation is secure.'

'Again,' said Kryuchkov, 'The Czech Army secures the country against anti-regime elements.'

'But Czechoslovakia is secure.'

'For the most part.'

Kryuchkov moved on. 'There is Romania.'

Ligachev groaned. The Ceausescu regime had long been a headache for the Soviet Union, and was even more so now that there was an actual war on.

'The question in Romania,' Kryuchkov began, 'is not anti-regime elements. The regime is stable and Ceausescu is in complete control. The issue is Ceausescu. Always delays with getting the Romanian Army in the field. Always delays clearing road and rail hubs for forces advancing to the Turkish front.

The Turkish Army had proven remarkably tough against the Soviet and Bulgarian drive against European Turkey and had held them up outside of Adrianople.

'Enough of this, 'said Ligachev. 'Poland is the key. It does not matter what happens in Romania or even Czechoslovakia or Hungary so long as we maintain control in Poland. If Poland goes...'Ligachev trailed off. All the assembled men knew if Poland revolted Soviet forces in the west would be cut off and the war would be doomed.

After a long silence, one of the two men under seventy on the Politburo spoke. 'Is the war not already lost?' asked the minister of agriculture.

'Defeatism,' said Lysenko.

Ligachev only glared.

'Excuse me,' Mikhail Gorbachev said. 'I spoke too bluntly and I apologize. I merely meant that I did not see the point of further fighting if we have already been pushed out of West Germany.'

Lysenko exploded in a rage of angry nostalgia for the battles of Moscow and Stalingrad. After a minute Ligachev regained control of the meeting. 'Comrades, let Minister Gorbachev speak. Please continue.' *There you are, Mikhail, always waiting for everyone else to speak before expressing yourself.*

'Thank you, Comrade Secretary. We are losing the campaign in West Germany. That is a fact.'

Lysenko almost exploded in rage again, but Ligachev held up his hand.

'Facts are facts comrades. NATO has stopped our best units, have they not? What do we have left, Comrade Secretary, Category B and C Divisions?'

Ligachev nodded.

'Let us be honest, Comrades. NATO will make minced meat of those forces.'

Lysenko flew into a rage, hurling epitaphs at Gorbachev and accusing him of being a fascist until finally he broke down in a fit of coughs. As Lysenko composed himself, Gorbachev continued.

'Comrade, communist zeal and proletarian spirit is nothing against NATO. They are getting stronger, are they not Comrade Kryuchkov?'

Kryuchkov nodded. 'Reinforcements are flooding in from the United States. We believe they have assembled enough regular army units to form an entirely new combat corps. Also, given the sudden appearance of older equipment, it is clear that the American National Guard is now arriving in Europe in strength.'

'So the Americans will soon be able to field an additional two combat corps?'

'Yes, Comrade Gorbachev. Also, intelligence assets in England tell us that British Territorial Army units are crossing the Channel and joining the British Army of the Rhine.'

Ligachev bit his lip in thought, 'Comrades Gorbachev is right,' he said, 'up to a point.'

Grishin scoffed.

'Let us say, and I think both comrades Grishin and Gorbachev would agree, our forces in West Germany have accomplished all they will accomplish.' He paused for effect. 'Yes, let us say the Red Army accomplished its mission.'

Lysenko exploded, 'Are we on the Rhine, Comrade!?' he thundered. 'Have we overrun West Germany, are our forces poised to invade France and the Low Countries?'

'We shall say, Comrade Lysenko, that our forces have accomplished their goal and are withdrawing.'

Having been shown a way out, the members of the Politburo nodded their heads.

'So that is all!?' Thundered Lysenko. 'Is this the end of the war?'

A young army lieutenant entered the room, a severe and concerned expression on his face. Ligachev knew the machinations of the Kremlin staff well. Whatever news the lieutenant brought, it could not be good, and being a young officer, he had been ordered to take it to the Politburo.

Annoyed Ligachev asked, 'What do you want?'

'Comrade Secretary. Minister Sokolov is in his office.'

'Does he have an explanation?'

Speechless, the young officer handed the Secretary General a piece of paper.

Ligachev took the note, it was written on Minister Sokolov's personal stationery.

If the Politburo needs more blood, let it have mine…

Ligachev realized blood was spattered on the note.

Vauxhall, London

Despite the war, Sir Colin McCall insisted on remaining at MI-6 head-quarters in London. He always loved the stately old building at Vauxhall Cross. MI-6 didn't run during the Second World War, and neither would he, Sir Colin had told his staff.

On the phone with the PM, Sir Colin was adamant. 'Prime Minister, I assure you it was not MI-6.'

'The Soviets are claiming the West Germans assassinated their defence minister. There is no way the Germans could have done this thing.'

'No, Prime Minister.'

'What about the CIA, Mr. Director?'

'Certainly not.'

Sir Colin thought he heard the prime minister laugh.

'Very well, Mr. Director. Thank you.'

The prime minister hung up the phone.

Sir Colin hadn't authorized anything like the assassination of Soviet Politburo members. He hadn't even conceived of something so bold, and preposterous. Sir Colin had been far more concerned with operations of his stay-behind forces in occupied West Germany, and lately his intelligence assets in Eastern Europe sending back a steady stream of reports about dissent in the Eastern Block. He didn't think much of assassination anyway, Sir Colin was interested in gathering intelligence. Assassination was not a tool of intelligence, and largely a myth anyway. Honey traps, however, were extremely useful. One of MI-6's honey traps had scored a tremendous intelligence coup, all be it, against the French….

UK 1 Armoured Division

General Cordingley issued the order dispassionately. 'Open Fire.'

A great fusillade of fire and smoke sprang up from the volley line, reduced by two days fighting to forty-three effective Challenger Tanks. Two forward battalions fired a volley of HE shells at the surging Soviet armor. Seconds later a score of explosions ripped through the Soviet advance. Further back of the Challengers, a line of Warrior APCs fired a volley of missiles. These reached out for the follow on forces. Seconds later another series of explosions tore through the Soviet advance. The division's artillery began another barrage, this impacted behind the lead Soviet armored elements.

Smith observed it all from the cupola of his own APC, placed several hundred yards in back of the volley line. He had experienced bullets flying past him earlier in his career, Smith saw no need to engage in 'lead from the front' heroics. Wellington hadn't after all. Neither had his personal hero, Slim, who positively bristled at heroics from generals.

'Fire at will,' ordered Cordingley.

En mass the Challenger Tanks sent a volley of shells screaming toward the Soviets. The battlefield lit up with more explosions and became choked with smoke, obscuring the ever-growing collection of destroyed Soviet vehicles.

'General Smith, report from quartermaster.'

'Thank you,' the General said. He took a piece of paper from his aide. It was a hand scrawled note from the colonel in charge of the division's logistics. *Reserves of ammunition exhausted. Load-outs carried by vehicles all that remain.* Signed…

Smith crumpled the note and put it in his pocket.

'General?' the aide asked.

'The rate of fire will be maintained, Colonel,' said Smith. 'Even the Soviets must run out of equipment.'

The artillery barrage rolled east into the rear of the Soviet push. At the same time one battery fired a volley of chemical shells at the lead Soviet units. Smith looked away. He felt no need to watch wheezing and dying Soviet soldiers.

'That was the last of our chemical rounds, sir.'

'Yes, Colonel, thank you.' Because he didn't want the colonel nagging him any longer, Smith said, 'Get me a cup of tea, would you?'

The division's remaining Lynx Helicopters joined the battle next. A line of gunships flew over 7 Armoured Brigade and threw up a wall of hell-fire missiles. When these were expended, they engaged individual targets with their 20 mm chain cannons. By the end all he could see was a line of burning Soviet vehicles, and here and there a burning British tank. That's when the division's CAC called in the American A-10s. And still the Soviets came.

'This has to be their final push,' Smith said.

'Sir?'

'Yes, Colonel?'

'Might we order 7 Armoured Brigade to withdraw, and conduct a defense in depth?'

Smith shook his head. 'No.'

'But, General, the Soviets are getting close…'

'They must have no hope. They must see us as a brick wall.'

'And if 7 Armoured Brigade depletes its supply of ammunition?'

'Then they do,' replied Smith. 'I've not yet heard General Cordingley ask for permission to withdraw, nor will I order him to do so.'

The Soviet advance finally ran out of steam, Smith couldn't see it through the fire and smoke, but he could hear the chatter across 7 Armoured's brigade net. While brigade reports filtered into his HQ, Smith waited for the battlefield to clear. When it did, he saw scores of smashed Soviet vehicles, tanks, APCs, towed artillery, soft skin trucks… a great flaming junk yard in the midst of the most advanced, high- tech economy in the world.

'General Cordingley requests permission to advance.'

'Tell him he doesn't have enough ammunition to advance.'

'Yes, sir.'

Through his binoculars Smith scanned 7 Armoured's line; here and there a knocked out Challenger, behind those burning Warriors. Ambulances were moving forward. In the air a quartet of British Jaguar fighter bombers made an attack run on the retreating Soviets.

'General, we have been contacted by someone claiming to be a Soviet colonel.'

'Really?'

'He says he represents a Soviet general, and he would like to discuss terms.'

The Kremlin

'Gentlemen of the Politburo, I give you our new Minister of Defense, Marshal Dimitry Yazov.'

The blue-coated marshal walked into the Walnut Room to polite applause from the other members. He took a seat next to Grishin. Ligachev nodded to both men. Yazov was the choice of Grishin and his block. For his part, Ligachev did not have a better suggestion.

Yazov opened his remarks by paying tribute to the late Marshal Sokolov and then giving a full briefing on the situation in his former command the Soviet Far Eastern Front.

'In short, Comrades, Soviet forces in the far east are strong and untouched by the war. I propose this is where we should take the war.'

'I thought we had a tacit understanding with the Americans about the Pacific,' said Gorbachev.

Lysenko said, 'We once had such an agreement with Hitler.'

'Yes,' said Kryuchkov, 'let us not repeat that mistake. We have significant forces in the Pacific and it is time we made use of them…'

UK 1 Armoured Division

Smith's chief of staff escorted the Soviet delegation into his headquarters. The four men were all generals and about Smith's age, though with rugged vitally infused by decades of military service. As the HQ didn't have an entrance per se, Smith waited for them at the edge of the tarp protecting his communications equipment. He wore simple combat fatigues, insignia and a beret. His chief of staff met the Soviet officers and motioned for them to proceed to General Smith. They walked up to him and saluted. Smith returned the salute.

'I am General Yuri Tsabrov, Chief of Staff to General Tevelec, commander of 3rd Shock Army.'

'General Rupert Smith, UK 1st Armoured.' Smith extended his hand. Tsabrov took it. 'Please come with me, gentlemen.'

A table had been found, but no chairs, so the men sat across from each other on crates. Smith looked at the men, they were stone faced. He wondered how much of that was the situation they found themselves in and how much was their typical Russian severity.

'Gentlemen, can I offer you tea?'

'Please,' said Tsabrov.

Smith nodded to his orderly.

'Let us not waste time,' he said.

'Your terms, General?' Tsabrov asked.

'Immediate surrender of all Soviet and Warsaw pact forces in the Hanover vicinity.'

'We need help with our wounded.'

'I can send medical personnel to you upon completion of this agreement.'

'Please, General. We need help urgently.'

Smith's chief of staff brought a tray of teacups and put them on the table. Smith passed out the cups and handed the men a tin full of English tea.

'We will need twelve hours for destruction of ammunition stocks.'

'You must cease firing immediately then.'

'Done,' Tsabrov said. 'And the destruction of equipment.'

'Unacceptable. You may spike your equipment but not destroy it.'

The Soviet officers looked at one another and spoke in Russian. Tsabrov held up a hand, 'Quiet,' he said in English. 'We accept that stipulation.'

'I will have the surrender typed up,' said Smith. 'Twelve hours from this moment, Agreed?'

'Da.'

The Kremlin

'How is this possible?!' Lysenko thundered.

Ligachev fought the urge to put his head in his hands. 'Is it true?'

'It is,' Yazov said. 'We were contacted by 3rd Shock Armies' commander this evening. He announced his intention to surrender. I ordered him not to. He said he would not obey the order.'

'Arrest him!' Lysenko yelled. 'Arrest the officers!'

The usually quiet Gorbachev said, 'How do you propose to do that when they are in West Germany, Comrade?'

'Then arrest their families!' he shouted.

Kryuchkov said, 'Comrade Secretary, you know what needs to be done.'

'What are you saying?' he asked the KGB director.

'Third Shock Army must not be allowed to surrender.'

'The general has already refused Yazov's order.'

Kryuchkov said, 'Comrade Secretary, then we must use all means at our disposal.'

'Any means?' Ligachev asked.

'Da, comrade secretary.'

UK 1 Armoured Division

'General Smith, what the bloody hell is happening?' asked the normally imperturbable NORTHAG.

'General, throughout the night, Soviet forces, as per our agreement, were spiking equipment. We had already received several hundred of their wounded. At 0600 hours Soviet personnel began coming over to our lines. Not long after that artillery impacted within Soviet lines.'

'Whose?' asked NORTHAG. 'Right now the Soviet government is claiming we fired on surrendering troops.'

'Absolutely not, General,' Smith said sternly. 'At no time did British forces fire on the Soviets within the Hanover Salient.'

'Then who did, General?'

'The Soviets,' said Smith.

'Preposterous.'

'General, they launched chemical armed Scud Missiles from East Germany.'

'At their own troops...' NORTHAG said as he pondered the implications.

'I'm afraid so, sir.'

'What is your current situation?'

'Some Soviet troops have returned to their lines, some have scattered. Thousands have continued turning themselves over to us.'

'Has there been any aggressive action by Soviet forces outside the Hanover Pocket?'

'Aside from the artillery fires, no, sir. They are standing pat.'

'Very well. Continue with the surrender operations as best you can.'

'Yes, sir.'

'I must brief the prime minister.'

PART II: THE BATTLE OF NOME, ALASKA

CHAPTER 1

The Pentagon

'General Powell, the Soviets claim British forces attacked their troops as they were trying to surrender,' said Bloviating Hair Maniac.

'Is there a question?'

'Did they?'

'That's ridiculous.'

'It's what the Soviets claim.'

'Do you believe everything the Soviets say?'

A more collected reporter from a rival network interjected. 'What will happen to the remaining Soviet prisoners?'

'They will be processed and detained in the manner proscribed by the Geneva Convention.'

'Where?'

'I'm afraid I can't reveal that.'

'Has the president decided what he is going to do next?'

'The president,' said Powell, 'is in constant contact with our NATO allies. NATO will decide what actions to take next.'

'Will NATO or the United States open negotiations with the Soviets?'

'That's a question for Secretary Baker.'

'What will you recommend?'

'I serve at the discretion of the president . Whatever orders he issues, I will carry out.'

The White House

President Bush had begun his day with the morning security briefing from Scowcroft followed by a direct phone call to Chancellor Kohl. Often the two leaders discussed military matters. Sometimes Bush's call was no more than a pep talk, a simple message to an ally whose country was being torn apart that he was not alone. His lunchtime phone calls went to Prime Minister Thatcher, and Bush had come to dread these. Every day she pestered him about the war; American management thereof, the pace of American reinforcements, and when American naval might would finally make itself felt in the North Atlantic.

Sununu had joked that to be sitting in the Oval Office with the president while he spoke to Thatcher was to hear steady recitations of, 'Yes, Maggie....no, Maggie, wouldn't think of it...you're absolutely right Maggie...'

This one time, Bush felt he had the upper hand. As he spoke to the prime minister, he looked at the morning edition of the *Washington Post*. 'Soviets Claim British Massacre of POWs', the headline read.

'Prime Minister, did your people do this?'

'Absolutely not, George,' she replied.

Bush hated it when she addressed him as 'George'.

'I personally spoke with NORTHAG this morning, Mr. President. He assures me his troops did not fire on surrendering Soviets.'

'Well, then who?'

'He speculated that the Soviets fired on their own troops. This is what officers on the ground believe.'

There was an urgent knock on the Oval Office door. Scowcroft came in and indicated that what he had was urgent. Bush excused himself and hung up the phone. Thatcher seemed annoyed with the phone call anyway.

'Yes, Brent.'

'Mr. President, I have just gotten off the phone with the DEW Line commander in Alaska.'

'DEW Line?' Bush replied, 'My God, it's started. Nuclear War.'

'No, sir, nothing that bad. But still not good.'

'Very well, what is it?'

'Soviet forces are making a move across the Bering Strait.'

'The Bering Strait?' Bush asked. 'They're attacking Alaska?'

'I'm afraid so.'

Uelen, Soviet Union

The Siberian Pacific coast was a desolate place. Here, just a few miles from Cape Deshnev, sheer cliffs dropped into the ocean, which in turn battered the cliffs. Colonel Kamyetsov couldn't imagine why anyone would live there, yet people did. Through his binoculars he examined the ruins of a native Chuchi village, long ago evacuated by the government. There were small fishing settlements up and down the Siberian coast, and of course, across the Bering Strait in Alaska. According to Soviet intelligence, there were more than 2000 people in Nome Alaska.

Looking at the bleak grayness all around him, Colonel Kamyetsov sipped his tea from a paper cup and absentmindedly said, 'I miss the Ukraine.'

He sighed in contentment at the thought of the warm Black Sea.

'Sorry, Colonel?' asked the helicopter pilot standing next to him.

'Nothing.'

Colonel Kamyetsov turned his attention to the battalion zampolit, a particularly loyal and ideological apparatchik named Netta. He was new to the airborne battalion. Young and committed, the Party had supplied all he ever needed.

The helicopter pilot said, 'Colonel, do you think that is actually doing any good?'

He pointed to Netta, who was reading quotations from the works of Lenin to the sergeants of the heliborne company.

Colonel Kamyetsov shrugged. 'It keeps him away from me.'

'Ah.'

When Netta finished there was furious applause from the assembled sergeants. He was too committed to Marxism to see the joke.

Lenin quotations tucked neatly under his arm, Netta bounded over to Colonel Kamyetsov. Nothing, he had noticed, gave Netta a shot in the arm like a good reading of Lenin. He saluted and said, 'Thank you, Comrade Colonel for allowing the reading. I believe it did the men much good. Did you see their applause.'

'I did, Comrade Major.'

Colonel Kamyetsov sipped his tea.

Netta looked at his watch. 'Colonel the hour is here. It is time to take this army of workers across…'

Colonel Kamyetsov held up his hand, 'Da, comrade, Da.' He sipped his tea, threw away the paper cup and looked at his watch. Colonel Kamyetsov nodded to the helicopter pilot. 'Signal the airstrip, get our planes up.'

He clapped his hands and shouted at the sergeants. 'Let's go comrades! Let's go! Time to visit the Americans!'

The sergeants cheered. This time they meant it.

Bering Strait

The people of Diomede, Alaska knew there was a war on, though it had not touched them in the slightest. Once a pair of Soviet Migs buzzed them. This had been cause for excitement not fear, as the children were particularly eager to watch the Migs as they flew overhead and across the Strait to the mainland.

On this morning though, they saw more than a few Migs. In fact, they saw a large flight of Soviet helicopters. Several made due east toward the Alaskan mainland.

'Wales,' said a knowing Eskimo. 'They're headed for Wales.'

The four Soviet helicopters were indeed heading for the small fishing and hunting community.

'What about those other eight?' another asked.

'East, southeast,' said the Eskimo.

'Same as those airplanes we heard before.'

'Yes.'

'Heading for Nome, then?'

Nome City Hall

Mayor Rick Banks was on his office couch. It was not a comfortable place to sleep, certainly not after his wife threw him out of the house. He opened his eyes and saw a stack of dredging permits. He laughed. They were, of course, the reason why he was sleeping in his office. Gold miner's wives were willing to do a lot to get those permits, and Banks was willing to oblige.

There was a noise.

'What the hell was that?' he asked.

He heard it again. A distant explosion, and what sounded like a rocket.

Banks pulled himself off the couch and staggered toward his office window. He pulled back the drapes. The window provided an excellent view of Anvil Mountain and the city's LORAN telephone array on top. Banks rubbed his eyes to make sure he wasn't seeing things. He wasn't. Hovering above the array, firing rockets into it, was a Soviet Hind helicopter.

Breaker's Bar, Nome

Big Tom Tomlinson, (his name was Edgar but nobody dared call him that) stumbled out of Breakers Bar into the cold grey dawn. Feeling the effects of four, (or so he thought), pitchers of beer, Big Tom made his way to his pickup and got in. Though a two tonner and adorned with a 500 pound steel plow up front, the truck actually dipped as Big Tom maneuvered his massive frame behind the wheel. He had always been big, big enough to play line in high school before they threw him out. Thirty beer and steak fueled years in Nome had brought his large frame up to nearly three hundred pounds. There was fat, of course, but also muscle massed from decades working around Nome on the dredges, fishing boats, lumber yards and even stints up at Prudhoe Bay. Which is why Big Tom sat wherever he wanted to at Breakers.

Big Tom heard helicopter rotors and thought it was odd. The Coast Guard didn't usually do patrols this early.

He looked at his dash clock, 5:32 am. He was due at the airport in half an hour. He started the truck and drove out of Nome for the airport. Just at the crossroads leading to the airport Big Tom saw headlights.

'Damn,' he said.

No doubt it was officer Grant. He had stated his intention to bust Big Tom ever since he'd put his truck in a ditch last winter, and given Grant's well known thoughts and actions on the whole issue of cruel and unusual punishment, Big Tom had no desire to be arrested by him. There was no turning around, Grant would just follow him. There was nothing to do but slow down and take it like a man, Big Tom decided. If he lost his license, he could always find a job inside Nome.

Big Tom stopped his truck and rolled down the window. He could hear a big airplane engine at the airport, which was unusual in this fog. Two men walked forward, one directly in front of the truck, the other made for the driver's side, which was also weird. To keep the witnesses to a minimum, Grant worked alone. The figures approaching weren't dressed like Grant and rather than service revolvers, they carried rifles.

Big Tom had spent three years in the United States Army, two of them in Korea during the war and he liked to think he survived by learning to spot trouble before it spotted him.

He took his .38 out of the glove compartment. It was small but it would get the job done.

The figures emerged out of the morning fog. They wore camouflage and the rifles they carried were AK-47s. They were soldiers. The one on the driver's side (he was just a few feet away now), raised his rifle.

'Russian?' Big Tom asked.

'Da, Ruski.'

Big Tom stuck his .38 out the window and squeezed off a pair of shots. The soldier went down. Then Big Tom floored the accelerator, his tires kicked up dirt and gravel and propelled the truck toward the other soldier, who never stood a chance. He was hit by the truck and impaled on the crest of his plow. Tom slammed on the brakes, flinging the now dead soldier forward and bringing him within view of the bridge that led to the airport. He could see more soldiers, and one of the airport security cars.

Big Tom didn't wait, he hung a U-turn and sped back down the road the way he came. He took his CB, 'Nome Police…Nome Police!'

There was a crackle and then, 'Who is this?'

'This is Tom Tomlinson.'

'Tomlinson?' it was Grant, 'Get off the air.'

'Look, Grant,' Tomlinson said as he barreled back into town, 'I just shot a Russian.'

A pause and then more static. 'A Russian? Where are you? You must be drunk and driving. I'm coming to arrest you.'

'Go ahead. The Russians are right behind me.'

'You better not be driving, Tomlinson.'

By then Big Tom was in the western end of town and approaching Anvil City Square. What he saw made him slam on the brakes. 'Red Dawn!' he shouted.

Sitting in the square next to the giant memorial gold pan were two Soviet Hind gunships. As Big Tom sat astonished at the sight of Soviet troops in his beloved Nome, two more helicopters roared overhead towards the east end of town. A soldier in the square saw Big Tom and squeezed a burst from his Ak-47. The rounds ricocheted off his steel plow. Big Tom put the truck in reverse and sped the opposite way down the street and whipped the big vehicle around the corner. He saw a quartet of Soviet soldiers following him. Not knowing where else to go, he spun and drove back toward Breakers.

Since the driver's side window was open, Big Tom heard more helicopters, and now gunfire.

When he got to Breakers, Big Tom didn't even take the keys out of the ignition. He ran inside, opening the door with his shoulder and nearly knocking it off the frame.

'Hold up!' the bartender shouted from behind a stack of dirty beer glasses. 'What the hell are you doing back here?…and put that .38 away!'

'Russians!" Big Tom shouted. 'The Russians are here, Bob!'

'You're drunk. Get the fuck out of my bar!'

'Listen!' Big Tom shouted. 'Come here and listen!'

'I'll come over there, but just to smack some sense back into you, big drunk…'

They both heard a rip of Ak-47 fire followed by a shotgun blast, then the pop-pop of a .45, then more Ak-47 fire.

Bob motioned toward the general store across the street. 'That sounded like it was coming from the Nugget,' said Bob.

Bob poked his head out the door and saw four Soviet soldiers running toward the bar.

'Holy shit!' he shouted.

There was a burst of gunfire, but Bob got his head back inside before the rounds slammed into the door.

'C'mon, Tom!'

Bob grabbed his best customer and dragged him behind the bar. 'Down!'

A moment later the Soviets kicked the door in. Something bounced off the floor. Bob, himself a WWII Vet recognized the sound and shouted, 'Grenade!'

The blast sent shrapnel flying through Breakers, but it wasn't enough to punch through the heavy mahogany bar.

'You alright?!' Bob shouted.

'Yeah!' replied Big Tom.

Bob crawled over to the cash register, his skill honed by the campaigns in Italy and France kicking back in, and grabbed his pump-action shotgun. He chambered a round and stood up just as the door burst open again. Bob saw a Soviet soldier running in, leveled his shotgun on him, and fired. The soldier flew back toward the door. Bob chambered another round and fired it at the door for good measure. He ducked down behind the bar.

'C'mon,' he shouted. 'Let's get out of here!'

The two vets crawled to the back room and ran out outside. They faced the seawall and beyond that the Bering Strait. The two ran around the bar to Front Street. They could hear gunfire coming from inside Breakers as the Russians shot up the bar. On the street they were passed by a pickup speeding east. Big Tom saw a bullet hole in the passenger door. That was when they heard sirens. They looked down Front Street and saw a police cruiser speeding toward them. Grant was behind the wheel. He pulled up to Breakers and got out just as a Soviet soldier exited the bar. As the Russian raised his AK-47 Grant dived behind his cruiser. Bullets slammed into the police car, exploding tires and shattering the windows. Bob raised his shotgun and fired. The Russian dived back inside the bar.

Bob and Big Tom ran behind the cruiser where they found Grant curled into a ball, his revolver drawn.

'C'mon!' the ex squad sergeant shouted.

Bob pulled Grant up and together the three men ran across the street and got behind a parked car. Someone shouted from above. They all recognized the voice. It was Jim Parsons. In most places he would have been the town nut, but in Nome he was utterly unremarkable.

'What are you doing here?!' he shouted to Grant.

Grant breathed hard, gulped for air, and said, 'Report of gun fire,' he gulped again.

'Hey you idiots, get away from my truck!'

Big Tom looked up and saw the owner angrily shaking a rifle at them.

'What are we supposed to do!?' Big Tom shouted.

'Yeah!' added Bob. 'We're being invaded and you're worried about your truck!'

The man above looked away and shouted 'Duck!' and fired two rounds at the bar. 'Ha-ha! You commie bastards!' he shouted. 'Got one!' He looked down at the three men behind his truck. 'You three gonna help or just hide behind my truck!?' He peered down at them. 'Is that you Officer Grant?! Any damage to my truck I'm billing to Nome PD.'

'Well that's just...'

'Look out!' Parsons fired another shot at the bar.

He ducked inside the window just before AK-47 fire bounced into the building. From under the cruiser, Bob fired a blast from his shotgun but only managed to explode the cruiser's tires.

'Why don't you guys do something useful?!'

'Like what?!' Bob shouted.

'Well, Bob, Mr. big fancy WWII sergeant. Rush the bar! I'll lay down covering fire!'

'With a shotgun, a .38 and a service revolver!'

'Hold on.' Parsons disappeared for a moment and reappeared with an M-14 rifle. 'Here!'

He dropped it down to Big Tom who caught it.

'That's the only magazine I have for that thing, so make 'em count.'

Parsons and Big Tom fired rounds in Breakers.

'C'mon, Grant,' Bob said.

He grabbed the cop by the scruff and pulled him into the street, the two men stumbled forward until they got to Big Tom's pickup. Bob peeked over the hood. The door to Breakers was open and the two windows on either side had been shot out. He ran to the left window and crouched, then he held up his shotgun and fired two blasts inside. Bob turned around and shouted, 'C'mon Tom!'

Big Tom made his way across the street as fast as his three hundred-pound frame would let him. On a count of three he and Officer Grant rushed inside the bar. They saw a dead Russian, the other three were gone.

'There they go!' Parson's shouted from his second story perch. He fired several rounds. 'Got one!' he shouted.

Big Tom and Grant ran back out in time to see two Russians turn the corner and run for the shore.

'Go after them!' Parsons shouted. 'I'm coming down!'

Parsons came down and ran across the street.

He peered around the corner. 'Follow me,' he said.

Without waiting Parsons ran around the corner. Big Tom and Officer Grant followed. When they got to the shore, they found the other two Russians. One was on the ground cradling the other's head. He held up his hands. Parson's walked forward and stuck his rifle barrel in the paratrooper's face. He motioned for him to stand. The now terrified Russian did as he was told.

'This one took a bullet to the stomach,' he said.

The wounded paratrooper screamed. The other one fell to his side and pressed his hands to his wounded comrade's stomach. He shouted in Russian.

'Help him!' Bob shouted.

Officer Grant, trained in first aid, got down next to the wounded Russian. He grabbed the other paratrooper's cap and pressed it to the wounded man's stomach, but it was no use. In a few more moments he bled out. Grant looked at the other paratrooper and said, 'I'm sorry.'

'No time for that,' Parson's said. 'Officer grant, cuff that man.'

Grant stood up and roughly spun the paratrooper around. He kicked his legs apart, grabbed his hands and cuffed him. Then he tripped him to the ground. The paratrooper looked at his friend and cried.

'A lot of people here will be doing that, you son of a bitch,' Parsons said right before he hit the paratrooper in the face with his rifle butt.

In the town center, the firing picked up.

Nome International Airport

The gunfire in town could clearly be heard from the airport control tower where Colonel Kamyetsov made his headquarters. Taking the airport had been no problem. A company of paratroopers had parachuted onto the tarmac and easily overpowered the personnel there, who were locked, in the airport's cafeteria. However, Nome itself was proving more problematic. Another company had landed helicopters on the east, west and north of town, with two helicopters putting down in the town square. The battalion zampolit was convinced that the socialist zeal of the paratroopers would overcome any bourgeoisie resistance.

'We shall defeat the imperialists!' he had proclaimed after the first gunshots, which Kamyetsov had noted, were American small arms. He had glared at Netta.

'You really don't know these people, do you?' Kamyetsov asked.

'You do?'

'I do,' he nodded. 'I spent two years as military a attaché in the New York Consulate. 'These people will not give up without a fight.' He said. 'Are you familiar with the expression *from my cold, dead hands?*'

The zampolit was silent.

Indeed. Half an hour into the assault on Nome, the reports were not good.

Listening in on the battalion radio net, Kamyetsov heard commanders report scattered but widespread resistance, and mounting casualties. The battle raged. Yes he thought, raged is the proper word. For every burst of AK-47 fire there was a response, single shooters, pistols, shotguns. And rather than lessen, with every minute the American rate of fire only increased. Only hand grenades and RPGs seemed to silence the fire. Several smoke plumes already rose from Nome.

'Fall back,' a sergeant ordered over the battalion net. 'Fall back to the square.'

'Fall back!' Netta repeated incredulously.

Kamyetsov furrowed his brow and pursed his lips. Given the way the assault on Nome was going, that seemed like a wise choice.

The battalion radioman said, 'Comrade Colonel, Captain Tsalalikin requests reinforcements.'

Kamyetsov nodded. 'Order the reserve platoon to ready. Send them into Nome, but I want the cordons to remain in place.'

'Da.'

'And tell the airborne Hinds that they are released. Provide fire support.'

'Da.'

'We need to control this situation before the freighter arrives with our heavy equipment.'

Nome, Alaska

Bob went back inside the bar and grabbed a roll of duct tape, which he used to tie the Russian's feet together. Then they took the Russian's weapons and ran back to Front Street. Grant got on his CB and called the station, but no one was answering. They did hear police sirens, though.

'Guess everyone is out, I should…'

Before he could finish a Soviet Hind roared overhead and fired a pair of rockets. They heard but did not see the explosion.

Someone shot at them, a single bullet slamming into the pavement at their feet. The three men dived to the ground. Parsons shouted. 'God damn it hold your fire!'

'Parsons?!' Someone shouted.

'That you, Kelly?!' Parsons shouted back.

'Yeah, I'm over here!'

A man stood up from behind a mailbox. 'Sorry, saw the AK-47s and figured you were Soviets.'

'Dressed in sweaters and blue jeans?!' Parsons shouted.

All four men hit the pavement as the firing over at the town square picked up.

'C'mon!' Parsons shouted.

The three men picked themselves up and ran down the street, hopping in and out of doorways for cover. As they approached Anvil City Square the gunfire intensified. Another run by a Soviet Hind sent the men to the ground, but the helicopter ignored them and instead strafed a target to the east. When they got near the square, Parsons motioned for the other three men to stay behind him. Over the din of AK-47 fire he peeked around the corner.

'What's happening?' Big Tom asked.

'I see a couple of dead Russians in the square. Rest of 'em are holed up in the church.'

Parsons laughed. 'Ha!' he shouted at the church. 'Take refuge in the house of God you commie bastards!' He leveled his M-14 at the Church and fired a round. 'Ha! He knows!'

Several cars were stopped in the street, all had been shot up by Russians. One person was slumped over the steering wheel. Another was sprawled on the ground next to the driver's side, an open shotgun in his hand.

'That's Tim Simpson,' Parsons said. He indicated the open shotgun. 'At least he needs to reload.' He fired another shot. 'You commie bastards!'

A Russian within the church fired at Parsons but missed wildly.

'Looks like they're exchanging fire with the trading company next door.'

'Sure,' Bob said. 'They have plenty of guns there.'

'Ha!' Parsons said. 'I have an idea.'

'An idea?' Bob asked.

'Yeah. You fellas wait here.'

Parsons slung his M-14 over his shoulder and ran down the street.

They waited for a moment, then Officer Grant's radio squawked, 'Any Nome PD units. Russian troops are coming out from the airport.'

Grant replied. 'That you, Jenner?'

'Grant? Yeah, it's me. I'm just on the east end of town. There's a bunch of Russians double-timing it into town. And they got a roadblock set up.'

'Bet that was the roadblock I ran into,' Big Tom said.

'We already have Russians in town.'

'Well you're about to get more.'

'How many?' asked Bob.

'How many?' Grant repeated.

'Uhh…ten…fifteen…I dunno, looked like maybe forty. Any other of our guys out there?'

'I don't know. '

'Well, I'm staying put'

'Alright. I gotta go.'

A cab was coming down the street. Joe Cummins, the owner of the local cab company was driving. Parsons was in the passenger seat.

Parsons got out.

'What are you going to do Parsons?' Bob asked, 'Give the commies a ride out of town?'

He opened up the back passenger door and took out a milk crate full of bottles. 'Na, I'm giving them a ride to hell.' He grinned. 'Molotov cocktails!'

Cummins got out of the cab reached in and grabbed an M-16 rifle. He had a couple of magazines stuffed in his pockets.

'And we got some more military hardware.'

There was an explosion in the distance and then another. Then a series of single shots coming from the Trading Post.

'Hey wait.' Grant said. He picked up his mic. 'Trading Post, this is Officer Grant anyone there?' he looked at Parsons. 'They have ham radio over there. This is Grant, anyone at the Trading Post?'

There was static and then, 'Hell yes we're here.' It was Rob Kelly the owner. 'Me and my staff are inside, trading shots with the commies.'

'How many?' Grant asked.

'Me, my two boys and my clerk. You know that nice girl who came here last summer?'

'Becky? Sure.'

'Give me that.' Parsons snatched the mic from Grant. 'Kelly, listen up.'

'Is that you, Parsons you nut?'

'Shut up. We got half a dozen Molotov Cocktails here.'

'Jesus.'

'Not for those godless commies. Watch out, cause here comes the fire.'

'OK.'

There was a flurry of shots from the Trading Post.

Parsons gave the mic back to Grant. 'Ok, Bob, there are two windows on this side of the church, ain't there?'

'Yeah.'

'Ok, take my M-14 and shoot them out. Then I'll toss one inside. Cummins, give me those rags.'

Cummins got some gas soaked rags from the cab, Parsons quickly stuffed them into the bottles. 'No point in waiting around. Let's get to it.

M-14 at the ready, Bob stepped around the corner and fired several shots. They all heard glass breaking. Parsons took a Zippo from his pocket and lit one of the cocktails. He stepped around the corner and hurled it toward the church. The Molotov hit just below the window and burst, flames cascaded down the side of the church.

'Give me another!' Parsons shouted as he ducked behind the corner. He lit the next bomb, stepped around the corner and hurled it toward the window. This one went through and exploded inside.

'Another! Don't bother with the rag!'

Parsons sent this one after the first. It exploded as well.

'Another!" he shouted without moving this time. Cummins tossed him a bomb. He caught it with both hands and threw.

Parsons jumped up and down and shouted 'Take that you Godless heathens!' He turned to the men, 'Get out here and cover me! Cummins, bring the whole crate and get the other one from the cab!'

Big Tom dropped next to Parsons and fired his captured AK-47, Grant did the same. Parsons threw one more through the window, they could see it explode inside.

'Stuff rags in those other two!' He shouted to Cummins.

With two more bombs ready, Parsons lit them both and sent them through the second window.

A Soviet stepped out the front door and sprayed fire at them.

'Retreat!' Parsons shouted.

The quartet scurried back behind the corner, Ak-47 rounds chasing them.

'Alright, Tom. Now just stick that AK around the corner and fire. After he fires, Grant, you come back around with me. Cummins, light that bomb up.'

When all was ready Tom squeezed off a along burst. Grant dived out into the street and fired. Parsons followed him, bomb alight and lobbed it through the air. It shattered and exploded on the roof of the church.

'Ha! Haaaaa!' he shouted in triumph. 'More bombs! Quickly, quickly.'

Cummins tossed Parsons another bomb, he threw it after the first, this one exploded right over the burgeoning fire on the roof and showered the tiles with flame. Parsons kept throwing bombs until he ran out.

'There's one!' he shouted. 'Get that commie!'

Another Russian stepped out the door and was cut down by Big Tom and Grant. Then from inside, one threw a grenade.

'Get back!'

Grant dived behind the corner, Big Tom rolled and tripped up Parsons, who fell down behind the wall.

The grenade exploded.

Parsons picked himself up and said, 'That was a stupid thing to do Tom!' he shouted.

'Sorry. This frame,' he shook his head. 'It was just easier to roll.'

Parsons took the M-14 and peeked around the corner.

'Ha! Haaaa!' he shouted again. 'The church is going up in flames! Ain't gonna be no Commie sermons in that church!' he shouted. 'Uh oh! Duck!'

More grenades exploded in the street. A moment later there was a burst of AK-47 fire and then another. Then quiet. After that there was renewed firing from the Trading Post.

Parsons looked around the corner. 'They're bugging out!'

Several Russian soldiers were coming out of the flaming church, two of them being carried by their squad mates. They took fire from the Trading Post. One took a bullet to the leg and fell to the pavement. A soldier stopped and helped him up and then collapsed in a heap. Cummins stepped into the street and squeezed off several shots but didn't hit anything. The Soviets fired wildly at the Trading Post.

'Uh oh,' Parsons said.

'What?' Grant asked.

'There's a whole bunch of commies at the far end of the street.'

'Let's go get that wounded commie before his pals do. C'mon!'

Parsons gave a shout and ran into the street, then three other men followed him.

Nome International Airport

The wounded platoon commander said, 'Comrade Colonel, it was like a hornet's nest.'

'Go on,' Colonel Kamyetsov said.

'When we landed, all was fine, for several minutes. We were able to stop a few vehicles. Then one mad man spotted us and accelerated right at us. My men shot up his car but then he got out with a pistol and opened fire.'

The lieutenant grimaced as the medic tending him taped a bandage to his shoulder wound.

'Then more people appeared, all with guns. At first just one or two of them, then it seemed like there was a whole squad in the building next to the square. As we took fire from them another group attacked us from across the street.'

'And burned down their own church,' Colonel Kamyetsov said.

'Yes.'

'What about you?' Colonel Kamyetsov looked at the other platoon commander, who had come to the rescue of the first.

'As we went into Nome, we were fired on by several people. Then, once we met with Lieutenant Slava's group they chased us out of town. People fired at us from windows, rooftops, and doorways as we passed.'

'I see, thank you gentlemen.'

The two officers saluted.

Colonel Kamyetsov went back to the control tower where the zam-polit was waiting. He didn't want him talking to the men so soon after the battle. Netta waited with great anticipation and shot up to his feet when Colonel Kamyetsov walked in.

'Well?' he demanded.

Colonel Kamyetsov sat down in thought. 'Interesting,' Colonel Kamyetsov said.

'Interesting!' Netta responded, 'I hardly think...'

Colonel held up his hand. 'This is like the battle of Lexington-Concord in their revolution. The same thing happened to the British. Of course, that was thousands of American militia against a regiment of redcoats.'

'What happened?'

'They killed hundreds of British,' he said. 'These Americans…anyone else would have run and hid, but not these people.'

Netta shook his head, 'This is what we are fighting against, Comrade Colonel. Who are these people to act without orders?'

'You see, Comrade Netta, they have their own ideological zeal. I have seen their movies.'

'Bourgeoisie trash.'

'Perhaps. But they have all seen countless westerns. A few lone men on the frontier…' Colonel Kamyetsov looked wistfully away as he remembered watching American westerns like *Big Jake*, *The Searchers*…

'Lenin would say these people are ideologically corrupted.'

'What do you suggest? That I bombard the town?'

'Yes.'

'We have no heavy artillery.'

'But the helicopters.'

'Hmmmm.'

'Is that how the Americans would put it. Big guns?'

'Yes.'

'And the freighter should arrive in the morning.'

'Yes it will.'

'With a battery of six heavy guns.'

'We wait, Comrade Netta.'

'Why wait, Colonel?'

'We are not the fascist Germans, Comrade. We will fight like soldiers, not fiends.'

CHAPTER 2

The Pentagon

Powell took a question from Bloviating Hair Maniac, 'General Powell, would you not say that the White House has lost control of the situation?'

Powell replied in his amiable but distant manner, 'What do you mean?'

'The Soviet attack on Alaska, for instance. The State Department was putting out peace feelers.'

'It's true, we did not anticipate this warrantless action. Attacking Alaska cannot help the Soviets, it cannot improve their position. It just prolongs the war.'

One of the more mild mannered reporters from CBS asked, 'General, what help is the president sending to Alaska?'

'I cannot, of course, divulge our specific moves, but the American people, and the people of Alaska should know that the government and the military are taking direct, concrete action.'

'General,' asked another reporter, this one from NBC, 'is it true that the British Army is fighting independently of NATO, on the Prime Minister's word alone?'

Powell flashed a disarming smile. 'Not true. British forces are, as we speak, fighting in West Germany with NATO's full support...'

Bloviating Hair Maniac asked another question, 'General Powell, does this mean the President supports further military action in Europe?'

The White House

'But how did it happen?' President Bush demanded.

'Mr. President,' Cheney began, 'we simply did not believe the Soviets would escalate in this way.'

'Escalate?' Bush said, 'This is an attack on American territory!'

'I did not believe they would take this action,' Baker said. 'Through contacts at the Indian Embassy in Geneva, my counterpart assured me the Soviets would leave American territory alone. An assurance I reciprocated.'

'I'm afraid it's much worse than Nome, Mr. President,' Cheney said.

'Worse?'

'Yes. At roughly the same time they attacked Nome, the Soviets launched an amphibious assault on Shemya.'

Scowcroft said, 'So right now, we've lost a major radar and recon installation.'

'Are we sure?' Bush asked.

'Shemya went off the air yesterday. It's an air and naval facility, sir. They have security, but no army or marines. So I'm afraid it's probably lost.'

Bush shook his head.

'The Coast Guard station on Attu is off line as well. And we've had no contact with the station on Kiska.'

Bush groaned.

'How did this happen?' he said to Scowcroft. 'You are the national security advisor, Brent. How did you not know this was happening?'

'Mr. President, our latest sat data shows Soviet main fleet units in port at Vladivostok and Petropavlovsk. There are surface units in the Sea of Okhotsk, but those we feel are defending the SSBN bastion there.'

'I'm sorry to say Mr. President, it looks like the Soviets pulled one over on us.'

Bush shook his head again. Then he looked at General Powell. 'I want plans to send help up there. To Nome, to retake Shemya.'

General Powell considered his words and said, 'I won't rush into anything, Mr. President.'

'Can't we send paratroopers into Shemya?' Bush asked.

'Mr. President,' replied Powell, 'If we rush into something it will be a disaster.'

'I'm afraid I agree with General Powell,' Cheney said.

'You're asking me to accept the occupation of American territory,' Bush said.

Cheney cleared his throat, 'Mr. President, we do have significant forces in the Pacific. The 25th Infantry Division in Hawaii, the 7th Light Division in Washington, the 3rd Marine Expeditionary Force on Okinawa. The *Midway* and *George Washington* carrier groups in the Pacific.'

'Why did we not send troops to defend Alaska?' Bush asked.

Scowcroft said, 'We did not want to do anything provocative.'

'Provocative?' Bush repeated incredulously. 'We're at war!'

He thumped the table with an open palm.

At the far end of the table, the Vice President, who had remained silent until then, said, 'Mr. President, please.'

'You're right, I'm sorry gentlemen.'

'Mr. President, this is my fault,' said Baker, 'If I no longer have your confidence…'

The president held up his hand, 'Don't even think about it, Jim.'

Baker nodded.

'What could they be hoping to accomplish in Nome?' the President asked.

'There is a small port there, Mr. President,' said Cheney, 'and an international airport.'

'Could they be trying to establish a base on American soil? For what?'

'Cut the Alaskan pipeline, Mr. President,' said Baker. 'Attack Prudhoe Bay. Perhaps take out the DEW radars on the Alaskan north shore.'

Powell said, 'Mr. President, there is still the matter of the rest of the Aleutians. Adak, Unalaska for starters.'

'Yes,' confirmed Scowcroft.

'We will have to defend them,' said the president. 'General Powell, I want plans for getting reinforcements to Alaska. I don't care what other operations it interrupts. I want reinforcements to Alaska. And I want those islands retaken.'

Cheney nodded to Powell. 'We'll have something for you Mr. President.'

'Yes, Mr. Secretary,' Powell said to Cheney. 'But I must insist on one thing, Mr. President.'

'Yes, General.'

'We can retake Shemya, Kiska, and Attu. But we'll need time. Time to assess. Time to plan. Time to assemble adequate force.'

Bush nodded. He shook his head. 'What could the Soviets be thinking? What could they be doing in the Aleutians?'

Shemya

'Sgt. Yegorovich, I do not know who gave private Petr that black eye.'

'I am sure you don't,' Yegorovich said.

He looked over at Private Petr, who sat in the corner with a plastic bag full of ice pressed to his eye. The Americans always had lots of ice.

The north Pacific wind blew, rattling the windows of the captured American barracks.

Yegorovich looked out the window. Windswept Shemya looked as desolate as ever. He saw mechanics and technicians swarming over a pair of captured American spy planes. Next to them, under camouflage tarps, was a squadron of Mig-23s. Their captain had sworn the company would only stay a week. Yegorovich was wondering if they'd last that long.

Yegorovich looked back at Private Petr.

'So who gave you the black eye?'

'It was an accident.'

'See, Sergeant?' said Private Kutta, 'Accident.'

'Sure,' said Yegorovich.

Without waiting to be dismissed, Private Kutta walked away.

'An accident, Petr?' Yegorovich asked.

The injured private shrugged.

Kutta was back in the lounge, the American lounge. Yegorovich would have gone himself, but he didn't want to see Kutta's smirking face. He thought about taking the incident to the lieutenant, but Yegorovich knew he was already at the captured officer's club, and no doubt drunk. The zampolit would be there too, and he would use it as an excuse to take away the squad's new found luxury. 'Ideologically disruptive,' the zampolit had called the captured American accommodations. Yegorovich did not want to lose his new found luxury.

From the lounge, Yegorovich could hear a woman moaning uncontrollably and most unrealistically, at least in his experience. The men had found the pornographic videotapes the Americans had kept in their quarters. Yegorovich already had to go to the lounge once and order three soldiers to zip up. He had no desire to do so again, not with Kutta there. So Yegorovich went to his temporary billet.

He lay down on the bed and closed his eyes, not in exhaustion but contentment. The room was nine by seven, more personal space than he had ever had back home in Smolensk, certainly more than in the army. The US Air Force issue mattress was also the most comfortable he had ever slept on. There was a radio with a tape player and hundreds of cassettes, and in a drawer in the corner, a half dozen issues of Playboy featuring pictures of well endowed American women. The billet had belonged to an American sergeant, a black man, the first Yegorovich had ever seen in person, who was now locked up in a hangar with the rest of Shemya's American personnel.

'That damn Kutta,' Yegorovich said.

He was older than the Yegorovich and had been in the unit twice as long as he had. The burley Siberian, Asian really, thought he had the right to ignore Yegorovich. He had waged a struggle for control of the squad since arriving six weeks before. Yegorovich sighed. *This is not what I thought the Red Army would be like.*

Yegorovich thought of his grandfather, who had raised him on tales of his exploits in the Great Patriotic War, carrying a rifle in the Red Army from the Donets to Berlin. Grandpa claimed to have killed over a hundred fascists, and when he got drunk on the fruity wine he liked, would talk about the German women he and his squad mates had raped in Berlin.

So far, Shemya had not been Berlin. They had parachuted onto the island expecting to be met by a hail of fire, instead only to find a few hundred stunned American Air Force personnel, middle-aged men, mostly, who wouldn't have been able to put up a fight, even if they had wanted to. Shemya was taken without a shot being fired.

Yegorovich heard shouting from the lounge. 'We watch what I want!' Kutta proclaimed.

Yegorovich ran down to the lounge in time to find Kutta choking Petr. He grabbed the large man, who turned around and socked him right in the chin. Yegorovich fell to the floor unconscious.

Nome

Nome Elementary School was filled with scared and angry people. Every one of them carried a gun of some kind, many carried multiple weapons. On the stage, Mayor Banks clutched the podium, which seemed to be the only thing holding him steady as the awful reality of what was happening threatened to crush him.

'Folks,' the mayor said, 'People!' he shouted louder.

To Mayor Banks It looked like most of Nome was there, save for the families at the hospital, and the morgue. So far, the meeting was not going well. People were scared, but also irate.

Behind the mayor, Chief Nicks sat with his arms folded and snorted through his bushy mustache. A long time resident of Nome, he knew there would be no quieting down the crowd.

'*How could this happen?*' People demanded.

The first fifteen minutes had been taken up by people screaming at the mayor.

Tiring of the cacophony before him, the mayor took out his own sidearm, a colt .45 and banged the handle on the podium.

'People, be quiet, goddamn it!' Finally, in frustration he chambered a round and fired it into the stage. This got everyone's attention.

First, he addressed the questions that had been asked before the meeting went over to the crowd. 'Listen. To answer the second-to-last question, I am not going to resign, and as for the last question, you can impeach me when this is over. We have more important things to worry about than my term of office.' There was an uproar from the crowd, but the mayor quieted them down by pointing his colt at the stage.

Someone shouted, 'Resign! And lose your kickbacks!? Ha!'

Banks couldn't see who shouted. If he had, he'd have ordered the police to tail him and come up with a moving violation.

'Well, what the hell happened?!' Someone shouted.

There was more shouting, people wanting to know how the mayor didn't know about the attack, as if he had a suite of complex sensors in his office.

'Here's what we know. The Russians have taken the airport and the seaport. They had road blocks east and north of us, but they pulled back.'

'What are you doing to keep them out?!' someone shouted.

'Why didn't you ask the governor for protection?!'

'How come no army troops?!'

'Yeah! Hundreds of thousands for the Krauts but none for us!'

Banks pounded the podium once.

'What are we doing to stop the Soviets?!'

There was more shouting from the crowd. When it died down Banks answered.

'We have roadblocks at the west edge of town and up at the Nome-Teller Road,' said Banks.

'What about help?!' asked someone else.

'The Soviets took out the LORAN array on Anvil Mountain, but we have our own radios. We are in contact with the governor. He knows what's happening here, and so do the Feds.'

'When is help coming?!'

'I don't know.'

There was another uproar from the crowd.

'Why can't they send help?!'

'In case you haven't noticed,' Banks began, 'there's a war on! The Feds have bigger things to worry about than us!'

There was more irate shouting.

'Well, we can all bitch and moan and wait for the Feds, or we can figure out what to do!' Banks shouted. 'People! People!' he shouted again.

'How many dead?!' Someone wanted to know.

'Eleven dead, eight wounded,' Banks said

The crowd hushed; that was a lot of people in a town of 3,000.

'Hey there, Mr. Mayor!' it was Parsons, 'Why don't you tell these folks what we did to the commies?!'

'You really think that matters, Mr. Parsons?' Banks asked.

'It does to me! We killed fourteen commies and captured two others! We got the bodies to prove it. And their weapons!'

'Yes, Mr. Parsons,' Banks replied.

'So what are we waiting for?' Parsons asked.

'What do you mean?' the Mayor asked.

'We can't just sit here!' he shouted.

The mayor held out his hands. 'Hold on. We have three thousand people here, women kids….'

A woman decked out in hunting camo and a fur cap stood up. 'I got a rifle right here!' she thrust a rifle into the air, 'Don't need to be worrying about us, Mayor.'

Another woman, wearing jeans, boots and a flannel shirt did the same. 'Twin colts on my hips, Mr. Mayor. If those commies bust into my trailer,… well, I wouldn't want to be the first couple of guys coming through the door.'

Parsons looked around the room and said. 'How many of you fellas are army vets?'

A few dozen raised their hands. Then someone shouted, 'Marines!" and raised his hands, another dozen did the same.

'Coast Guard here!'

'Me too!'

'Me and my brother here were both airmen!'

'So was I!'

'Canadian Armour, here!'

'And I was in the Princess Pats!'

Parsons shouted, 'And there's a bunch more guys in town that aint here, not to mention the ones at the roadblock!'

'Alright, alright,' the Mayor said. 'I see your point.'

'Yeah!' Parsons shouted. 'We don't have to wait around for the Feds! We ain't helpless!'

'So what do you want to do?' Banks asked.

Parsons shouted, 'Fuck with the commies!'

Shemya

Yegorovich was wondering how he was going to tell his already bored and angry men that they would definitely be staying on the island longer. The company commander had delivered the news to the assembled officers and noncoms, who even then were telling their men. Yegorovich was working up the nerve to tell his own squad when he heard someone yelling in the lounge. He got up from his commandeered bunk and ran down there, expecting to see Kutta beating up someone. Instead, Private Lavrov was punching the door and cursing.

'What's wrong, Lavrov?' Yegorovich demanded.

'This! Fucking! Thing!' he slammed the door with each punch.

'Private!'

Lavrov finally stopped.

'This fucking game.' He pointed to the TV.

'Game?'

'Yes, the game. This video game the Americans have.'

Yegorovich walked over to the 30 inch color TV, another luxury he wouldn't even dream of having back home. On the stand beneath the television was a grey box, he read the English words, 'Nintendo,' he said.

'Da,' Lavrov said. 'I have been playing this fun game, it is called Super Mario Brothers.'

'Super Mario Brothers?'

'Yes, you control this man named Mario and have to rescue a princess by overcoming turtles and mushrooms.'

'I see.'

'But I can't get past Level 3!'

Lavrov was about to slam the door again, but a glare from Yegorovich was enough to stop him. Sitting in the chair in front of the TV was Private Leovich, Lavrov's best friend in the squad. 'Da, Sergeant,' he said. 'I have trouble with Level 3 myself.'

'What is this?' Yegorovich said more than asked. 'You are sitting here worrying about a video game?'

'Comrade Sergeant,' Lavrov said; as he spoke, another plane landed on the runway, they had been coming in every hour or so. 'We have secured this base. There is little else for us to do while not on duty.'

'Very well, soldiers,' said Yegorovich. 'But try not to get so mad.'

'Da,' both replied. Then, 'Sergeant, would you like to try?' Leovich held out the rectangular controller. 'It is fun, Sergeant.'

Yegorovich took the controller and began playing. Leovich told him what the various buttons and arrows did, and within minutes, the squad sergeant was happily bouncing his Mario character around the game, pouncing on turtles and battling gnomes.

When he was finished more than an hour had gone by, Yegorovich realized. Leovich was right. The game was fun. 'Thank you, Leovich,' Yegorovich said.

'You know, Sergeant, there are more games.'

'More?'

'Yes.'

Leovich held up a grey cartridge that read *The Legend of Zelda*, and another labeled *Super Tecmo Bowl*.

'Tecmo Bowl?'

'It is the American version of football.'

'Ah, I do not like the sport.'

'Yes, Sergeant, but the game is fun. Want to give it a try?'

Yegorovich shrugged, why not? If they were going to be stuck on the island for a few more days, might as well have some fun.

He and Leovich played a game of Tecmo Bowl. Leovich took the Kansas City Chiefs because they were red, and also because he had seen a few American cowboy and Indian movies in his time and he had a soft spot for the later. Yegorovich took the New York Jets, because he had an uncle living in Brooklyn. The ins and outs of the sport were easy to learn, though the game was hard to master. Yegorich had already played a few matches, and so he beat his sergeant thirty-one to ten. They played another. They got into the third quarter, before the game was interrupted by Kutta screaming at someone. Yegorovich ran down the hall to quell things, never noticing that another transport had landed and a line of paratroopers were marching out of the hold.

Nome International Airport

Colonel Kamyetsov was not surprised at the citizens' aggressiveness. All night they had harassed the battalion's perimeter, the roadblock just east of town, and the block on the north end of the airport toward Anvil Mountain. The partisans, (Netta insisted on calling them fascist reactionaries) had just taken scattered shots at the Soviet positions. Colonel Kamyetsov was thankful for that. He had been to Afghanistan, those people knew how to lay down fire. Colonel Kamyetsov doubted his men had killed any Americans either.

Still, the resistance was worrisome. A student of warfare as well as American films, Kamyetsov knew that an advance into Nome would be a bloodbath. Netta seemed to view the possibility as a necessary result of ideological purification... idiot. Colonel Kamyetsov was more concerned with the aftermath. He would need the people of Nome if he was to fulfill his mission there. Slaughtering them in the name of Marx would not make allies of them.

At least the airport and docks were secure, but the freighter was late, held up by reports of American submarines.

The battalion's executive officer said, 'The freighter should be able to dock within twelve hours.'

'Very good,' replied Colonel Kamyetsov.

'But there are problems.'

'Such as?'

'The port workers all fled. There are neither longshoremen nor pilots for the tugs.'

'Our men and the sailors aboard should be able to unload.'

'Yes, Comrade.'

Now, with the transport approaching, Colonel Kamyetsov thought, *perhaps I have some leverage with these people.*

'Communications, see if you can raise authorities in Nome. Tell them I would like to speak with them.'

Nome

'This is the Mayor,' Banks said into the receiver.

'Ah, Mr. Mayor,' said a Russian accented voice. 'This is Colonel Kamyetsov, commander of the Soviet Nome Expeditionary Force. I would like to talk to you.'

Banks looked at Chief Nicks, who shrugged. 'Yes,' said Banks, 'Go ahead.'

'First, we are missing two soldiers.'

'Yes, we have captured two of your men.' Banks wondered if he should be telling the Colonel that.

'I trust they are being well cared for.'

'One is at the hospital, one is at the jail.'

'If possible, Mr. Mayor, could you have a doctor there give a report to our doctor?'

Banks felt a wave of annoyance rise up within him. 'You attacked us, Colonel. An awful lot of citizens of Nome are dead because of you.'

'I understand, Mr. Mayor,' Colonel Kamyetsov replied. 'And I would like to make a proposal to end the fighting.'

Banks looked at the chief, 'He wants to talk. I don't know anything about this sort of thing,' Banks protested.

'Weren't you one of the union reps during your time at Prudhoe?'

The radio squawked. 'Mr. Mayor?'

'One moment please, Colonel,' Banks replied. He looked to the chief. 'You know, you're right, why that one time, I got a man triple pay for working on his kid's birthday…. and also got a kickback from the company for ending the strike.'

'Then go to it,' the chief said.

Banks said, 'Alright, Colonel, what are you proposing?'

'Leave us alone at the port and airport, remain in your homes, and we will occupy Nome.'

'In exchange for what?' *That's a tough opening offer,* Banks thought, *but there's some room in there.*

'I will guarantee your persons and property.'

'And for this we are to leave you alone to fly in more troops?'

'I may not divulge our plans. Look, Mr. Mayor. Why do I not come to Nome, we can negotiate in person.'

'Negotiate? Are you serious?'

'I am. I am willing to talk with you, and meet with your townspeople.'

Banks put down the receiver and looked at the chief, who shrugged again. 'You're the mayor.'

He thought for a moment. 'Alright. Colonel. Come to Nome and we'll listen to what you have to say.'

The White House

'Mr. President,' said General Powell, 'One battalion of the 7th Light Infantry Division has landed at Anchorage, Alaska. Another is en route to Fairbanks.'

Sununu said, 'I've already informed local media in Anchorage and Fairbanks.'

Powell's eyes turned toward Sununu. 'You what?'

'The media has been informed.'

'Mr. Sununu,' began Powell, 'am I to understand that you have leaked military movements to the media?'

'It's not a leak,' Sununu countered, 'it's public relations. People in Alaska should know we are defending them.'

'And now the Soviets know.'

Bush held up his hands, 'Now, now, boys.' He looked at Cheney. 'Dick, what do you think?'

'I don't believe announcing the troop movements puts them at risk. And I think John is right, the people of Alaska should know we are defending them.'

Powell said. 'Very well, but when we further move troops I must insist the chief of staff not be informed.'

Sununu growled.

'Dick, General Powell,' the president began 'what have you come up with so far?'

Cheney looked at Powell and nodded for him to proceed. 'We still have two battalions of the 7th Light Division uncommitted. We'd like to send them to Adak and Unalaska.'

Bush nodded. 'What about re-taking Shemya, Kiska, and Attu?'

Sununu interjected, 'The Soviets should not be allowed to hang onto American territory, and there is the issue of Nome.'

'Mr. President, we do have options in that regard. As you know, the 3rd Marine Division is still in Okinawa, partly as a reserve, partly as a threat, partly in case the North Koreans get cute.'

'Uh huh,' the president said.

Cheney said. 'As you recall, sir, the 2nd Marine Division was sent from Pendleton to Panama to defend the canal.'

Bush nodded.

Cheney said, 'General Powell and I agree that re-taking Kiska, Attu and Shemya would be a tough job. At least a regiment of Soviet paratroopers attacked the islands. And we know they've flown in reinforcements.'

'Probably some fighters and fighter bombers as well,' said Powell. 'There is also the matter of the Soviet Pacific fleet. We know a battle group based on the *Frunze*, that's one of their big *Kirov*-class ships…'

Bush interrupted, 'I know what it is.'

'Sorry, sir.'

'I don't understand. Don't we have naval forces available?' Bush asked.

'Of course, Mr. President,' said Cheney. 'We have *Midway* and her group in the Sea of Japan, *George Washington* is in Yokohama now with *Missouri* and her group.'

'I don't understand,' said Sununu. 'We have all this force in the Pacific, yet you gentlemen are reluctant to liberate Shemya?'

Powell did not look in Sununu's direction, Cheney glared but said nothing.

'General Powell,' began the president, 'have you consulted with the joint chiefs?'

'I have. The chiefs and I talked things over and then I met with Secretary Cheney. We are in agreement. A move to retake Shemya and the rest of the Aleutians would be unwise.'

'I think you should meet with the chiefs independently, Mr. President.'

Cheney was now slightly annoyed, but could see Powell was fuming. Before the Chairman exploded, Cheney said, 'That won't be necessary Mr. President. General Powell has already met with the chiefs, and they concur.'

'I see,' said the president. 'What I want, gentlemen, is a formal plan for retaking Shemya.'

General Powell nodded, 'We can do that Mr. President.'

'What about helping Nome?' Sununu asked.

'We need more information,' General Powell said. 'But since the Soviets hold the airport, I don't know what we can do, directly.'

Cheney added, 'Maybe some airdrops of weapons,' he shook his head. 'I don't know yet.'

The president said, 'So you're telling me that Nome is on its own.'

'For now, Mr. President, yes.'

Nome

Because Colonel Kamyetsov was blindfolded, a policeman led him onto the stage. The citizens of Nome booed Colonel Kamyetsov, and hurled invective that he found impressive. *This is what it must have felt like to be in one of Beria's show trials*, he thought. Colonel Kamyetsov was placed in front of a podium, at which time the policeman removed the blindfold. The boo-ing became louder and the insults more pronounced. Colonel Kamyetsov actually smiled, and then shouted, 'I do not think it would be possible to do that to a polar bear!'

The crowd suddenly fell silent, as if they were shocked to find out that a Russian was human, and in fact, had a sense of humor.

The mayor began, 'People, I invited the Colonel here. Let's just listen to what he has to say.'

Colonel Kamyetsov nodded to the Mayor. 'Thank you, Mayor Banks.' He turned to the crowd. 'People of Nome, I'd like to thank you for inviting me here and listening to my offer.'

A woman screamed. 'You killed my husband! You killed him!' she sobbed. A woman sitting with her grabbed her by the arm and hustled her out of the auditorium.

'I truly regret the death of that woman's husband, and the pain I have brought her.'

There were a few hisses.

'My men and I are fulfilling our duty. I suppose many of you men here served in your own nation's armed forces. In fact, given the fight you gave my men, I am sure of it. Surely you know a soldier's duty is to follow orders and stay with his…' Colonel Kamyetsov did not want to use the word com-rade, he searched for the right word for a few moments until awkwardly choosing an English colloquialism, 'your duty to fight with your …buddies, regardless of your personal feelings.'

Colonel Kamyetsov saw many of the men in the audience nod their heads. 'If you will permit me, I would like to tell you a few things about myself.'

More nodding.

'I am from the Ukraine. I attended the Frunze Military Academy, which is like your West Point. I fought two terms in Afghanistan and was with the Soviet consulate in New York.'

As Banks watched he nodded his head and thought, *he's good.*

For his part Colonel Kamyetsov saw faces in the crowd softening a bit. Inwardly he nodded. *Americans like the personal touch.*

'You do not want me here, people of Nome, and I do not wish to be here, but I must. I do not know how this conflict will end. All I ask is that you listen to my offer.'

'Go ahead!' someone shouted.

'My offer, the offer of the Soviet government is simple. Take what you need from your stores. Then remain in your homes. My men will stay out of Nome.'

'And what do you want?!' Someone shouted.

'All we want is the port and airport.'

'C'mon!' someone else shouted. 'After you attacked us?!'

'Landing in Nome was a mistake. One I regret. We should have left the town alone. But please understand, it was a mistake my men paid dearly for.'

Playing up sympathy, Banks thought, *interesting ploy.*

'Leave us the port and airport and we will leave you alone. That is all, that is all I have to say. My word of honor.'

'The word of a Communist!' an angry man shouted.

'Please, sir,' Colonel Kamyetsov responded. 'We may be enemies now, but once we were united in a war against the Germans, were we not?'

People nodded.

'My word is as a Soviet Army officer. That is all I have.'

More nodding especially from the military vets.

'That is all I have to say. If the mayor doesn't mind I would like to return to my men. They need me.'

Mayor Banks nodded to the chief. He and the other police officer blind folded Colonel Kamyetsov and led him off stage.

Mayor Banks took to the podium. 'Alright, folks. I'm going to let you all talk about this. I suggest forming a line for the podium and everyone taking a minute or so to get their say in. The council and I will stay out of it.'

Banks caught snippets of conversation in the crowd, 'Made some sense,' one man said, 'He seemed like a nice Russian man,' said an old lady.

Mayor Banks went back to his office with the chief.

'Well, Mr. Mayor,' Chief Nicks said. 'You think all that did any good?'

'Couldn't hurt,' said the Mayor.

The discussion lasted more than three hours. The Mayor didn't really expect the three hundred or so citizens of Nome to vote in favor of Colonel Kamyetsov's plan, though he was surprised at how long it took them to formally reject it. How was a Communist so good at retail politics?

'All right then,' Banks asked once things had settled down. 'What do we do?'

One man stood up and said he was leaving.

'Where to?' Banks asked. 'Are you going to drive to Fairbanks?'

'You can just get in your truck and leave,' someone else said. 'I have a family to think about. What are we supposed to do?'

'Yeah! I've built a life here. I ain't just gonna leave it now!' Banks recognized Mr. P. He was one of the gold dredgers, and operated a successful mining company as well. His tall, lanky 14 year old son, sporting a .22 rifle, sat next to him.

Someone else shouted, 'You want to stay and fight the Russians?'

'Yeah,' another shouted 'with rockets and machine guns?'

Parsons stood up next. He was mad, 'We already pushed the commies out of here once! You saying we can't do it again?'

There was more shouting as the room quickly split into those who thought they could fight the Soviets, and those who figured they didn't have a chance. There was lots of talk of mortars and rockets and the advisability of fighting trained paratroopers.

'But we outnumber them!' Parsons shouted.

'What's your plan then, Parsons?' a skeptic asked, 'throw ourselves at the Russians till they run out of bullets.'

For once, Parsons had nothing to say.

There was more shouting.

Mr. P. stood up again. 'Now hold on folks, hold on!' he proclaimed in a voice that dominated the room in land-use auctions. 'We may not have rockets but we have plenty of guns.'

'What about their RPGs?!'

'I was getting to that. Ok, we can't make a 105 mm howitzer but we can fashion our own cannons and air guns.'

'What are we going to shoot at them? Potatoes? This aint the A-Team!'

Mr. P. laughed. 'How about dynamite? I got boxes of the stuff back at my garage.'

'Oh come on, dynamite?'

'I use it to blow holes in rocks,' said Mr. P. 'We build a C02 gun, we could fling a stick...heck I dunno, a couple of hundred feet.'

'A couple of hundred feet? They'll shoot you before you get that close.'

Sitting next to Parsons, Big Tom nodded as he heard these words, but then remembered the AK-47 rounds bouncing off his plow. 'Hey wait a minute!' he said. 'One of them Ruskis emptied a magazine at my truck, but the rounds all bounced off my plow.'

Mr. P. said, 'Well sure! Steel plows. How many we got in Nome? There must be dozens.'

'So what do you want to do? Attack the airport behind a bunch of steel plows?'

'Yeah, throwing dynamite at the Ruskis.' Mr. P. said. 'In fact I have a better idea. Let's head down to my shop...'

Nome International Airport

Netta said, 'I do not see the point of what you have done, Comrade Colonel.'

'I talked to the Americans.'

'Was that wise?'

'You wanted to read them quotations from Marx and Lenin?'

'I thought if they only knew…'

Colonel Kamyetsov dismissed Netta with a wave of his hand. 'They do not care.'

'Do you really think they will accept your offer?'

Colonel Kamyetsov shook his head. 'I doubt it.'

'What was the point of you talking to them, Comrade Colonel?'

'Churchill once said, jaw-jaw is better than war-war.'

'You quote Churchill but not Marx?'

'Are you insinuating something, Comrade?'

'Not at all.'

'One other thing, Comrade,' said Colonel Kamyetsov. 'By talking to them, I delay them. And that gives us time for the freighter to arrive.'

Nome

Mr. P. showed off the gun, 'Oughta get the job done. This can fling a stick 200 feet.'

Parsons nodded.

'I can build a couple more at least. May not be heavy artillery, but it can make a big boom.' He put the CO_2 gun down.

'Well it looks good, I…'

The Mayor's radio squawked. It was Banks. 'You better get up here, Mr. Mayor. We got trouble. Ship coming in, and it isn't ours.'

'Where are you?'

'Orthodox Church.'

'Be right there.'

The Mayor got back in his truck and drove over to the Orthodox Church. Banks was in the bell tower. He climbed up to the top, the chief pointed out to the overcast Bering Sea, partially shrouded in morning fog.

The ship grew larger by the minute as it made for Nome. Using a range finder every few minutes the chief relayed the freighter's distance over to the station.

Parsons and Mayor Banks watched as the freighter pulled alongside the quay on the outer harbor. They saw dozens of men, looking tiny in the distance, scurrying along the quay. Sailors fore and aft tossed ropes down to the soldiers on the quay. Above them hovered a pair of helicopters.

They left a pair of policeman in the bell tower to watch the freighter.

'What do you suppose is in the ship?' Banks asked. 'More men?'

Parsons thought for a moment. 'Nah. If there were more men inside, they'd be getting out of it now. '

'We have some Soviet prisoners. Why don't we go ask them?'

'Good idea.'

The chief called the station. 'We're coming in.'

'OK, Chief,' said the dispatcher on the other end.

'Make sure Grant is there. I need him for something.'

They drove to the police station. People were already moving quickly along the streets, as word of the Soviet freighter made its way through town. When they got to the station, Grant was waiting outside. He waved. Together the four men walked into the station.

Grant grinned and said, 'Been a long time since you said you needed me like that, Chief.'

The chief looked at Parson's and the mayor. 'You two better wait here.'

'I'm the mayor,' said Banks.

'Which is why you don't want to be in on what we're about to do.'

The chief and Grant went down the steps to the basement jail. The wounded Soviet was in the hospital, but his companion was unhurt and had been kept in the jail. Private Peneva had been no trouble during his day long incarceration. In fact, he had been imminently bribable with American cigarettes. When the Chief and Grant got to his cell, he was laying on his bunk listening to Madonna tapes on a Walkman one of the other cops had lent him.

When he saw them, Private Peneva sat up and took his headphones off. They could hear *Like a Prayer*, blaring.

The chief opened the cell and nodded to Grant. He handed the chief his holster and walked in. The chief closed the cell behind them.

'How are you, private?' Grant asked.

'I well, thank you,' Peneva said in heavily accented English.

'I have some questions for you.'

Peneva said nothing.

'A Russian freighter came into port. Since you're Russian, I thought you could tell me what's onboard.'

'I am not Russian,' Peneva said. 'I am from Byelorussia.

'I couldn't care less. What's in the freighter?'

'All I have to tell you is name, rank, number.'

Grant smacked him across the face so hard he slammed back down to the bunk. Then Grant grabbed him by the hair. 'Let's go for a swim, boy....'

CHAPTER 3

Nome

'Can't you shoot the dynamite sticks onto the deck of the freighter?' Banks asked.

'Don't matter,' Mr. P. said. 'Getting a couple of sticks of dynamite onto the ship won't do no good. You'd have to get a bunch; a dozen, two dozen, all in one spot. If they're scattered all over the place it'd just make a big bang. Won't do no damage to the ship.'

'Then what can we do?' Banks asked. 'All this dynamite, there must be some use for it.'

Shawn tried to interject, 'Dad.'

Banks said, 'We could try to take out the crane.' He inwardly winced at the thought. That crane was a wonderful opportunity for graft.

Mr. P shook his head. 'Nah, these things don't have the range, and we'd never get close enough.

Shawn tried again. 'Dad.'

Parsons and Mr. P. bickered for another moment.

'Dad!' Shawn shouted.

'What, Shawny?' Mr. P. said.

'Why don't I scuba over there and throw some dynamite at the ship?'

'Shawny! What the hell, I mean that's…' then Mr. P. stopped talking. 'Not a half bad idea.'

Mr. P. sat down and rubbed his chin in thought.

'My God!" Parson's grinned 'The kid's got an idea.'

Mr. P. held up his hand. 'You couldn't toss them up there.'

'What about the air guns you built?'

Mr. P. shook his head. 'Naaaa, they'd get waterlogged.'

'Wouldn't the dynamite?' asked Bob.

'You could use a watertight container…hell, you could put them in Ziploc bags….and a timer….' Mr. P. looked at this son, 'You got a hell of an idea, kid.'

'I can get my stuff at the garage and get in the water…'

'Hold on, Shawny,' said Mr. P. 'What makes you think you're getting in there?'

'I worked on my scuba all summer Dad. I was the best guy on the dredge.'

'Yeah, but we weren't talking about explosives!' he yelled. 'No way.'

'Most of the rest of the divers left Nome weeks ago,' said Shawn.

'I don't think, from the water, you could toss a big bag of dynamite up there.'

Banks had an idea and was about to speak, but didn't.

'What?' Mr. P asked.

'Well,' Banks said. 'I don't want to get your son killed….'

'Oh go ahead and say your idea,' Mr. P. said. 'We have Ruskis all over Nome. Time to grow up fast.'

'Ok, couldn't he scuba over there and just stick the explosives to the ship?'

Mr. P. held up his hand and then stopped. 'Wait a minute…you might be…you are right!' Mr. P. turned to his son, 'Shawny, get your gear!'

Shemya

'Would you idiots put those controllers down and come see this?'

The two paratroopers didn't look up from their game of Super Tecmo Bowl.

Yegorovich turned away in disgust. He had never been much of a communist, but he was beginning to wonder if the Party had not been right about the trappings of capitalism. He hadn't been able to keep his men away from the damn American video game. Yegorovich looked out the window to the choppy Bering Sea.

Several miles north, he could make out a pair of assault transports, each carrying a battalion of naval infantry. At first he had thought and hoped they carried his battalion's relief. But no. They pressed on east through the rough, choppy water. After a time he spotted another silhouette. Then he could see it, the Pacific Fleet's *Kirov* class nuclear battle cruiser and trailing a kilometer behind that, a *Minsk* class aircraft carrier.

'You guys are going to miss it,' Yegorovich admonished.

'Excuse me, Sergeant, but we are playing for league championship. Americans call it Super Bowl....come on! How could he drop that?' the soldier said in frustration as his wide receiver dropped an easy catch... The other soldier said, 'By the way, Sergeant, comrade Kutta was looking for you. He seemed mad.'

Yegorovich cursed.

Nome

At Breakers Bar, Banks and the Chief waited while Mr. P. helped his son into the scuba gear.

'Good thing your mother is back home, Shawny.'

Shawn tucked his longish locks inside his swim cap and smiled. 'Yeah, she'd kill me for trying this.'

'Yeah, and then she'd kill me.'

Then Mr. P. helped his son put on the oxygen tank. The flippers went on last.

'Now, you got three hours of air in here, Shawny.'

'I know dad,' Shawn said.

'You got to swim a mile there and back.'

'Dad, I know.'

'So don't waste no time.'

'Dad, do you think I was going to hang out with the Russians?"

Mr. P. picked up a bag. 'This is a watertight bag. Just swim over to that ship, and use this rubber cement to glue it to the hull.

Shawn nodded.

'Make sure you extend the antenna on the detonator.'

'Jeez, Dad, I know. Would you stop.'

'And swim right back here.'

You ready Shawny?'

The boy nodded.

Mr. P. and Shawn crept down to the sea wall.

'Need help getting in?'

'Dad! I can do it, OK?'

'Alright.'

'You be careful, boy.' Mr. P. hugged his son. 'Your mother and I love you.'

'Aww, jeez, Dad, knock it off.'

Nome International Airport

'No air assets?' Colonel Kamyetsov asked.

'None are available,' replied the logistics officer on the other end of the line in Petropavlovsk.

'Why?'

'They have all been allocated to the upcoming airborne operation.'

'But I need technicians. I need people who can repair the dock-crane here.'

'I am sorry, comrade colonel,' was the reply.

'I have a ship full of armored vehicles and no way to unload them and all you can say is that you are sorry?'

'Would you like me to apologize again?'

'That will not be necessary.'

Colonel Kamyetsov replaced the radio receiver in disgust.

'No?' Colonel Netta asked.

Colonel Kamyetsov shook his head in annoyance. 'Pacific Command is beginning a new operation as we speak.'

'Another attack on the Aleutians?'

'We are not supposed to know, but most likely. The base at Adak I think.'

Colonel Netta shrugged.

'Could we not just use all our troops and storm the town?'

Colonel Kamyetsov raised an eyebrow. 'We?' He grimaced. 'Doing so would get many of my men killed, unnecessarily.'

'Then what do you propose, Comrade Colonel?'

'I want my armored vehicles unloaded. Then even these people,' he motioned to Nome, 'will come to their senses.'

Netta nodded his head.

'Damn Americans,' Colonel Kamyetsov said, 'Damn Americans and John Wayne, and their Second Amendment and their Revolution and...'

Colonel Kamyetsov's frustrated diatribe was cut off by an explosion.

'What was that?' he asked.

'I think it came from the port.'

'Oh no.'

The White House

The men assembled in the White House Situation Room stood as the president entered. When Bush sat at the table, Scowcroft began the briefing. He nodded, and one of the White House aides turned on the projection TV at the far end of the room. A map of the Aleutians appeared on the screen.

'The Soviet Pacific Fleet is making its move. A large task force, containing at least one carrier, one missile cruiser and several amphibious assault ships was spotted east of Shemya by one of our submarines cruising west, southwest. We believe the target is Adak.'

Bush looked at Cheney, 'Dick?'

'Yes, Mr. President. Adak was reinforced by one infantry battalion of the 7th Light Division. We have a squadron of F-16s there too, Air National Guard.'

'Is it enough?'

'Mr. President,' the secretary of defense began, 'I just don't think the Soviets will be bringing enough manpower to dislodge an infantry battalion, not to mention the bases' garrison.'

'What is this going to be, Wake Island all over again?'

'Hopefully not, sir,' said Cheney. 'USS *Midway* and her battle-group are on the way.'

'So maybe like Midway?!' Sununu said all too cheerfully.

'I hope so,' Bush said.

Cheney said, 'After this, Mr. President, I'd like to talk to you about some contingency plans for winning things in the North Pacific.'

'That's what I like to hear,' Sununu said. 'Look great in the papers. Shemya, Kiska and Attu should be retaken as soon as possible.'

The President nodded.

'Actually, sir,' said Cheney, 'I was thinking something bigger.'

'Bigger?' Scowcroft looked over at Cheney.

'Much bigger.'

Nome

'How'd you get the black eye, Mr. P.?' asked the mayor.

His son laughed.

'The boy's mother heard what I allowed him to do and punched me.'

'Well, the boy is ok, ain't he?'

In the wind blown darkness, the mayor couldn't see Mr. P. scowl. 'Can we get back to business please?'

Banks spoke into his walkie-talkie. 'Chief, your men in position?'

'Atop the mountain,' the chief replied.

'Ready whenever you are, Mr. P.'

'Alright,' Mr. P. said, 'We got two of these guns mounted on the pick-ups there,' he said to the gathering of men and a few women. 'We'll get as close as we can and then fire. Won't be accurate or worth a shit, but they'll get the job done. Make some noise.'

The mayor added. 'Don't no one fire until Mr. P. says so. We want a few sticks of dynamite in the air before we let the Ruskis have it.'

'Everybody got that?' Mr. P. said.

There were grunts of affirmation.

'Got that, Parsons?'

'Sure thing,' Parsons replied. 'But when the shootin' starts, I'm letting those commie bastards have it with everything I got.'

'I still say we oughta come in on boats!' one of the dredgers shouted.

'We've been over this,' Mr. P. Replied. 'They'll just catch us on the water and shoot us up. We'd be sitting ducks.'

The man grumbled. Someone said, 'He's right.'

'And if their choppers come, just scatter, the trucks will.'

'Ok?' Banks said.

The men grunted and nodded again.

'Well, no point in waiting around, Mr. Mayor.'

The two pick up drivers started their engines and advanced north out of Nome to the airport. Behind them a line of seventy people, armed with a hodgepodge of weapons walked.

Nome International Airport

Kamyetsov heard an explosion and then another. It was dynamite he knew now. All day he had sat in his confiscated office and wondered what to do next, the plan didn't call for taking the town without heavy equipment, and if he sent his men into Nome on foot they'd get shot to pieces. The towns-people weren't going to hear anymore offers from him, that was for sure.

By the time a second round of explosions pierced the night he was outside and running for the roadblock on the bridge to Nome. When he got outside he heard the windows of the control tower shatter from American fire. He listened. It was scattered but constant, a mix of American rifles and captured Soviet Ak-47s. There was another pair of explosions. He got to the roadblock, the lieutenant commanding reported. 'Comrade Colonel. The Americans are perhaps 200 yards from us.'

They ducked down behind an empty steel barrel as bullets whizzed past them.

'The dynamite?!' he shouted over his men's return fire.

'They keep missing. Landing in front of us,' he pointed ahead. 'Or behind over there.'

'I don't understand. Even these Americans can't throw a stick of dynamite that far.'

'I do not know, comrade, I…'

There was another explosion, this one landed in the water beside the bridge.

'And they have trucks out there.'

'Why haven't you disabled them?'

'One of my men fired an RPG, but it bounced right off.'

More firing from the Americans. This time a Russian paratrooper fell to the ground screaming.

Damn, Kamyetsov thought.

'Very well. Stay here, I will send reinforcements and get the helicopters in the air.'

Nome

'Get those men out of here!' Mr. P. shouted. He pointed to the two wounded men laying behind one of the trucks. 'Get them out!'

Another rocket streaked in and hit the plow of one of the trucks. It exploded, shattering the windshield and rocking the truck back on its shocks.

'You alright, there, Edgar?' Mr. P. asked.

Big Tom wiped blood off his face. 'Yeah, yeah, I'm ok. Just a few cuts. And don't call me Edgar!'

'What are we, about a hundred fifty yards?'

Mr. P. ducked as bullets ricochet off the steel plow.

'I'd say so.'

'Let's get closer.'

'Time for Billy'

'Yes,' replied Mr. P. He shouted behind him, 'Billy! Get up here!'

A moment later Billy got in the back of Big Tom's truck. He was a young man, a native of Nome, who, because of his athletic skill, had gone to high school in Anchorage where he was a starting quarterback, and later went to college in Oregon where he played Division II football, again starting quarterback. Upon graduation he had matriculated back to Nome.

Mr. P. got in the back of the truck with Billy. Out of a lock box, he took a bundle of four dynamite sticks. 'You sure you can throw these?'

'Been practicing all day Mr P.' a rocket exploded nearby.

'How far?'

Danny hefted a bundle in his hand. 'Sixty, no problem.'

Mr. P. slapped the back of the cab. 'Alright, Edgar. Get us close. Fifty- yards.'

'Ok!'

Mr. P. hooted at the other truck and twirled his finger. 'You know the plan! Let's go!'

The other truck raised its plow and drove ahead of Big Tom's. The driver took it forward at fifty miles per hour. Four men with automatic rifles stood in the back of the cab and fired forward. Big Tom brought his truck behind the first one and followed closely.

'Down in the bed,' Mr. P. said as he pushed Billy down.

Under cover of fire and another volley of dynamite from the air cannons, they raced forward. The two trucks zigged and zagged in the dark against Soviet fire.

'I think here is good!' Mr. P shouted.

Big Tom spoke into the CB and told the lead truck to stop.

'Make it quick, Billy.'

Mr. P. handed Billy a dynamite bundle. 'Where?'

'Right on 'em!' he shouted as a burst of machine gun fire slammed into the plow. 'Now!'

Billy heaved the dynamite forward. Mr. P. tossed him another bundle. 'Spread 'em around!'

Billy launched it to the left and the next one to the right.

'Keep them coming, Mr. P.!' Billy said.

He tossed the last two directly forward.

'That's it!' Mr. P. shouted. 'Duck! Everyone down!'

He reached into his pants pocket and took out a radio controller. He extended the antenna and pressed the big red button. The blast wave rocked the truck on its shocks.

Nome International Airport

The blast knocked Kamyetsov forward onto his face. He sat up to see the road block. It was shattered. The barriers were blasted to bits, the men manning the block scattered about, some alive, many dead, or crying in agony from their wounds. He had just gotten to his feet when a pickup truck barreled through the roadblock and burst onto the road to the airport. Dozens of men followed on foot, they randomly and wildly fired their motley collections of weapons and the dazed Soviet soldiers around the block, killing them without mercy.

'Get those AKs!' Someone shouted. Then, 'Follow the trucks! Move!'

The men proceeded on foot. After them came more pickup trucks and then taxi cabs full of armed men. Kamyetsov hoped the platoon he sent to reinforce the roadblock would be able to stop the tide, but the lead trucks caught them in the open. Kamyetsov cursed. Lieutenant Korda should have deployed his men in a skirmish line and waited for the Americans. Instead he pushed forward and tried to reach the roadblock before the Americans. The result was they were caught on flat open ground. Many were shot where they stood. He tried to take solace when someone got off an RPG and blew up one of the American cabs, but that drew fire and

Kamyetsov saw the man who fired the rocket go down in a hail of small arms fire. The platoon quickly scattered.

Kamyetsov stayed low on the ground. He didn't dare stand. The Americans weren't even taking prisoners. There was more small arms fire, this time from the eastern edge of the airport. At least someone was keeping their head.

Nome

Big Tom slammed on the brakes so hard that he threw Billy out of the truck-bed. He landed on the ground with a thump and a scream, 'My leg!' he shouted over the hail of gunfire coming from the airport.

Even though the plow deflected the Soviet bullets, Big Tom dived down in the seat. Mr. P. lay flat on the bed and clutched his rifle.

'Stay down!' he shouted to Billy.

'I ain't goin' nowhere!' He shouted back as he clutched his leg.

All around Mr. P's men fell to the ground and returned fire. The other two trucks came in line with Big Tom.

'Shoot some dynamite at them!' Mr. P. shouted.

One of the gunners gave him a thumbs up.

Mr. P. grabbed his walkie-talkie. 'Alright, Green. Come on in!'

Nome International Airport

Netta was worried. They had lost Colonel Kamyetsov, presumed dead at the roadblock, and now the better part of two platoons were out of the fight. The Americans for the time being were stopped outside the east edge of the airport but Netta heard the explosions again, those damn explosives the Americans were using. He had heard that the government was lenient about gun ownership, but explosives? Where did they get those? And those dammed plows of theirs. Netta shook his head. *The Bourgeoisie...* More explosions from the east, and then more gunfire, this time from the north.

'Now what?' Netta asked out loud.

He looked north and could see gun flashes. He felt a sinking feeling in the pit of his stomach. There were just a few sentries on the north end of the airport. If the Americans were hitting them from the north as well…

Nome

Bullets continued to slam into the plow. The line of trucks and cars waited a few dozen yards behind Mr. P. Besides them were dozens of armed men some wounded and a few dead. The two gun trucks lobbed dynamite at the eastern edge of the airport, but couldn't seem to hit anything of consequence. Mr. P. was beginning to get discouraged when he saw muzzle flashes to the north.

Mr. P. grabbed his walkie-talkie. 'Greene is that you guys?'

'What do you mean, is that you guys?!' Greene replied. 'Can't you hear us!'

'Where are you?'

'We blew right through their sentries!' Greene shouted. Mr. P. heard gunfire over the radio. 'We're on the tarmac!'

'You're on the tarmac?!'

'Yes!' Greene replied. There was a shotgun blast. 'Send more guys! Send reinforcements!'

'Alright, hold on.'

'Their choppers are up ahead, we're going right after them.'

Mr. P. raised the cabs. 'That's right go north and then turn due east on the airfield, ok?'

'Alright, will do.'

'When you get on the tarmac turn on your lights. Greene will know it's you.'

'Roger. Can I take one of the dynamite guns?'

Mr. P. looked at the trucks, which continued to lob dynamite at the Soviets to little effect.' 'Sure. Now just drive up there and then onto the tarmac.'

'Right, and we'll come right down behind the Russians!'

Nome International Airport

Kamyetsov saw that the pace of the fighting was favoring the Americans, as was the direction, which moved consistently west toward the airport.

You cannot sit here while the battle is lost, he said to himself.

He crawled forward toward the Soviet line. Fortunately the fighting had moved far enough west that no one was looking in his direction. He was getting close to the tarmac when he heard a new round of explosions, dynamite, he knew. Then he realized they were coming from further up the tarmac, near the control tower. There was another explosion, then another. After a third explosion Kamyetsov heard a wrenching, twisting sound and saw that the control tower was aflame. There was more firing, this time all along the tarmac. Suddenly, the Americans east of the tarmac surged forward, their steel plowed trucks leading the way, and onto the airport proper.

With nothing else for him to do, Kamyetsov kept crawling forward until he reached the old Soviet line. There were bodies all around, some American, but mostly Russian. The Americans hadn't left anybody to occupy the positions. Professional soldiers would have. They did take every AK-47, as Kamyetsov found to his chagrin while he was looking for a weapon. There were more explosions, then more firing. Then the shooting died down and stopped entirely.

Kamyetsov waited. After several minutes, he heard cheering and hooting coming from the Americans. Then he could see a flashlight pointed toward one of the hangars, and then men coming out with their hands in the air. There was still some shooting even further in the distance, but it was clear to Kamyetsov that the battle for Nome Airport was over.

The White House

'Mr. President.'

'Huh?' Bush said as he shot up from the couch.

'Are you awake, sir?' the Secret Service agent asked.

Bush rubbed his face. Beside him on the couch was a folder, the previous day's casualty list, 172 confirmed dead 412 confirmed wounded, as well as several other reports.

'I was asleep?'

'Yes, sir.'

'For how long?'

The agent looked at his watch, 'Fifty-seven minutes, sir.'

'You let me nap?' he asked, somewhat annoyed.

'Yes, sir. You drifted off. We thought it for the best.'

Bush glared at the agent, who betrayed no emotion at all. *Just doing his job, I suppose.*

'The National Security Advisor is on the line, sir.'

'Alright.'

The President got up and went to his desk. He picked up the phone. 'Hello, Brent.'

'Mr. President. I wanted to share the news with you right away.'

'Uh oh.'

'No sir, good news. The Soviets in Nome have surrendered.'

'Surrendered?'

'That's right, sir.'

'What happened?'

'Quite a story Mr. President. It seems the people of Nome attacked the Soviets holding the airport and beat them.'

'Towns people against the Soviet Army?'

'Yes, sir. They contacted Ft. Richardson with a captured Soviet radio. The airport is theirs, the Soviets are kaput.'

'Well that's great news. We need to get them help, right away.'

'Yes, sir. General Powell has already ordered an infantry company out of Ft. Richardson to Nome. They should be arriving within the hour.'

Nome

Kamyetsov stayed in the brush until daylight. During that time he had heard no more firing. He had watched for hours as the townspeople gathered his men near one of the hangars. He counted fifty-three Soviets. Many of them were wounded. To Kamyetsov's relief a pair of

PART II: The Battle of Nome, Alaska

ambulances came from the hospital and picked up some of the more badly wounded. The rest of the men sat cross-legged in a circle, bathed in the lights of three police cars. He was glad to see the Nome police, now the townspeople were standing guard. He hadn't seen Netta. *Was he dead? Most likely*, Kamyetsov thought. The zampolit would no doubt have insisted that the paratroopers fight on to the death. It seemed the surviving officers and NCOs had better sense. Kamyetsov was thankful for that.

He had wondered what to do with himself until daylight. That's when he heard the drone of propellers. Kamyetsov hoped they were Soviet reinforcements, a hope that was dashed when he saw the plane coming low over the tarmac. It was an American C-130. As the plane taxied down the runway, the Soviet colonel considered his options. He looked around. There was no place to run. He'd be spotted. He could crawl to the marina, he supposed and maybe steal a boat. Then what? Kamyetsov shook his head. 'No,' he said aloud. *My men are at the airport, and that is where I should be.*

Kamyetsov unhooked his belt, leaving a walkie-talkie and pistol on the ground. Then he stood, held his hands over his head, and walked toward the tarmac.

'Hey, there's another one!' someone shouted.

Two police officers ran over to Kamyetsov.

'Just stand still,' one of them said. He held a shotgun at the ready. The other frisked him.

'He's clean,' he said.

'I am Colonel Kamyetsov, and I demand to be taken to my men.'

'No problem,' said the cop with the shotgun. He nudged Kamyetsov forward. 'Move.'

'No need for that,' the Colonel said.

As the trio approached the Soviet POWs one of the sergeants stood up and pointed. 'The Colonel. It's the Colonel!'

Other Soviet soldiers stood up and pointed.

'Alright, everyone back down,' one of the police officers said.

But it was no use. The POWs broke ranks and ran over to the Colonel, sweeping aside the two officers guarding him. They surrounded Kamyetsov and patted him on the back.

'The Colonel! The Colonel!' the men shouted.

There was a shotgun blast and everyone ducked, except Kamyetsov.

'Everyone back over to the circle, Godamit!'

It was the Chief of Police.

'Back now!'

'Back over, men,' Kamyetsov said.

The POWs went back to the circle. Kamyetsov walked over to the chief and saluted. 'I am Colonel Kamyetsov and I am here to surrender.'

'Yes, Colonel, the chief said. 'Over with the other POWs.'

'Of course,' he replied. 'I trust my men are being treated in accordance with the Geneva Convention.'

'I don't know anything about that, Colonel. But we ain't killing anyone.'

'I am glad to hear that.'

Kamyetsov walked over to his men. They clapped as he made his way to the center of the circle. There was more clapping and cheering.

'Down, Colonel,' the chief said.

'One moment, please.' He turned to his men. 'Well, men, you all look worse for wear.'

There were nods and a chorus of 'Da's.'

'You should all be proud.'

The POWs looked at one another in confusion.

'Yes, proud. We had an impossible mission, I tell you. Impossible.'

'No!' someone shouted.

He held out his hand, 'Da. Impossible. But we did our best. We acted like soldiers. We fought our battle, and we lost. We fought as soldiers of the Soviet Union.'

More nods and affirmations.

'We did our duty for the motherland. Sometimes the enemy just beats you. There is no shame in that. We did our best, but it wasn't enough. We fought with courage. And you should be proud. We fought with honor. Did we massacre these people here?'

'No!' someone shouted.

'Did we act as the fascist beasts from the Great Patriotic War?'

'No!'

'We acted as honorable soldiers. We fought on as best and as long as we could. And then we acted with honor. We made the choice honorable soldiers make. We chose to live. We chose to spare our own lives and the lives of our enemy. We are proud!' He pumped his fist.

The men gave a great cheer.

'We are now in the care of the Americans. Do not fear. I have lived among them, remember. And like us, the Americans are honorable. Have no doubt, you will be treated well. I suspect I and the other officers will be separated from you. I have one last order. Cooperate. Your duty now is to survive. To survive and return to your families. That is all we can do. Like Russians!'

Another great cheer. The men stood up against and hoisted the Colonel upon their shoulders. They carried him around as the rest clapped.

'What's all that about,' one of the cops asked.

The Chief said, 'Nice for them to get some good news, I guess.' He nodded to the C-130 which even then was disgorging regular army troops. 'They're the army's problem now.'

The Pentagon

'General Powell,' began Bloviating Hair Maniac, 'what steps is the president taking to secure Alaska?'

'We have troops stationed at important places throughout the state.'

'Where?'

'I won't reveal military details.'

'We know there are troops in Anchorage and Juneau. Are there troops anywhere else?'

'Please…'

'What about the bases in the Aleutians,' asked the less egotistical correspondent from NBC, 'are they still held by the Soviets?'

'Yes, at this time they…'

Bloviating Hair Maniac jumped in, 'Do you have any plans to retake them?'

'As I said, we do not discuss future military operations.'

'So there is a plan to retake the lost Aleutian bases?' concluded Bloviating Hair Maniac.

'Sam all I can say is that we are considering our options in the Pacific…'

Powell let the word hang on its own for a moment. *Let them wonder what* that *means*, he thought.

Shemya

Yegorovitch had assembled his squad in the lounge. He looked the men over, and in the week they had been on Shemya, could see that he had really let things get out of control. None were in full uniform, many wore captured American clothes. Netta wore an American Air Force jacket and no pants. Yegorovich shook his head. He couldn't blame himself entirely. The officers had practically abandoned their men, spending most of their time in the Americans' lavish, (by Soviet standards) officer's club. They had even called the non-coms over there to deliver the bad news, bad news which Yegorovich was now passing on to his men.

'Bad news, from Nome, men,' said Yegorovich. He told them about the defeat suffered there by Soviet forces.

'So what the fuck do we care?' asked Netta.

Yegorovich smirked and said, 'Because, you ape, it means we have to stay here.'

There was a groan from the assembled men. 'What the fuck!' Netta shouted. In rage he pushed one of his squad-mates out of the way and punched a hole in the wall. 'I don't fucking believe this!'

The man pushed down by Netta sprung to his feet and jumped on his back. Seeing the squad bully finally being confronted, two other men attacked Netta, one punched him rather ineffectively in the face, the other kicking him in the shins. One of Netta's friends joined the scuffle, punching out one of the men and turning to face the other, however, he himself taken down by yet another trooper.

By then the entire squad was brawling. Yegorovitch shouted for order and calm to no avail until Netta stalked toward him, his assailant still holding on to his back. Yegorovitch held up his hands in defense as Netta swung at him. As he hit the floor, Yegorovitch knew his arm was broken, which is the last thing he knew before Netta stomped on his neck.

PART III: THE BATTLE OF THE NORWEGIAN SEA

CNN– Los Angeles

Larry: And we're back. Now Tom, maybe you can explain to our viewers what I think is one of the most surprising aspects of the naval war.

Tom: Sure Larry.

Larry: Why did the Soviets pick on Scandinavia?

Tom: Ha ha ha. Larry, Scandinavia is crucial.

Larry: Norway?

Tom: Absolutely, Larry. The Soviets have occupied about half of Norway. The bases they seized have made NATO's job of keeping the Atlantic sea-lanes open very difficult.

Harold: Soviet amphibious operations were well executed, and I don't think NATO anticipated the ferocity of their attacks in Norway.

Larry: How so?

Tom: The Soviets posses a trio of carriers, two heavy cruisers, big missile ships. NATO planners seemed obsessed with bringing about a surface engagement. The Soviets used those assets to facilitate and cover their operations in Norway. They weren't interested in a large surface engagement.

Harold: And don't forget Iceland. Critical.

Tom: That's why the Soviets hit it twice.

Larry: Now, gentlemen, What we have seen here over three weeks is basically a repeat of the Battle of Atlantic.

Tom: I think that's exactly right, Larry. The Soviets had to close the trans-Atlantic sea lane to stop American reinforcements from getting to Europe.

Larry: And they failed.

Tom: Yes, absolutely. We held onto Iceland. Anti-sub aircraft out of Keflavik were able to harass Soviet subs as they came down through the north Atlantic.

Harold: Yes, and because we held Iceland, NATO hunter-killer groups were able to patrol the GIUK Gap.

Larry: Hunter killer groups?

Harold: Surface groups usually numbering two or three ships.

Tom: And the submarine line. In all three cases, air, surface and submarine, the British were essential

Larry: How so?

Tom: We know British forces in the GIUK Gap badly damaged the Soviet submarine effort.

Larry: So we have won the new Battle of the Atlantic.

Tom: Well, the first phase of it, Larry.

Larry: First phase. What is the next phase?

Tom: Counterattack.

CHAPTER 1

New York City

Even though the sun was setting on the East Coast, the Brooklyn Naval Yard was packed with workers. Two dry-docks were occupied by damaged US Navy ships, one a destroyer, the *USS Arthur W. Radford* and the other a frigate, *USS Paul.* Men swarmed over the damaged hulls, repairing bulkheads, swapping out damaged and often saltwater- logged equipment. Batteries of klieg lights had been rigged up on the adjoining piers to ensure work continued through the night.

In the Hudson River a tug towed the *USS Long Beach* west toward its temporary berth up the Hudson at Tompkins Cove, a transitory stop for ships deemed too badly damaged to get back in action. Seven other navy ships were already anchored there. The tug passed one of its brethren bringing the badly damaged *USS Belknap* to dock. Waiting for the ship were a hundred workers, welders, electricians, and electronics experts. Because there was so much work to be done, many of the workers were independent contractors, a problem for the union, smoothed over with a small adjustment to their health insurance plan co-pay.

As the ship approached, they stood in awe of the damage. The entire fore superstructure had been blasted away by a Backfire launched missile. The aft superstructure had been engulfed in flame and ninety- two sailors had lost their lives. A few men whistled in amazement that the ship had reached port at all. As she passed by the workers all removed their hard-hats. Many placed them over their hearts. Several men bowed their heads in prayer. When the stricken warship finally docked, the men walked over the gangplank and got to work.

On the west side of Manhattan, the docks were filled with undamaged navy ships, and thousands of sailors after ten days of arduous convoy duty had spilled ashore. Times Square and 42nd Street were washed over by a sea of naval whites and blues. By 1700 hours the bars on 2nd Avenue were bustling and CBGB's was packed. The Hard Rock was overrun with sailors. By 1830 the first bar was closed down by the NYPD and Shore Patrol. The former's resources were already stretched, as extra units were needed to keep an eye on the heavily 'Russified' Brighton Beach section of Brooklyn, mostly to guard against vandalism, wrongheaded hooliganism and idiocy. Already a few Russian restaurants had been torched by yahoos. The FBI was active in the neighborhood though, just to be on the safe side. By informal agreement midtown was reserved for officers. The Shore Patrol studiously prevented lower ratings in various states of inebriation to cross the invisible line at 42nd street. In the higher-end establishments, officers checked into rooms with their wives. Single men, or those whose families who couldn't make it to New York congregated in hotel bars.

The officers of the *USS Stirling* decamped at the Algonquin on 44th street. Those who hadn't retreated to the rooms upstairs with their wives or girlfriends gathered in the Oak Room where a seasoned Jazz pianist worked her way through the Sondheim catalogue. Most of the officers were too young to really appreciate jazz, but they didn't care. It was nice to listen to something that wasn't the hum of turbine engines, or alerts of incoming Soviet bombers, or the screams of waterlogged merchantmen sailors. The pianist actually led the officers in a sing along. 'That's how we did it during the last war,' she explained.

At the bar outside the Oak Room, Captain Lauring finished off his beer and handed the glass to the bartender. 'Another,' he said.

'Yes, sir,' the bartender said.

Lauring took a fresh beer and drank. He watched the men gathered around the piano as they began a rendition of Sweeney Todd. Most didn't even know the words, but just hummed along with the pianist. Lauring took a healthy swig of beer.

'Captain!'

Lauring was nearly knocked over by his executive officer, who tripped into the bar and collapsed onto a stool. He looked at Lt. Commander Stewart. His hair was disheveled, cheeks red, shirt un-tucked and blazer worn awkwardly. He ordered a whiskey and smiled at his captain.

'That was, fast, Stew,' said Lauring.

'I don't need a lot of time.'

'And what did Vicki say?'

'She said she wanted to go shopping.'

'In Manhattan? Hide the credit card.'

'She's already at Saks,' Stewart grinned. 'Said she'll pick up a little welcome home present while she was out. I told her to make sure it comes off easily.' Stewart nudged the Captain.

'She came all the way here from Norfolk to get fucked and go shopping?'

Stewart grinned again.

Lauring shook his head and polished off his beer. He handed the glass to the bartender for another. Lauring downed about half of it.

'Easy there, Captain,' Stewart said.

'Why?' he asked. 'Unlike you, I can hold my liquor.'

Which explained why Lauring, a simple USNR officer, had surpassed Stewart, a graduate of Annapolis.

'Hey, Captain,' Stewart replied, 'I've earned it.'

Lauring patted his XO on the shoulder, 'After the last convoy, you certainly have.'

He polished off his beer and asked for another.

Stewart pounded the bar with his open palm, 'We bagged one Sierra class boat! Wooooo!'

'And probably a Kilo class too.'

Even then the chief of the boat was painting a third submarine silhouette on the ship's smoke stack. They had come up empty on the first convoy run, but definitely bagged two Soviet subs on the second.

The maitre'd approached. 'Gentleman I do apologize, but the officer here will have to quiet down.'

Stewart barred his teeth like a bearcat. The maitre'd took a step back. 'That's Ok...,' he strained to read the maitre de's name tag, 'Roul,' he patted the man on the shoulder. 'I was heading out anyway.' He shot his class of whisky and walked out of the bar.

As Stewart left, Lauring said, 'Sorry about that.'

'Not at all, sir.'

Lauring drained his mug and held it aloft for another.

The bartender took the glass and refilled. 'So what's it like out there?' he asked.

For the first time Lauring looked at the bartender. He was an older man in black pants, vest and white shirt. The sleeves were rolled up revealing a tattoo of a ship with the words *Four Stackers* above a rendering of a four- stack destroyer. So Lauring answered.

'Bad.'

'It can't be that bad,' said the man, 'I was at the battle of Java Sea, that was bad.'

'Your tin-can make it?'

'No. We was in Manila when the Japs bombed it. Then my ship went down, spent the rest of the war in a POW camp.' He paused for a moment. 'They say we're winning.'

Lauring took another long pull. 'We are,' he said. 'Didn't look good for a while. First convoy, when we weren't taking it from the subs, we were getting it from Soviet Backfire Bombers. Brass won't say so, but we were bait.'

'Bastards.'

'Yeah, the Backfires would come out of Russia, fly through the GIUK Gap. The air force out of Iceland would take out a few at a time on the way in and on the way back. But they got through. I watched a frigate take a couple of missiles and just explode.'

'All hands?'

'Yep.' Lauring drank. 'Off the Irish coast I saw them nab a merchantman. Damn ship blew up. You could actually see M-1 tanks flying through the air.'

'Hope it was worth it.'

Lauring shrugged. 'Second convoy run, Ivan hit us with a wolf-pack of subs about four days out of Le Havre. It was a running battle. Four boats we think. Got two of 'em. They got five of us.'

'Jesus.'

'We'd detect a sub, swarm it with choppers and bring in a frigate. They got the frigate we sent in, but the choppers put three fish in the water. We got him.'

'Got into Le Havre, unloaded in 12 hours, then turned right around and came back.' He finished off his beer. Without a word the bartender refilled it.

'Third convoy things were better. The Backfire threat was gone. I guess we made Ivan pay too heavily for those raids. Sub threat subsided. By then the Brits had thrown up a really good cordon along the GIUK Gap, subs, Nimrod anti-sub planes, surface action groups. The Brits were sinking a sub a day. Ivan tried to push some of their big boats through, but we know the Brits nabbed several of them.'

There was silence for a few moments.

The bartender said, 'There were a bunch of navy guys here three days ago. Carriers. Said something big was up. The carriers are gone now. And all the marines that were in town have disappeared.'

'Hey, loose lips…' Lauring admonished

'Give me a break,' the bartender said. 'You think the Ruskis ain't got people in NYC?'

'Probably right.' He sipped his beer. 'Hey, how do I know you're not a Ruski spy?'

The bartender started cursing in Italian. 'Born in Sicily, came here in '28. If I'm a Ruski spy, they've done a damn good job, ain't they?'

Lauring gave a non-committal shrug. 'We'll be shoving off…' he looked at his watch, 'in 41 hours.'

'So something big is up?'

'I wouldn't know. Just know my orders.'

A group of officers from another ship walked in and approached the bar, 'Excuse me.'

Indeed, Lauring knew something big was coming. His orders were to proceed North for a rendezvous off the Scottish coast. With whom and for what reason he did not know.

When the bartender was done with the new officers, Lauring said, 'Hey, got a phone I could use?'

'Sure.'

He reached down, grabbed a phone and put it on the bar. Lauring began dialing Cynthia to try to talk her one last time into coming up from Norfolk. He wasn't optimistic.

Faslane, Scotland

As HMS *Tenacious* put out to sea, Chief Torby guffawed.

Captain Lovelette took his attention away from the receding Scottish coast and looked at his chief.

'What's so funny?'

'I'm sorry, sir, it's just that Bernard Manning.'

'I don't like...that man.'

'Oh, come now, sir. He came down to the yard yesterday and put on a great show.' He guffawed again. In the dim light of the North Sea night, all Lovelette could see was the chief's unruly beard.

'I don't like his use of that word.'

'What, sir. Paki?'

'Yes.'

'Now, sir, Manning says his own neighbor is one and don't mind at all.'

In the dim light, Chief Torby couldn't see the captain's glare.

'I don't see any of those public school toff comedians coming down to entertain the lads....sir.'

Lovelette didn't respond.

'Excuse me, sir,' said the young ensign. He pointed to the headphones over his ears. 'XO says it's time to submerge.'

'Very well,' said Lovelette. 'Clear bridge.'

'Clear the bridge!' bellowed the chief.

When Lovelette got to the control room he gave the order, 'Take her down, XO. One hundred feet.'

'Yes, Captain.'

'I'll be in my quarters.'

Lovelette retired to his quarters by the control room. He removed his cap and placed it on the stateroom's tiny desk. Then he reached into his shirt and took out the key that he had hung around his neck. Lovelette opened up his safe and took out the orders from fleet. He opened and quickly read. No surprises. With the navy assembling a large amphibious task force in the Irish Sea, every man aboard *Tenacious* knew where they were headed.

Lovelette picked up his intercom and raised the control room. 'This is the captain,' he said. 'Give me the XO.'

A moment later, 'Griffin here.'

'Set course zero-five-five, speed ten knots, Mr. Griffin.'

'Yes, Captain.'

'I'm going to try to get some rest, XO. You have the control room.'

'Yes, sir.'

'And give the kid sometime in the control room,' said Lovelette, referring to *Tenacious'* young and enthusiastic ensign.'

'Yes, sir.'

Lovelette thought he heard the sound of dejection in his XO's voice. He replaced the receiver and lay on his bunk and kicked off his shoes. He had a pair of slippers he kept at the foot of the bunk in case he needed to get out in a hurry.

Lovelette sighed and closed his eyes. In three days at Faslane they had topped off the boat's stores and replaced her torpedoes. Lovelette smiled. In two patrols *Tenacious* had fired off twelve of her sixteen fish. The first in an aggressive patrol north of the GIUK Gap against the Soviet's attack boat assembly area, the second in the defense of Iceland. Chief Torby had already painted three submarine silhouettes on the boat's coning tower.

Come on, old boy, Lovelette said to himself. *Stop thinking shop.*

Then he laughed.

'Paki neighbor,' Lovelette said aloud. 'That is funny, isn't it?"

Tromso, Norway

The men at Tromso put on a brave face.

Admiral Romanov walked the paratrooper ranks, thinned out from the recent assault on Iceland. Weather beaten faces of stone looked back at him. Many had fresh scars. The casualties among the officers had been heavy. One company was led by a Lieutenant. A platoon was being commanded by a sergeant. When he finished walking the ranks, Romanov was given a quick tour of the fighter squadron stationed there. Here too the ranks were thinner. Three weeks of campaigning had cost them nine Mig-29s. The accompanying squadron of Mig-25s had lost seven. Pilot fatigue was severe. Behind the revetments smashed Norwegian aircraft, F-16s and P-3s had been bulldozed aside. Beside the junk pile was a graveyard for the Norwegian Air Force and Army personnel killed in the Soviet Spetznaz assault on the base.

The base commander gave Romanov a quick briefing on the squadrons there, but he wasn't really interested. Inspection of the air force and army personnel was his real purpose for the visit.

When Romanov asked about morale, the commander had replied, 'The men are proud and excited to be fulfilling their international duty. Morale is high.'

Romanov knew that was a lie but he pretended it was true. He didn't blame the commander for telling such a lie. The lie was convenient;, the truth could get him denounced. Later Romanov met with some of the surviving NCOs, informally on the tarmac before he boarded his plane. They were young men, not much older than the recruits they led in battle. The fight for Iceland had seemed to age them.

'Tell me, men,' Romanov began, 'did you have everything you needed on Iceland?'

The NCOs looked at each other, seemingly reluctant to speak.

'Come now, I am the commander of the Red Banner Northern Fleet. I will not even remember your names. You can, you must speak freely.'

A young man with his left hand bandaged finally said, 'I am sorry, Admiral. But air support was often lacking.'

Another sergeant nodded. 'Air support was hard to get, and often the Americans intercepted it before it even arrived.'

Said another, 'It seemed as if the Americans had air support whenever they needed it.'

Romanov nodded.

'And all the artillery they wanted,' said yet another.

'Do you feel that at any point you could have won the battle?' asked Romanov.

The sergeants shook their heads.

The first sergeant spoke again. 'Please do not misunderstand, Admiral. Our men fought like heroes. Our officers led us well.'

'Da,' added another. 'Many of our officers are not here.'

Romanov spoke with the sergeants for several more minutes, thanked them for their candor and then boarded his plane.

As the Tupolov took off, Romanov shook his head. After the first failed attack on Iceland; a combined amphibious-airborne assault that had cost the Northern Fleet most of its amphibious lift capability, Stavka had insisted on a second effort. He had warned Stavka that the Americans would have reinforced Iceland making a successful attack unlikely. Indeed, intelligence thought that the two Soviet airborne brigades dropped on Iceland had been met by at least a division of American marines. After a two-day fight on the northern coast, Romanov had ordered that the paratroopers be evacuated.

The Tupolov reached cruising altitude and headed northeast. Romanov had wanted to visit Andoya, a captured Norwegian airfield on the coast, but it had recently been visited by British Buccaneer Bombers, and his staff insisted it was too risky. So instead, the pilot turned for Polyarni, the great Soviet naval base on the Kola Peninsula. Romanov sat back in his chair and flipped through his evening briefing.

Acid welled up in Romanov's throat and he sent an aide for the last of his American antacid pills.

Three weeks of war have robbed you of your youthful vigor, Pavel, he thought to himself. *You wanted the job,* he admonished.

Romanov read. All of the half dozen captured Norwegian airfields were intact and operational. The squadrons there were another matter. Most were down to fifty percent strength. The bases themselves were subject to periodic, though ineffective harassment by Norwegian partisans, most likely the remains of the units that had garrisoned those bases. The center and south of the country, beyond the southernmost captured airfield of Bodo was doggedly held by the Norwegian Army and what was left of their air force.

The naval situation had stalemated. The *Kirov* and *Frunze* surface action groups were on station off Norway's Nord Capp. The defense minister had ordered him to preserve them at all costs. *What was the point*, he wondered, *of having capital ships like* Kirov *and* Frunze *if they weren't going to be committed to battle?* Get me those sub transit estimates,' said Romanov.

An aide handed him another folder. As he read the estimates, acid welled up again in his esophagus.

In the last week, eleven subs had been delegated for transit through the GIUK Gap. Northern Fleet knew for a fact that two were lost, and two had been turned back by persistent British anti-sub patrols. The other seven they didn't know but were presuming three got through and four lost.

'That's not enough,' he murmured as he downed the last of his American Pepto-Bismol. 'Those damn British Nimrods. So effective.'

Romanov gave a couple of light slaps to his chest and burped. An aide handed him another folder.

'Hmm,' he thought as he read, 'increased activity in the North Sea.... many contacts...unidentified....' *If NATO is gathering naval forces in the North Sea, that can mean only one thing.*

Romanov burped again.

Norwegian Sea

For forty-eight hours *USS Stirling* had been on station in Area Xavier with HMS *Exeter* of the Royal Navy, running rectangular search patterns ahead of the advancing task force.

On the bridge Lt. Commander Stewart pressed a button on the intercom. 'Captain Lauring to the bridge.' Stewart sipped coffee while he waited for the Captain. When Lauring arrived he wore pajama bottoms and a robe and his captain's hat. Tucked into his left pocket was a bottle of Nyquil. 'They're here, Captain.'

Stewart pointed to the radar.

Coming up from the Irish Sea was a line of blips about 40 nautical miles off *Stirling's* starboard aft. Stewart pointed, 'That's *Illustrious* there behind those two British destroyers.'

'Yeah,' Lauring nodded. 'And that's *Indomitable* ten nautical miles south...three, no... four more destroyers. And two assault ships.'

'Must be all of 3 Commando on the move.'

'Yes, Captain,' replied Stewart. 'Also plenty of air support. Four pairs of Tornado G4s overhead. Limey Phantoms too.'

'Impressive.' Lauring rubbed his face, picked up the phone, and rang up the radio room, let me have that message from CINCLANT.'

'Yes, sir.'

Lieutenant Conner came up from the radio shack, she saluted and handed the captain a message. As Lauring read the message he absentmindedly took the Nyquil out of his pocket, opened it and sipped.

STIRLING TO MANEUVER WITH HMS EXETER10-15 NM NW TASK FORCE 60MAINTAINING PORT FLANK.

SUBMARINE THREAT CONSIDERED SEVERE.

PROTECTION OF LANDING FORCE OVERRIDING CONSIDERATION.

COORDINATE WITH CAPTAIN, HMS EXETER AS NEEDED.

Lauring showed the order to his XO, 'What do you think, Stewart?' Stewart was staring at Conner, who tried hard not to notice. 'Stew?!'

'Thank you, Lieutenant,' Lauring said.

'Sir.'

The XO took the message and read. 'I think I'm tired of CINCLANT thinking Spruance destroyers are expendable.'

'Watch it, Stew,' Lauring said.

Stewart gritted his teeth and left the bridge. Lauring heard him punch a bulkhead.

Hope that helped, Lauring said sarcastically to himself. *He's been moody ever since we put out to sea.*

'Helm, begin working on search patterns.'

'Aye, aye, Captain.'

'Get me the latest situation report and threat estimates on the Norwegian Coast.'

'Aye, aye.'

'New Contacts,' Radar reported. 'Captain…look at this.'

Coming onto the readout were two battle-groups, big ones. 'Captain,' said the radar tech, 'That's *USS New Jersey*.'

'Yeah,' Lauring replied.

With word of the new contacts, Stewart came back to the bridge and looked at the sensor display like a kid in front of a Christmas tree.

'This one here,' Sonar pointed to the readout. 'That's *USS Nimitz*…'

Stewart said, 'Look, coming parallel.'

'Yes, said Lauring, '*USS Enterprise*.'

'And there's a another, sir,' said the tech. '*USS Eisenhower*.'

They watched the radar readout for some time, then yet another group emerged.

'Well lookie here,' Stewart said, 'Marine assault ships…'

'American Marines and Royal Marines,' Lauring said. 'Jesus.'

'Captain, this is the biggest amphibious operation since the Pacific War.'

Lauring looked north.

Comm reported, 'Signal from *HMS Exeter*, skipper.'

Lauring took the hand scrawled note.

CAPTAIN, PAUL BRYCE RN, HMS EXETER SENDS COMPLIMENTS.

Compliments, Lauring thought. *Maybe a dinner can be arranged.* After all, the Royal Navy allowed booze onboard….

Bardufoss Airbase, Norway

'I haven't felt warmth in a week,' Sgt. Clarke muttered to himself.

'Sorry?' his Norwegian counterpart, lying next to him said.

'Nothing,' Clarke replied. *You signed up for it, mate.*

Clarke trained his binoculars back on the target.

From the hill overlooking the airbase they were no more than half a mile away. The Norwegian revetments, occupied by Soviet aircraft the last two weeks, were below them. Through his binoculars, Clarke saw the last of the Soviet aircraft landing.

'I count eight Flankers,' Clarke said. 'And seven Sukhois.'

'So they lost three on that mission,' Sgt. Gudmundson said.

'Unless they landed somewhere else.'

Clarke had been jotting down the tail numbers in a small black notepad, later they would be transmitted via secure radio link to RAF Stornoway.

After a week in the field, Clarke had yet to fire a shot, the need for which he understood all too well. He had witnessed several incidents in which Norwegians, raised on semi-mythical stories of anti-Nazi resistance, had attacked the Soviets and been slaughtered. One group had struck a Soviet convoy, almost as if they were in *Red Dawn*. Clarke had watched as the Soviets simply turned their heavy machine guns on the attackers and mowed them down. Gudmundson had been disgusted. 'Idiots' he had remarked as the Soviet slaughtered his countrymen. A few scattered bands of Norwegian soldiers, the remnants of the regiment that had garrisoned Bardufoss, had managed to inflict some casualties. Clarke doubted the effort did any good.

'Aye, mate,' Clarke said. 'Looks like that's the last of them.'

'Think so,' Gudmundson agreed.

After waiting several minutes, no other jets landed. The pair made their way back to their hide, a clump of rocks beneath a stand of tall pines. Waiting there were three other SAS men and another member of the Norwegian Special Forces. There was no fire and only cold rations.

Clarke handed his notebook to his section radioman and said, 'Call it in. Terry'

'Right.'

Specialist Terry unpacked his secure satellite radio and relayed the report back to AUSTRALIA, SAS command. Clarke's team was call sign DINGO. Other groups were in Norway, he knew, with call signs like WALLABY and BOOMERANG he supposed.

Clarke sat down, his back up against a rock, closed his eyes and thought of Liverpool. He smirked. The weather wouldn't be much better there, this time of year, he thought. But there would be the pub, and Guinness, and Jenny. Well maybe not Jenny, who no doubt was going out with some other lad. Still…

'Sergeant,' it was Specialist Simon. 'I have people on the base of the hill.'

'People?'

'Aye. Norwegians, and they have guns. And they're headed this way.'

'Great,' Clarke said sarcastically. He looked at Gudmundson. 'What do you think?'

'I say we shoot them,' Simon said.

'Piss off, you,' Clarke said.

Gudmundson turned his binoculars on the two Norwegians coming up the hill.

'They are headed right here. Hmmmm,' he said. 'Those are hunting rifles.'

'Looking for food?' Clarke asked.

'We know the food situation is pretty bad, at least up in Tromso,' Gudmundson said. 'They will be here in a minute.'

Clarke pursed his lips in thought and said, 'bollocks! Right. Everyone behind the rocks. Gudmundson, you meet them.'

'Right.'

Gudmundson waved to the two men just as they reached the crest of the hill. One was old, a tall wiry man with a thin, beat up face. The man and Gudmundson spoke to each other in Norwegian. When he waved, Clarke stood up.

In English the old man said, 'Thank God, the British.' He elbowed the other man next to him, a boy really, by Clarke's reckoning. 'See Hans, I told you the British would come.'

Gudmundson said, 'This is Sven Venson and his grandson.'

'Yes,' Venson said. He stepped forward and extended his hand to Clarke, he shook it. His fingers were long and thin. To Clarke it was almost like gripping bone. His grip was like iron. Venson reminded Clarke of his granddad, a lifelong dock worker. Venson slapped Clarke on the back, 'It is good to see you British again. So good.'

'I'm sorry, sir?' Clarke said.

'Ah. I was in the Norwegian resistance in World War II. I worked with your MI-6. I have been coordinating resistance efforts in this area.'

'You mean you're the bloke that caused all this trouble?'

Venson scowled.

Simon finally spoke. 'Sergeant, we should shoot them both.'

Venson looked askance at Simon. Clarke knew that look. It was the same one his grandfather used to give him when he was a boy.

'Shut up,' he told Simon.

'We have to fight back,' Venson said.

Gudmundson replied. 'You are getting a lot of people killed.'

'And not doing much good,' Clarke added. 'What are you doing up here?'

'Hunting,' Venson said. 'I own this land. You are trespassing.'

Clarke lifted his eyebrows. 'Trespassing? You've compromised this whole team. What if Ivan catches you?'

'Oy,' Simon said. 'We already have 'ta move. And this was a good hide.'

'He is right,' Gudmundson said.

'Start packing up, lads,' Clarke said.

'I am sorry for that,' Gudmundson said.

Simon replied, 'Don't be sorry, mate. Just stay away from us.'

As the team packed up, Clarke said. 'I am sorry to be trespassing here, Mr. Venson. I won't tell you where we are going. But try not to wonder too much, right?'

Gudmundson nodded. 'I think it's also good if you stop attacking Ivan, you're just getting people killed.'

Venson said nothing.

Clarke and his team walked down the hill into the subarctic forest.

'Think he'll stop?' he asked Gudmundson.

'I do not know.'

Clarke thought of his granddad.

'I think I do.'

North Sea

'Run Ivan,' Lt. Commander Stewart said.

Lauring winced at the XO's enthusiasm.

Sensors reported, 'Contact making 25 knots, due north. Have a reading now, Captain. Sounds like a *Kilo*.'

'*Kilo*, huh?' said Lauring.

'Yes, sir.'

Lauring picked up the ship-to-ship receiver. 'We have a contact, probably Kilo.'

'Excellent, will pursue,' replied Captain Bryce.

They had learned the hard way that a Russian sub running, and making noise sometimes was trying to distract their attention. On *Stirling's* first convoy run, That trick had worked twice, costing the convoy a pair of *Perry*-Class Frigates. The *Kilo* kept running and didn't go quiet until a Navy Viking pounced on it, flooding a one kilometer square box with sono-buoys. Lauring listened in on the fleet radio net. After a few minutes the Viking pilot said, 'Contact acquired,' and dropped a fish in the water. Moments later the *Kilo* sped up again.

The ship-to-ship buzzed. Bryce said, 'Captain, bearing hard to port. Follow my lead.'

'Will do.'

Lauring gave the order.

As the two destroyers executed the maneuver, Stewart said, 'What if they fire on us or *Exeter?*'

'It's a risk. But they don't want us, they want the battle group to the south.'

They steamed west as the fight to catch the *Kilo* went on. The boat avoided two torpedoes from the Viking, then a pair of Sea Sprites joined the attack, bracketing the northern approach and forcing the *Kilo* west. *Exeter* steamed ahead five kilometers. For more than an hour nothing.

Lauring sat in his chair and sipped Gatorade. Finally, the Viking dropped a sono-buoy right on top of the *Kilo*. A torpedo followed. The Sea Sprites rushed to the target area as well and each dropped a torpedo.

Stewart watched on the sonar and said, 'She's not getting away this time.'

The ship to ship buzzed. 'Captain, faint contact, possible Delta boat.'

'We'll slow and listen for it.'

'Contact!' sonar said. 'Four kilometers, bearing three-three five, picking up speed. Ten knots…fifteen. Acquired.'

'Weapons, lock on.'

'Target acquired.'

As *Exeter* fired a torpedo, Lauring gave the order. 'ASROC, fire-one.'

The weapons tech pressed a button launching an ASROC torpedo. 'One fired, sir.'

'Twenty knots, now sir, running due north.'

'At this range, won't take long,' said Stewart.

Exeter's torpedo hit first, but didn't kill the Delta. A minute later *Stirling's* ASROC impacted with a tremendous explosion that sent a water geyser into the air visible a few kilometers away.

'Breaking up,' Sonar reported. 'Contact breaking up.'

'Yeah!' Stewart exclaimed with a fist pump.

Lauring glared at his XO. 'We just killed a hundred men, you know.'

Stewart looked back, 'So I...'

'Contact!' reported radar. 'Missiles, two, now four, now six. Bearing one zero three, range two twelve plus kilometers!'

'Targeted us?' Lauring asked.

'Negative...looks like the fleet.'

'Recover our helicopter.'

'Aye, aye.'

At that range the battle group had less than a minute to bring down the incoming missiles. One of the escorting Ticonderoga Class cruisers pumped missiles into the air, as did the two nearest frigates. Stewart watched the radar readout as oncoming blips merged with the incoming contacts. The last exploded within a few hundred yards of a frigate, showering it with fragments but doing no real damage.

Stewart said, 'Captain, might I suggest...'

'Yes. Make for the launch area, ten knots.'

He was about to signal *Exeter* when sonar reported, 'Contact, torpedoes in the water. Two contacts, now three. Range four kilometers, bearing one-seven-five. Torpedoes heading away from us.'

'Looks like we found the boat escorting the Delta,' said Stewart. 'Shall we divert?'

Lauring said. 'Helm, twenty knots.'

'Twenty knots, aye.'

'Captain, look,' sensors reported. To the west of the battle group, pickets reported a new contact, six missiles in the air, followed by another six.

Lauring shook his head, 'Too close, missiles are going to get through.'

Indeed, the western most picket, another *Spruance*Class, USS *Comte De Grasse*, took a pair of missiles aft. From *Stirling's* position they could see the growing smoke plumes.

'Contact!' reported sonar. 'Torpedo! Bearing One-Seven-five, course Three-five-five.'

'That's right toward us,' Lauring said, 'All ahead full. Right full rudder.'

'All ahead full.'

'Right full rudder, aye.'

Stirling's gas turbines spun to maximum capacity, accelerating her to 30 knots.

'Captain!' Stewart exclaimed.

'Contact! Sonar said, 'Bearing One-Five-Seven, range, four knots.'

'Vector our chopper to the target,' said Lauring. 'Type?'

'Unclear, Captain.'

'Torpedo still closing, Two kilometers.'

'Deploying counter measures.'

Weapons deployed a towed Nixie electronic noisemaker. The device activated and mimicked the noise generated by a ship.

'C'mon, Nixie,' Stewart said,.

There was no point in watching the incoming torpedo, so Lauring followed *Exeter's* attack. She fired a torpedo and increased speed to 20 knots.

'Torpedo has broken contact,' reported Sonar.

Stewart breathed, Lauring said, 'Helm, bring us up to 30 knots. Get us away from here.'

'30 knots, aye.'

'We'll lose the contact,' said Stewart.

'But we'll get away from whoever is firing torpedoes at us.'

To the west, *Stirling's* Sea Sprite hovered over the water, dipping its sonar into the ocean at the contacts last reported location. Despite several passes, neither *Exeter* nor the Sea Sprite could locate the attack boat. *Stirling* continued east. After five nautical miles east, northeast away from the attack boat, Lauring ordered. 'Helm, five knots. And let's listen.'

'Five knots, aye.'

Stirling slowed, sonar pinged away, but didn't reacquire the missile boat. They circled for twenty minutes and still found nothing.

'She's hiding,' Sonar said.

'If they don't make a move we won't find him,' said Lauring.

Over the battle-group net they heard reports of more torpedo contacts from the west. Minutes later *USS Thatch*, an Oliver Hazard Perry class frigate took a torpedo beneath the keel and broke in two.

'Jesus, trading Ivan one for one,' Stewart said.

A pair of Vikings sortied out from the fleet to look for the contact, joined by another frigate which steamed before a line of three anti-sub helicopters.

Task Force 60 was still ten nautical miles south of *Stirling*, it had slowed to five knots but had not halted or changed course.

'Contacts. Incoming bearing seven-zero. Backfire bombers.'

The fleet CAC diverted F-14 patrols to deal with the threat.

'Two groups, numbers undermined, now four...now six...'

Lauring and Stewart looked askance at one another.

'New contacts. Bearing one-five. Positively identified mixed group, Soviet fighters, fighter bombers. Twelve contacts....nineteen contacts....'

'Captain,' Stewart began. 'You get the feeling we're heading into an ambush?'

Lauring grunted.

Polyarni

A tray of tea and pastries accompanied the morning report. Admiral Romanov had only gotten a few hours of sleep. He tossed and turned with worry, which brought back the indigestion with renewed vigor. NATO had steamed into the Norwegian Sea quicker than the fleet had anticipated and before the entire submarine force had assembled off the Norwegian Coast. Three missile boats and their attack boat escorts were in transit when NATO had steamed into the battle zone designated by Romanov.

We were not ready he thought.

Even so, they had sunk at least two American ships, but contact had already been lost with two boats.

We cannot trade the Americans loss for loss, he thought. *Not at this stage in the war. And not when the Politburo has ordered me to divert missile boats to the Arctic.*

The Anglo-American naval group steaming north was massive, intelligence knew that. They thought there were at least two American and one British carrier. There were no doubt marine assault ships coming up behind the carriers. Up until that point the Americans hadn't sent their vaunted carriers into the Norwegian Sea. Romanov wouldn't have done so either. The risk from subs and Backfire Bombers was too great. But now the Americans didn't seem to care.

This is it, Romanov thought. *I think I understand what the Americans are trying to do.*

He looked over at his bookshelf. It contained the works of Lenin, and histories of the Red and Tsarist navies. The rest of the cabinet was occupied by history books on naval warfare, in English. Every volume of Samuel Elliot Morrison's naval history of the Second World War was there, as was Clay Blair's detailed study of the German U-Boat campaign. He had recently read and enjoyed John Costello's *Pacific War*. His eyes fell on the immensely important *The Influence of Sea Power Upon History*.

They're Mahanists, they believe in the big, decisive naval battle. Romanov shook his head. *Even their experience in the Pacific war has not shaken them of this notion. Rather one massive naval battle, the USN had destroyed the Japanese Navy through a series of engagements, each building upon the other, whittling the Japanese Navy down to nothing by 1945.* Romanov sighed.

But all the Americans remember is Midway.

Romanov pondered the map.

I could send my two battle groups south, but that would just be giving the Americans what they want. He pondered the map again. *Not yet. Let the subs and aircraft whittle them down. Then I'll send in my surface forces.*

He thought again about the order sending missile boats to the arctic. There was only one reason to do so. Romanov shook his head.

Norwegian Sea

Exeter burned. Lauring doubted she could be saved, but Captain Bryce was determined to try. He would have done the same thing, Lauring knew. Four nautical miles north of *Exeter*, *Stirling's* chopper dipped its sonar in the water once more. A line of sono-buoys trailed north to south. Stewart followed through his binoculars.

'Got him!' sensors reported. 'Bearing zero-five-three, speed nine knots….ten knots.'

'Class?'

'Working on it, skipper….Tango. It's a Tango class.'

Lauring picked up the phone. 'Weapons get me a firing solution.'

'Target acquired,' the weapons officer said.

'Fire.'

'ASROC away.'

To the north, the chopper dropped a torpedo in the water as well.

'No,' Lauring said to the Soviet attack boat that had already eluded them once. 'Not this time.'

Stirling's ASROC detonated beneath the Tango's keel, crippling the boat. It was already sinking when the chopper launched torpedo impacted. There was clapping on the bridge.

'That's two boats in two days, Captain,' Stewart said.

'Get back to work, Stew,' Lauring said. 'Recover chopper,' Lauring ordered.

He pondered the sonar readout. 'Helm, make zero-zero-zero and zig-zag, ten knots.'

'Aye, aye.'

'The missile boat that Tango was escorting is still out there. Let's see if we can find it.' Lauring said. 'You have the bridge. I'm going to doze on the wing.'

'Aye, aye, Captain.'

Lauring walked over to the bridge wing and lay on the cot he had placed there. He pulled a bottle of Nyquil out of his pocket and polished it off. Then Lauring pulled his cap over his eyes and tried to doze. He'd been up for twenty hours, a long time when one was making do with cat naps rather than sustained sleep. In that time the Task Force 60 had been fighting a running battle against Soviet subs, sinking two others besides the *Tango* sunk by *Stirling*. They had lost two more ships, a frigate and destroyer, besides the burning *Exeter*. Task Force 60 had aggressively deployed anti-sub helicopters and S-3 Vikings, driving Soviet subs away from the task force. In response, the Soviets had launched several sustained air attacks, shooting down a trio of helicopters and at least one Viking that Lauring knew of. Not an hour had gone by without Soviet aircraft from captured bases in Norway pressing Task Force 60's defenses. Stewart had no idea how the air battle was going, but all hell had broke lose when the dreaded Backfire Bombers had punched through and put two dozen missiles in the air. One of the task force's Ticonderogas had taken a hit but survived.

And still Task Force 60 steamed north.

Lauring ran his hands over his beard and sighed. *Get some sleep, idiot*, he thought to himself.

He had dozed off for only a few minutes when a sailor woke him. 'Sorry, Captain. Commander Stewart thought you'd want to know, *Exeter* is going down.'

Lauring rose from the cot and shuffled over to the bridge. From there he could clearly see the flaming ship slowly listing into the water by its starboard side. Lifeboats were out and a pair of helicopters were in the air already, recovering sailors.

'I hate watching ships go down,' Lauring said.

'Kind of hard to turn away though, isn't it?' Stewart said.

Lauring looked at his XO. 'You are a macabre bastard, aren't you?'

The phone squawked. It was the radio room. 'Message from fleet, sir,' said Lieutenant Conner.

'I'll be right over.'

When he arrived Lauring took the message and read:

STIRLING TO CONTINUE LEAD ANTI-SUB OPERATIONS.
WILL BE JOINED BUY USS THATCH PROCEED

CONGRATS, TWO SINKINGS.

'Well that's good of them.'

'Sorry, Captain?'

'Nothing.'

He handed the message back to Conner and went back to the bridge wing. After dozing for a few more minutes he was awakened by the air raid alarm. At the CIC the officer of the watch said, 'Looks like a big one, Captain. We have Soviet jets coming in from the north and east.'

'Any orders from task force?'

'Negative, Captain. Proceed North. Our own anti-sub pickets are coming in.'

Stewart pondered the sonar readout. 'Not surprising. Can't lose those Vikings to Soviet jets. Sprucans on the other hand….' He didn't complete the sentence. 'Very well. Make 20 knots. Let's get out ahead.'

'Aye, aye, Captain.'

'And get the chopper back up.'

'Aye.'

'In an air raid?'

Lauring smirked. 'Aviation ain't for the timid,' he said. 'Maybe we'll get lucky and catch Ivan trying to sneak forward under cover of this raid.'

Over the Kola Peninsula

'Damn fools,' said Romanov.

'I'm sorry, Admiral?'

Romanov was about to expound but the jet hit some turbulence. The cabin shook. Romanov waved his hand. 'Never mind.'

Under the escort of four Mig-27 Flankers, Romanov was flying down to Bodo to meet with commanders there. He doubted the escort was really necessary. At that very moment a squadron of Migs were screening half a dozen backfire bombers in yet another raid against the NATO task force with at least a dozen more aircraft flying various missions in central

Norway and off the coast. The Americans and British had their hands full. For the moment.

'You are going to use up our bombers!' the division commander had said when Romanov ordered another round of air strikes. *They are making preparations for nuclear war and using up our Backfires in the Norwegian sea.*

Romanov had let his old student rage at him for a few minutes before cutting him off and reiterating orders. 'Press your attacks,' Romanov told him 'and inflict losses.'

The admiral shook his head and went back to the morning action reports.

Stavka had tied his hands, Romanov knew. They were demanding bloody losses be inflicted upon NATO, especially the Americans. *And they will bleed us as well*, he thought.

General Davydov sat next to him. He was naval infantry, but Romanov liked having such men on his staff. One needed reminding that the purpose of controlling the seas was to control the land.

'May I ask how the reports seem, comrade Admiral?'

'We are inflicting losses.'

'This is good, no?'

'Da, but we are suffering as well. Several submarines have failed to reestablish contact.'

He held a sheaf of papers to Davydov, who took it and read.

'Tell me, General Davydov, are you familiar with the American's Guadalcanal campaign?'

'Admiral, I am naval infantry. Of course I am.'

'I mean, did you study the naval action?'

'Some.'

'It took the Americans a year to win the island from the Japanese. They fought not one major naval battle, but dozens of small and a few medium sized engagements.'

'Medium sized?'

Romanov held out his hand and wagged it. 'Perhaps a carrier or two.'

'Ah.'

'There were so many small naval battles, that the Americans came to call the sea around the Solomon Islands "Iron Bottom Sound."'

'I see.'

'The Americans bled the Japanese Navy white.'

'And you think this is what they are trying to do to us, Admiral?'

'I do.'

'Then would not the proper course of action be withdrawal?'

'I would do so, if Stavka would permit me.'

Davydov nodded his head in comprehension.

'So we fight and hope to bleed the Americans until they get tired and stop.'

'Will they?'

'Do you know their mind, General? I do not think so.'

Romanov leaned back in his seat and sighed. 'At least we have a dozen more missile boats and their escorts along the coast.' He burped as the indigestion welled up in his chest. 'I shall take a cat nap. Maybe our disposition will change by the time I wake.'

Norwegian Sea

A pair of S-3 Vikings had honed in on a Soviet missile boat, believed to be a Delta-IV and mercilessly dropped torpedo after torpedo into the water. It took five torpedoes, three of which impacted, to finally kill the sub. Stewart had cheered on the Vikings, while Lauring watched morbidly.

'Do you have to be so happy about it?' Lauring asked as one of *Eisenhower's* helicopters circled the area in search of debris and survivors.

'They're trying to kill us.'

Lauring shook his head in disgust. Seeing that his CO was pissed, Stewart said, 'I'm going down to the wardroom to get a sandwich.'

'Fine.'

'Maybe I'll check in on radio room.'

'Lieutenant Conner is off duty.'

'Interesting. She in her bunk?'

'Watch it, Stew.'

'Fuck you…sir.'

Stewart left the bridge.

Lauring walked out into the open air bridge to get some air. He watched the silhouette of ships behind *Stirling* and then spat into the choppy Norwegian Sea below. He yawned but knew not to bother to try to get some sleep. Lauring knew he couldn't. He was just too tired to go through the routine of trying to wind down and actually close his eyes, only to be woken a few minutes later.

A thousand yards to the fore *USS Reuben James* cut ahead of *Stirling* and zigzagged. He followed the ship for a few minutes until a steady drone overhead caught his attention. He looked up and saw a quartet of F-14 Tomcats flying north, northeast.

Must be another incoming raid, he thought.

Then another quartet raced overhead, then another and another.

Must be an entire squadron. Hmm They've never done that before. This is more than an air raid alert. *Something's up.*

Lauring pondered this for a few seconds. Then he heard over the PA 'Contact.' He went back to the bridge.

Bardufoss Airbase, Norway

'Well,' Clarke said, 'something sure as 'ell has Ivan spooked.'

'That's the last of their Flankers,' said Gudmundson.

'Aye,' Clarke said. 'Whole squadron is in the air.'

'They never do that unless they're attacking.'

'They ain't attacking,' Clarke said. 'Those pilots ran right out of their barracks into their jets, right? I saw enough RAF movies to know, that when pilots do that, they are the ones under attack.'

Simon called in the new report to AUSTRALIA. Clarke lay down against his Bergen and closed his eyes.

He didn't know how long he'd been asleep when the sonic booms woke him up.

Clarke scrambled from his sleeping bag 'Ay!' he said. He looked up into the fading day sky and saw several jets streaking east.

'Those are ours,' Gudmundson said.

'Norwegian?' Clarke asked as he cleared the sleep from his eyes.

'No, I mean our side. Look.' Gudmundson pointed to the sky. Clarke saw a pair of jets with large swept wings, and dual tails and engines. 'American F-14s. Two of them.'

Before Gudmundson finished the sentence, one was blown out of the air by a Soviet missile. The other banked hard left and climbed, leaving a trio of flares in its wake. Two more F-14s came into view from the east. They each unleashed a pair of missiles, which streaked across the sky, right over Bardufoss, and over the east slope of the mountain. Clarke could hear an explosion and then another. Then, several miles to the east in the direction of the missiles, they saw smoke plumes trailing down toward the ground.

Gudmundson turned his binoculars east and saw another jet.

'Look', he said to Clarke, 'running north, low off the slope, see it? The light is glinting off it.'

Clarke turned his own binoculars to where Gudmundson was pointing and saw a large jet, running north. The nearby F-14s fired another volley of missiles and peeled off to the west, their sonic booms tearing the air open. Clarke followed the missiles until they impacted near the jet. It spiraled and plowed into the mountain.

'No explosion?' Clarke asked.

'Flying low. Maybe the pilot survived and crash landed.'

'Whatever, mate,' he said. 'I'm gonna try to get some more sleep.' Clarke went back to his Bergen and leaned up against it. He took a Walkman out of his pocket and pressed play. Brian May's guitar riffs blocked out all other sound.

More F-14s came in. 'I think the American Navy is serious.' Gudmundson said.

But Clarke was already asleep.

Gudmundson trained his binoculars on the crash site, and could see the jet shimmering in the setting sun. *Wonder what that was*, he thought.

The White House

'Two issues this morning Mr. President,' Cheney began. 'First, we have completed the re-deployment of the 7th Light Division. One battalion is at Adak, another at Unalaska in addition to the two at Fairbanks and Anchorage.'

Much to the annoyance of Scowcroft, Cheney and General Powell, Sununu spoke. 'Ok, they've been redeployed. What about retaking Shemya, Kiska and Attu?'

Scowcroft looked over to General Powell, who answered. 'I'm afraid the 7th Light Division isn't equipped for an amphibious or airborne assault. We will need the 3rd Marine Division, possibly the 82nd Airborne for that.'

Cheney added, 'Plans are being drawn up.'

'Good,' the President said.

'But I don't believe that will be a good allocation of resources,' Cheney said.

Sununu glared at Cheney. 'Liberating American territory isn't a good allocation of resources?'

'Not at this time,' Cheney said.

'General Powell,' Bush asked, 'Do you agree?'

'I do, Mr. President.'

'I don't understand,' Sununu said. 'We have these resources, why don't we use them?'

Powell was annoyed but remained calm. 'These resources, as you say, Mr. Sununu are equipment and men. If they are to fight and die they should do so for an objective that will shorten the war.'

'Retaking those islands won't do that?' Sununu asked in a tone Powell didn't care for.

'I do not believe so.'

The president asked, 'The chiefs agree, General Powell?'

'Yes, Mr. President.'

Bush looked at Sununu, 'Then we wait, John. I will not micro-manage this war.'

'Now, Mr. President,' Cheney began. 'As to operations in the Norwegian Sea. There was heavy fighting last night. I'm happy to say it all went our way.' He extended a hand to Powell, 'General.'

'Yes, I must say I am pleased and optimistic, cautiously.' He held up his index finger with a note of caution. 'Last night the fleet began more aggressive operations into Soviet controlled air space. A major aerial battle ensued and we got the better of it. The fleet reports nineteen confirmed kills, mostly of Soviet front line aircraft.'

'Our losses?' Bush asked.

'Five Tomcats and one Hornet.'

The old navy flier winced at the losses.

'It is an excellent ratio,' Powell said. 'I'm sorry to say no pilots were recovered. We lost another destroyer last night, the *Comte de Grasse*, and the British lost one as well. In the air battle three of our anti-submarine helicopters were lost as were a quartet of Vikings. Right now we control the airspace above Task Force 60, and are contesting the space above Soviet occupied Norway. That is where the battle has shifted.'

'What did we do to the Soviet Navy?' Bush asked.

'We got one of their missile boats and one attack boat. I checked the reports before I came here, sir. There have been no new Soviet attacks on the fleet in the last six hours.'

'We can't have gotten all their subs,' the president said.

'No sir,' Powell replied. 'But the anti-submarine picket may be keeping them away from the fleet. Or perhaps the Soviets are regrouping. The battle is not over. Expect more losses I'm afraid.'

The president looked visibly pained. 'What next?'

'The amphibious groups are positioning themselves now, Mr. President.' Powell looked at his watch. 'In ten hours they will be poised to begin landing. Unless you give the order to hold back.'

'No,' Bush shook his head. 'I promised the Norwegian Prime Minister help. I gave him my word. I will see this through.'

Bardufoss Airbase, Norway

'I don't bloody believe this,' Simon said.

'What?' asked Clarke.

'Look down the slope,' he pointed.

Clarke took out his binoculars and pointed them down the slope. Coming up toward them were two men and a horse. A large object was tethered to the horse Indian style, and was being dragged up the hill.

'I'm going down there,' Clarke said, annoyed that they had been found.

'I am coming with you,' Gudmundson said.

The pair walked down the hill, weapons at the ready. As they approached, one of the men raised his hand. It was Venson.

'How the bloody hell did you find us?' Clarke asked.

'I have hunted these lands all my life,' Venson replied. 'Do you think you can hide yourself here? Do you think I will not see small changes in the land? Many Germans thought that in the last war. I killed them.'

Gudmundson said something in Norwegian. Venson replied in Norwegian, it sounded like cursing to Clarke.

'Well,' Clarke asked, 'What the hell do you want?'

'That plane crash yesterday. My grandson and I investigated. Look.'

Clarke walked over to the horse. It towed a stretcher. On it was a man. He was hogtied with a rag stuffed in his mouth. Clarke looked closely. 'Jesus Christ,' he said. 'That's a bleedin' admiral.'

They hurried back up the slope.

CHAPTER 2

RAF Stornoway, Scotland

On orders, SAS Headquarters at Hereford had been abandoned the night the war began. Indeed, two days later the Soviets bombed it with such ferocity that locals at first believed a nuclear exchange had begun. For four weeks, General Peter de la Billiere had made his headquarters at Stornoway, with a squadron there under his personal command and the other three SAS squadrons dispersed throughout the isles. B Squadron, of course was on mission in Soviet occupied Norway, relaying daily reports of Soviet air, sea and land movements. No team had been caught.

So far, he was satisfied. Information had been gathered by his SAS teams. Intelligence was gained, facts discerned. Right then facts about Soviet dispositions in occupied Norway were being passed on to the Anglo-American fleet fighting its way through the Norwegian Sea. As far as de la Billiere was concerned, the SAS was accomplishing its mission. This did not prevent Fleet Street from running gaudy covers featuring the spectacular SAS seizure of the Iranian Embassy in 1981 and asking, 'Where are the Commandos?'

Sitting in his makeshift office at Stornoway de la Billiere thought of that incident. 'Bloody Fleet Street,' he grumbled. 'Get all their ideas about Special Forces from movies…'

There was a knock on the door, 'General?'

It was his chief of operations, General Paul, an old colleague who had been with him in Aden and Oman. 'Interesting message from DINGO.'

De la Billiere looked up from his desk, 'Unscheduled? What do they want?'

'He says they have a prisoner.'

'A prisoner?' de la Billiere said. 'They bloody well know they're not supposed to have any contacts with the enemy.'

'Yes, sir, that is why I came to get you. DINGO says he has an admiral.'

De la Billiere raised his eyebrows at that. 'Alright, let's see about this.'

The two generals went over to the regiment's communications shack. A pair of card tables held several radios. Maps of Norway, Denmark and West Germany adorned the walls. Several antennas and a satellite dish had been attached to the roof. A pair of armed guards waited at the door. He entered without saluting.

'What's all this?' de la Billiere asked.

The officer of the watch said, 'Sir, ten minutes ago we were contacted by DINGO.'

'Unscheduled.'

'Yes. DINGO says there was an air battle over the target and the Americans shot down some kind of military passenger jet.'

'DINGO didn't investigate the crash did he?'

'No, sir. Some Norwegians did, though. They found a survivor and brought them to DINGO.'

'How on earth did they find DINGO?'

'I asked, General. DINGO says the Norwegian is an old hunter, resistance fighter from the Nazi occupation as well.'

De la Billiere nodded in understanding. During his time in the Middle East, he had met Bedouins quite capable of tracking SAS men and uncovering their best, most professional hides.

De la Billiere asked, 'And this Norwegian just brought DINGO a Soviet admiral?'

'Yes, sir.'

'Let me talk to him,' de la Billiere took the radio receiver.

'DINGO this is AUSTRALIA.'

'I have you, AUSTRALIA.'

'What's this about having a Soviet admiral?'

'Yes, AUSTRALIA, that is what I have. Come see for yourself.'

Modern soldiers were a bit less formal than de la Billiere cared for, he had to remind himself of that. 'What color is the uniform?'

'Dress uni, AUSTRALIA? It's blue.'

'What's this man's name, DINGO.'

'Don't know, AUSTRALIA. None of us speak Russian.'

De la Billiere clenched his jaw. 'Bloody hell,' he said.

'Excuse me, sir,' the watch officer said. 'I speak Russian.'

'Well damn all good that will do here.'

'Sir,' the watch officer said, 'Can't DINGO describe the letters?'

De la Billiere's eyes went wide. He handed him the receiver. 'Tell DINGO to do it now.'

After DINGO described the first three letters, de la Billiere knew who they had. 'Give me the receiver back.' He said. 'DINGO, you have Admiral Sergei Romanov, the commander of the Northern Fleet.'

'Bloody 'ell,' said DINGO.

'Yes, DINGO, my thoughts as well. I am going to give you back to the officer of the watch now. Excellent work, DINGO, excellent.'

'Thank you, AUSTRALIA.'

De la Billiere looked at the map. 'We have to interrogate him,' General Paul said. He looked at the map some more. An idea came into his head. After turning it over in his head for a few minutes, the idea became a plan. 'Let's head on over to Leeds and visit with 23 Reserve Regiment, shall we?'

Bodo, Norway

As Task Force 60 continued North, Task Force Rounders broke off from the main group and steamed east past the rocky islands fifteen miles off Bodo Cape. Clearing the skies above Bodo had proven to be a less arduous task than British planners had anticipated. After an air battle in which two American F-14s and an F-18 were exchanged for four Soviet Mig-29s the remaining Soviet aircraft at Bodo had flown off to the north, abandoning the air space to the Anglo-American Force. Even so the sky was patrolled by an entire squadron of Tomcats off of *USS Eisenhower*. As the flotilla advanced it was preceded by a screen of anti-sub helicopters and S-3 Vikings. Their search produced no contacts. A further screen of two British Type-42 destroyers also found nothing.

Standing on the Bridge of *HMS Illustrious*, Admiral Clapp observed distant Bodo through his binoculars. 'I just don't like it,' he said.

'I'm sorry, sir?' the officer of the deck asked.

'The Argentines gave us a much stiffer fight at the Falklands.'

The OOD thought back to the five ships lost in the last three days. 'Sir?'

'Oh, I don't mean the losses we've already incurred,' Clapp said. 'I mean as we approached the landing zones and after, we were beset by Argentine air attacks.'

'Yes, sir.'

He looked at Bodo again, two miles away.

'Perhaps I am just being overly cautious.'

'Yes sir,' said the OOD. 'Sir?'

'Yes?'

'The landing force, sir.'

'The order is given.'

'Sir.'

'Signal *New Jersey's* battle-group, landings underway.'

'Sir.'

And so the largest allied amphibious landing since the Normandy Invasion began.

From the Norwegian resistance in town they knew a reinforced battalion of Soviet Spetznaz was occupying Bodo. Naval infantry occupied the pair of small fishing villages further up the peninsula and positions even further north. As soon as the first wave of American and Royal Marines were ashore, *New Jersey* would turn her massive guns on suspected Soviet positions to the north.

New Jersey's nine 16 inch guns belched fire and hurled one ton projectiles toward Bodo's southern shore, blasting the sand and smashing the puny obstacles there. A British Harrier above relayed the results to *New Jersey*, whose gunnery officer adjusted fire as needed.

Admiral Clapp watched through his binoculars as the next volley smashed the beach. 'Remarkable gunnery. Just remarkable.'

The massive guns boomed again. Even inside the bridge of *Illustrious* they could hear the shells scream through the air toward the beach.

At the same time a formation of six British Harrier jump jets took off from *Illustrious'* deck. These buzzed the town of Bodo proper with the goal of scaring the Norwegians there. They also attacked targets of opportunity, catching a few Soviet BMPs and trucks in the streets.

New Jersey shifted its fire to the road leading out of Bodo, exploding airburst shells above as a deterrent to any Soviet forces that might attempt to enter the town.

South of Bodo Cape, 3 Commando's boats left their assault ships and made for the peninsula's south shore. Aboard were three companies of 40 Commando Battalion, many veterans of the Falkland's campaign. At the same time, the assault boats of the 2nd Marine Amphibious Assault Battalion put in the water and made for the peninsula's north shore. These were accompanied by the choppers of the 2nd Marine Recon Battalion who carried the marines to several points inside Bodo including the town square, the marina on the north edge of town, the city hall and the stadium.

Clapp saw tracer rounds reach up from the airbase at the approaching helicopters. Escorting Cobras swooped down and engaged the anti-aircraft guns. Something in the air exploded, Clapp couldn't tell what. The Marine choppers pressed on into the fire. Below the first wave of British landing boats reached the shore. Royal Marines spilled out of the holds and flopped down on the sand. They peppered the beach with small arms fire. No enemy fire returned. Within two minutes, the first company advanced and took the dunes. The second company advanced past the beach and broke into the Norwegian Air Force base. Here they encountered resistance from Soviet troops, who had taken positions atop and within Bodo's revetments.

On the north side of the peninsula the U.S. Marines hit the beach in two waves, the first securing the landing area, the second advancing inland. Within minutes, Marines had stormed onto the airstrip. Leaving one platoon to secure the beach, the rest of the battalion push north into the base. They encountered stiff resistance at the operations terminal at the center of the strip. By then the British had fought through from the south beach and linked up with the Americans. The tarmac was in NATO hands, though the maze of revetments south were not secure.

At this point, 3 Commando's second wave and 42 Commando Battalion came ashore and attacked Soviet positions within the myriad of aircraft revetments; a complex of hardened concrete bunkers dug into the ground. The Soviet's had prepared well, blasting firing slits through the walls and placing snipers and machine gun nests atop. The first attack on a revetment was met by a hail of fire and was bloodily repulsed, the lead squad was cut to pieces. From then on, the Royal Marines took on the Soviet positions one by one, laying down mortar fire and calling in American Cobra attack helicopters for support. Even so, it took the Royal Marines more than an hour to take the first revetment concentrated rocket fire from the Cobras who reduced it to rubble. Forty-two Commando's GOC hit upon the enterprising tactic of simply using rocket launchers to batter a hole through one side of the position and then sportingly offering the Soviets within the chance to surrender. Seeing what had happened to the first revetment, the Soviets inside the next two gave up. In this way 42 Commando Battalion secured the revetments.

By the time the sun reached the horizon, the airbase was in NATO hands, though there were Soviet holdouts in the line of trees on the south side of the base. When a British captain threatened to turn *New Jersey's* guns on them, the twenty or so Soviet paratroopers in the woods surrendered.

In the town of Bodo the Marines encountered stiff resistance, but it was localized as Soviet troops were scattered throughout. The Spetznaz had planned to contest every house, but once the battle began they found many people in Bodo had locked their doors, a few even fired on the Soviets as they tried to enter. With their plan thrown into chaos, Soviet troops retreated deeper into town, in many cases running right into Marines who had landed in the town square.

Admiral Clapp received the verbal reports from the GOCs of the American and Royal Marines and said, 'Very good. Consolidate the beachhead and make ready landings further up the peninsula. We'll press home the attack.'

The Kremlin

'What has happened?' Ligachev demanded.

Yazov said, 'The NATO fleet sailing through the Norwegian Sea landed troops at Bodo. We have lost contact with our forces there.'

'So we presume Bodo is no longer under our control?'

'Da.'

'What does this mean exactly for the war?'

Yazov said, 'NATO will be able to intercept our bombers long before they enter the Atlantic. They are of course poised for moves deeper into the Norwegian Sea and against our bases in Norway.' Yazov cleared his throat. 'Additionally NATO executed an airborne assault on our base at Andoya. We believe it was the Canadians. Here too, we have lost contact with our forces.'

Asked Kryuchkov, 'Should we not then, Comrade Secretary Yazov, be launching a counterattack against NATO forces around Bodo?'

The octogenarians around the table nodded.

'Da,' said Grishin. 'And reinforce Tromso.'

'Comrade Minister,' Yazov said. 'I have already ordered additional air units to Tromso. And arrangements are now being made for a Spetznaz brigade to be sent as well.'

Ligachev said. 'I want attacks on Bodo.'

Yazov interjected. 'It can be done, comrade secretary, but with Bodo already in their hands...'

'Do so, Minister Yazov.'

'Da, Comrade Secretary.'

'And we must recall Admiral Romanov.'

There were more nods .

'Comrade, Secretary,' Yazov said, 'I am afraid Admiral Romanov is missing.'

'Missing?'

'Yes, we believe his plane was shot down.'

'Then who is in command?'

'His deputy is already in command.'

Ligachev said, 'I do not understand how this has come to happen. Why did Romanov not commit greater force to the defense of Bodo?'

Yazov said, 'I was not privy to the admiral's thinking, comrade secretary. Minister Sokolov before his...' Yazov searched for the appropriate word, 'demise,' he cleared his throat, 'left no orders saying to the effect that Romanov felt Bodo was vulnerable and therefore expendable and seems to have favored an inner ring of defenses around Tromso closer to our own bases on the Kola Peninsula.'

Ligachev thought of the gathering NATO strength in West Germany. We must hold on to NATO territory,' he said. Bodo must be held and defended.'

'Da.'

'Our own surface forces,' Ligachev asked. 'What is their current location?'

'General Romanov positioned them just South of the Polar Ice Cap off of Nord Capp.'

'Two battle cruisers and two carriers?' Ligachev asked.

'Da, Comrade Secretary. I believe he was saving them for a crisis.'

'The crisis is here.'

'Da.'

'Move them south at once.'

'Da.'

Bodo, Norway

The Soviet aerial attacks began just after sunrise. The USN had maintained its F-14 CAP. But they had underestimated the ferocity of the Soviet effort, and two different raids had been able to fight through the F-14s and launch standoff missile attacks on Task Force Rounders. The first launch had been stopped by the task force's Ticonderoga cruiser and ship's point defenses. The second effort had been more successful, scoring a hit upon and sinking *HMS Glasgow a*nd annihilating one of the cargo-container vessels in a spectacular explosion which showered the fjord with debris. *USS New Jersey* had taken a hit as well, but the old armored dreadnought had seemingly yawned at the missile hit and suffered no damage more serious than shattered bridge windows and scorch marks on the fore.

Admiral Clapp sipped his morning tea and watched the smoke from the mountains above Bodo. Soviet forces there were resisting 3 Commando's push. He was summoned to *Illustrious'* radio room.

Through the ship's PA system the CAC announced, 'Incoming contacts...Incoming contacts.'

Alarm claxons sounded throughout the ship.

It would be the job of *Illustrious'* skipper to fight the ship in the CIC, so Clapp simply went back to the bridge.

Below him, the deck crew scrambled to get the ship's Harriers in the air. Above F-14s streamed north toward the incoming Soviet aircraft.

'Three-one contacts,' radar reported. 'At least twelve Backfires.'

A big one, Clapp thought. He did some quick arithmetic in his head. Twelve aircraft times ten missiles each...

'Second contacts,' radar reported. 'Twelve Backfires.'

Clapp clutched a clenched fist to his mouth as more F-14s roared overhead.

They mean it this time, he thought.

Within minutes the Backfires were in range. The bridge morbidly reported the bevy of new contacts, Soviet missiles heading for the task force.

Right away *USS Chosin* fired SAMs into the air, one after another the small escort ships launched SAMS as well, creating a zigzag of missile contrails over Bodo. Clapp saw some explosions in the air over the peninsula and then flashes of light in the bay as the ship's point defenses went to work. The Gatling guns on *Illustrious* fired, spitting out bullets at incoming targets. Clapp saw something explode over the water. The flight deck was showered with debris and he could actually see a man there get shredded to bits. The guns kept firing, a second burst over the water then a third. This time the bridge's windows shattered, Clapp was knocked to the deck . He was just wondering if he was hurt when a missile slammed into *Illustrious'* bow. He never felt the other missile, which cracked the carrier in two...

Vauxhall, London

Sitting in his office, over morning tea, Sir Colin read assessments from his various field commands discussing topics as wide ranging as estimates on Soviet forces in Eastern Europe, to Soviet grain production models, to reports from field agents behind enemy lines. He was taking the most interest in these. Agents were reporting extreme disillusionment in the Warsaw Pact countries, especially Poland, which was no surprise. Sir Colin wondered absentmindedly if the bourgeoning NATO air campaign against Soviet supply lines there would harden Polish resolve against the west. He quickly dismissed the notion. The Poles hated the Soviets. They were no doubt cheering as American aircraft pummeled their own nation.

He finally came to an emergency brief from the SAS, received just that morning.

'I don't believe this for a moment,' Sir Colin said. He sipped his tea. 'A Soviet admiral. They're daft over there at Hereford...Stornoway.'

Still, he thought.

He picked up his phone and buzzed his secretary. 'Won't you please ring SAS headquarters?'

'Certainly, Sir Colin,' his matronly secretary replied.

'General de la Billiere,' said the MI-6 director, 'this report of yours is fantastic. The Soviets have tricked you.'

'Now, Sir Colin, why would you say such a thing?'

'A Soviet admiral, General, the commander of their Northern Fleet no less, just happens to fall into your lap. It's too fantastic to believe.'

'Sir, Colin,' began de la Billiere, 'didn't Rudolph Hesse just fall into our laps?'

For a moment, Sir Colin had nothing to say. Then, 'Can you get him out? I'd rather not risk sending one of my men into Norway.'

'Not at this time, we have a major battle developing and I don't want to risk losing him to Soviet aircraft.'

'Good point.'

'Could you get someone in?'

Sir Colin thought for a moment. 'Are you saying you can't risk getting the admiral out but you are willing to risk getting one of my men in?'

'Well, when you put it that way.'

'Relax, General, I agree with you.'

'Ah, good.'

'I have just the man, an old interrogator of mine.'

RAF Stornoway

The makeshift office was filled with SAS, RAF, and RN officers. On the table before them were maps of the Norwegian Sea, Northern Norway, and Bardufoss.

General de la Billiere looked at the assembled commanders.

'Give me your plan.'

'Sir,' said Lt. Colonel Dawson, SAS Reserve, '*HMS Tenacious* to cruise from station northwest of fleet to coastal Norway. One section Tornado bombers escorted by one section Tornado G4s to fly from Stornoway and attack targets around Bordufuss. *HMS Tenacious* then launches Tomahawk missile strike on same. Air element to land at Andoya and refuel before returning to Stornoway. A Squadron, 21 SAS

Regiment then makes freefall drop on Bordufuss, secures objective and makes contact with DINGO.'

De la Billiere looked at Dawson. 'Your thoughts?'

'We can do it, sir.'

The General looked to the assembled RAF and RN officers. 'You all agree?'

The RN liaison stepped forward and said, 'It's a bit short notice, General. I know *Tenacious*' skipper. I washed out of Perisher and he didn't. Captain Lovelette can get there.'

'He can?'

'Yes.' The RN officer looked at his watch. 'He should be coming up for his daily messages within 45 minutes. So we need a decision.'

'RAF?' the General asked.

'Aircraft available. We have transports and refueling aircraft available too.'

De la Billiere looked at his chief of staff. 'You have heard from MI-6?'

'Yes, General. They are flying a man up from London. They say he's very good.'

General de la Billiere furrowed his brow.

'General,' the chief of staff said, 'Should we not bring the Americans in on this?'

'No,' de la Billiere said. 'This involves no American assets and will take nothing away from operations in the Norwegian Sea.'

There was a low murmur, all had seen the images of the shattered *Illustrious* on the news.

'Besides, the Americans are too prone to leaks.'

There were nods of agreement.

The RN officer pressed. 'General, I will need to begin encoding the message to *Tenacious*. We need a decision.'

De la Billiere looked at the map. 'Do it.'

HMS Tenacious

Chief Torby was not to be dissuaded from completing the Bernard Manning bit. '...So after the third time Hymie goes to synagogue and begs God to let him win the lottery, God finally says,' Chief Torby cleared his throat, 'Hymie, meet me halfway. Buy a ticket!'

Chief Torby's laughter filled the wardroom.

Lovelette sipped his whisky and tried to change the subject. 'There is one thing I will never understand about the American Navy, their no alcohol policy.'

Sitting across the table in the wardroom the chief laughed and took a pull off his mug of beer. 'Yes, sir,' he said.

Chief Torby began a diatribe about the inadequacies of the USN. He went on at length creatively questioning their mettle, ancestry and sexual orientation. For his part, Lovelette had nothing against the USN, especially their surface forces, but he felt their own submariners were far too cautious.

Lovelette listened as the control room operations were relayed over the PA. 'Depth, 50 feet....40...'

'Stop at thirty,' the chief said under his breath.

'All stop,' the ensign said over the PA.

'That's a good boy,' the chief said.

'Now, now, Chief,' Lovelette said. 'Be kind to Ensign Bobrick.'

'Be kind, sir?' the chief asked. 'You put a child in charge of the boat... sir.'

'He can do it.'

The chief looked skeptically at the skipper, said nothing, and sipped his beer.

'He did plot that extraordinary firing solution, Chief.'

Over the PA, 'Deploy cable.'

Lovelette sipped his whisky and smiled with pride at that one.

They had been cruising maybe one hundred miles off Iceland's east coast. Sonar had picked up a faint signal. It had reminded the boat's weapons officer of a Soviet boat he had been involved in tracking a few years ago on *HMS Trenchant*. That boat had been a big missile sub, and this contact sounded exactly like that one. Based on this, Lovelette had acted decisively and ordered two torpedoes fired. One located the target and hit, revealing a Soviet Sierra III. Two torpedoes later, the sub was destroyed.

'That was our third kill, chief.'

'We got two other of Ivan's boats without the wunderkind up there,' with a shoulder he indicated the control room, 'performing magic tricks.'

Over the PA, 'Reel in cable.'

'Ah, so that's it then?' Lovelette said.

'Sorry, sir.'

The captain breezily waved his hand about. 'You don't like Bobrick because he's young, ambitious, and coming up fast.'

The chief said, 'He can go through channels and procedures like the rest of the navy, Captain.'

Lovelette laughed.

Over the PA, 'Captain to the communications room.'

'Excuse me.'

Lovelette walked forward to the communications room, passing various ratings at their stations. He nodded to them, patting a few on the shoulder as he went, and noting the enthusiasm with which the crew was growing their beards. Young Bobrick bristled at the lax discipline, but it was fine with Lovelette. Chief Torby mostly scoffed at the young swabbies, many of whom could not yet grow a beard.

At the communications room, Ensign Bobrick handed Lovelette the message print out.

'Well this is all good,' Lovelette said.

He went up to the control room. 'Helm, steer course…' he quickly consulted a chart. 'Eight Zero. Ten knots.'

'Ten knots, Captain? Isn't that a bit fast?'

'Yes, but we have a new target and have less than twenty- four hours to get there.'

'Sir.'

'Ensign Bobrick!'

Bobrick came over from the control room.

'Begin working on Tomahawk firing solutions for the target noted here.' He handed Bobrick the message.

'Yes, sir.'

Bardufoss Airbase, Norway

'What's happening?' Gudmundson asked.

'Don't know,' Clarke replied. 'They told me to take cover and, get this, to be prepared to make contact with friendly forces.'

'So they are coming?'

Clarke shrugged. 'Sounds like it.' He said. 'Call sign VIKING .'

'Well who are they?'

'They didn't say, boyo.'

A few minutes later Bardufoss' air raid sirens blared. From their perch above, the team saw Soviet troops running to and fro across the base. Before anyone was in position, there was an explosion within.

'They just destroyed that radar dish,' Gudmundson said, 'And...'

Before he could finish there was a second explosion at the edge of the runway. 'They got one of the mobile SAMs,' Gudmundson said.

There was another explosion, then another, all before any of the Soviet SAMs even had a chance to fire. By then Soviet crews had gotten to the AAA batteries around the airstrip and were pointlessly firing, filling the air above them with a half dozen streams of tracers.

'Any SAMs left?' Clarke asked as he scanned the base through his binoculars.

'I do not think so,' Gudmundson said. 'In fact...'

There was another explosion, this time over the base buildings, a large burst in the air which showered everyone below with shrapnel. A second missile came in and impacted at the base of one of the long barracks, blowing a massive hole near the middle and setting the remainder of the building on fire. Another missile followed, and then another.

'Tomahawks?' Gudmundson asked.

'I think so.'

Another explosion amongst the buildings, followed by another and then another, each sending fireballs into the sky. Nearly a minute passed without an explosion. By then even the AAA batteries had ceased firing.

'Hear that?' Clarke asked.

'No?'

'Listen.'

High up in the air they heard propellers.

'What is that?' Gudmundson asked.

'Sounds like a C-130. We use them and…'

They saw shapes falling from the sky. Clarke knew what they were. Even though he knew better, he thought they would slam into the ground. Instead, a thousand feet above the runway shoots opened. The sky was full of them.

'Jaysus!' Simon exclaimed. 'That must be an entire squadron!'

Clarke hooted. Simon shouted down to the base, 'Who dares wins! You Soviet fuckers!'

One of the AAA guns opened up again. Clarke winced as he saw one of the chutes fold in on itself and fall to the ground. Another was cut in half and Clarke could actually see a figure plunging to the tarmac.

'God damn it!' he shouted.

He located the gun, and the edge of the strip, just below their position.

'Simon!' Clarke shouted. 'Your grenade launcher.'

'Already on it.' Simon ran back to his pack and took out his grenade launcher. He inserted a round and quickly judged the distance to the AAA battery.

'Can just reach it,' he said.

He held the launcher aloft and fired a round. It arced through the air and impact about 20 meters before the gun.

The firing stopped.

'I can get 'em,' he said.

He loaded another round, fired and landed this one just five meters away.

'That oughta get 'em,' Simon exclaimed.

By then at least two dozen SAS troopers were on the ground, dropping their chutes, and un-shouldering their weapons. They hit the ground and lay down fire as more of their comrades parachuted in. A trooper stood up and waved, several more stood up with him, they all ran toward the terminal firing their .203s as they went. The leader went down, the rest hit the tarmac and tossed grenades, then they got up and advanced off the tarmac, disappearing from Clarke's view. When the rest of the squadron was on the ground they followed, except for one section which went south forming a skirmish line there and firing into the tree line to their front.

The SAS troopers established a cordon around the field. The firing from within the base peeked and then tapered off. Finally, the radio spoke.

'DINGO, DINGO, this is VIKING, over.'

Simon replied. 'VIKING this is DINGO.'

'Please reveal location.'

Simon looked at Clarke who nodded approval.

'We're atop the hill south of the airfield. Will pop purple smoke, VIKING, over.'

'Roger, DINGO.'

Clarke reached into his pack and popped a canister of purple smoke. He waved it around then threw it down the hill.

'We see the smoke, DINGO. Stay there, we'll come to you.'

'Will do, VIKING.'

'And prepare your friend. We have someone who wants to talk to him.'

CHAPTER 3

Washington D.C.

Since the war began, Bull Feathers had remained open 24 hours a day. Located down the street from the Cannon House Office Building, the owner felt it was his patriotic duty to remain open so congressional staff had a place to unwind after Congress' marathon sessions. Besides, he was making a small fortune.

The time approached midnight as the Vice President's chief of staff sat down at a table in the back corner, far away from the chattering young congressional staffers. The chief watched in amusement. Young people dropped shot glasses into beer classes and chugged. One young man did a Jell-O shot from between the breasts of a young woman, the pair shouted 'bipartisanship!' and high fived. The chief wasn't surprised by the display. His colleagues at the District's major universities, George Washington and Georgetown, reported that students were skipping class, ignoring course work and generally enjoying themselves. A certain fatalism had set in amongst the young, he had noticed, a consequence he supposed of being raised on tales of nuclear Armageddon. He wondered what he would do if he was twenty years old.

The chief finally saw the rest of his party. The undersecretary of defense walked past the gaggle of young drunks and sat down. The two shook hands.

'Bill,' the undersecretary said, 'Thanks for meeting me here.'

'Not at all, Paul,' Bill replied. He pointed to his drink, 'Want one?'

'Sure.'

Paul flagged down a waitress and ordered a whisky.

Bill nodded to the young people at the bar and said, 'You think they know something we don't?'

Paul smirked, 'I think they're acting like young people.'

Bill shook his head. 'The whole city is paralyzed. Those who haven't left town stay indoors. It took me ten minutes to get here from my house in Northern Virginia.'

'I think those kids,' Paul nodded to the bar again, 'are using this as an excuse.'

Bill sipped his drink and shook his head. 'I think if you had seen movies like *The Day After* as a kid, you might be fatalistic about the war.'

'Eh. I saw *On the Beach* as a kid.' Paul sipped his drink. 'Business?'

'Business,' Bill agreed.

'Tell me, what does your boss think about the war?'

'He doesn't,' said Bill. 'The vice president is grateful that the president has found a role for him.'

'I think inviting him to the NSA meetings is the right thing,' Paul said. 'I know the president insisted, in case something happens to him, he wants Quayle up to speed.'

Bill nodded.

'Let me ask you, what does the vice president think should happen next?'

Bill laughed. 'So that's what this is about.'

Paul nodded.

'The vice president is not in the policy loop and he hasn't expressed one way or the other what he thinks should happen next.'

'Do you know what transpired at the meeting at St. John's last week?'

'No.'

'Thatcher wants to invade Eastern Europe.'

'Jesus.'

'So does Kohl.'

'They're serious?' Bill asked.

Paul nodded.

'What does the president think?'

'He's cautious as you know.'

'Is that bad?'

'I didn't say it was bad. Just that he is cautious.'

'What do you think?'

'Think about this, Bill. Thatcher made this point at St. John's. What if the war stops, the Soviets recoup, and we have to do this all over again?'

'Mmmmm,' Bill said in thought.

'What if it's like 1918 and the Soviet Army feels it's been stabbed in the back?'

'I see where you're headed.'

'Now think about this, and I think you'll agree. What if we win the war decisively? What if we took away the Soviet's ability to wage war on the west?'

'You mean, what if we free Eastern Europe?'

Paul nodded.

For a moment, Bill imagined the possibilities.

'We can go even further, I think.'

Bardufoss Airbase, Norway

Admiral Romanov had received excellent medical care, his leg had been put in a cast and the open wound on his shoulder had been stitched. In the last twelve hours he had been given two doses of antibiotics to fight an infection and fed two meals. All in all he was doing pretty well considering. Frankly, the most disconcerting part of the last twelve hours was the quiet. He had hoped that after losing the airfield, his subordinates would have ordered a raid on Bardufoss. But so far nothing. All he had heard was the sound of jets landing. Romanov wondered what was happening. His captors had been pleasant enough, though distant. They were British, Romanov had realized, no doubt members of their dreaded SAS. Romanov's only complaint was that he had sat on a cot with nothing to do.

That ended when the door opened and in walked a average looking man with a trim beard and expensive suit, dark blue with a light blue shirt and blue tie. His hair was immaculate.

'Admiral Romanov?' he asked in perfect Queen's English.

Romanov nodded.

'My name is Ingham. I'm with…a government agency.' He smiled quaintly.

'You are MI-6? MI-5?'

'I prefer not to say, Admiral.' Ingham looked around. 'Would you agree that you have been well treated?'

'I would,' Romanov replied.

Good, 'I'm so glad,' Ingham said. 'Now, you are the commander of the Soviet Northern Fleet.'

Romanov said nothing.

'Admiral, silence will do you no good.' Ingham reached into his pocket and took out a small envelope. 'I have your photograph right here. You are the commander of the Soviet Northern Fleet.'

'Then why do you need me to acknowledge that?'

'Because I would like to get you into the habit of answering my questions.'

'By yourself? Romanov asked. 'No guards?'

'Admiral, let me assure you, I could kill you with my bare hands any-time I wish.'

'I see.'

'You are going nowhere unless it is my wish. Do you understand?'

'I do.'

'Now, I will pay you the respect of being blunt. You *will* tell me what I want to know.'

'Do you think we do not train our personnel in resisting torture?'

Ingham smiled ever so slightly. 'Admiral,' he began. 'You are in a posi-tion few of us are ever in. What happens next is entirely up to you. You have complete control. In the end I will find out everything I want, the only question is time. How much time will it take?'

Romanov said nothing.

Ingham began pacing the room. 'I suppose we all have notions about duty, torture. We all like to think we can resist. You, Admiral, are experienced enough to know better.'

Romanov said nothing.

'Will you give me the information I require?'

Romanov shook his head.

'Well then,' Ingham said as he reached into his pocket and took out a pair of leather gloves. 'We had better begin. Up with you now.'

Norwegian Sea

Lauring read the decoded message from the radio-room. 'Proceed... north....northwest...ten knots...be prepared...to rescue...downed flyers Pass that along to the helicopter crews.'

'I ain't no messenger,' Stewart said.

Lauring raised an eyebrow.

Stewart reluctantly left the bridge and headed down to the hangar. Lauring sat down in the captain's chair and breathed. *I can't stand being around him lately*, Lauring thought. *Must be all his cracks about the Soviets.* He took a bottle of Nyquil out of his pocket and swigged.

Lauring looked behind him to the east; he could just barely make out the silhouettes of *Nimitz*, *Eisenhower* and *Enterprise*. Just beyond them was a haze of smoke from the wrecks of the *Saipan* and *Illustrious*. Lauring winced. He got up from the chair and meandered throughout the bridge, looking over the shoulders of the sailors there. Then he left the OOD in charge and wandered around the ship, exchanging brief pleasantries with the crew

Tired but content, he thought, *I wonder if...*

His thoughts were interrupted by the klaxon. 'General quarters, general quarters.'

Lauring trotted to radar shack. 'What you got?' he asked.

'Incoming,' said the OOD. 'Incoming aircraft. A lot of them.'

Overhead he could hear Navy F-14s.

'Headed west, sir,' the OOD said . 'Soviet aircraft are to the northwest.'

Stewart said, 'Looks like we found the Soviet surface fleet.'

The Pentagon

During the opening days of the war, when the American Army had been engaged in a massive battle with the Soviets for Fulda Gap, Cheney had found it excruciating to follow battles blow by blow as messages came in. So as the next stage in the Battle of the Norwegian Sea unfolded, rather than wait for reports he met with General Powell. There were plenty of officials Cheney preferred to meet with across the desk, but not General Powell. The two had worked well together since taking office and had even come to like one another personally. Instead, the two sat in a pair of cushioned chairs in the corner. A pot of coffee lay on the small table between them. Feeling at ease, Cheney sat back in his chair.

'General, I've asked you here because I want to know your thoughts about the proposal my under secretary for policy has been circulating throughout the department.'

'I haven't seen anything specific. However, it is my understanding that he is backing Prime Minister Thatcher's idea of attacking Eastern Europe.'

'He is,' Cheney said.

Powell considered his words and said, 'My thoughts are these. First, I do not necessary agree that peace now will lead to further war.'

'Ok.'

'That said, if we were to attack Eastern Europe, this could not solely be an American effort.'

Cheney shook his head. 'No, but let me ask you this. Do we have sufficient force?'

'I spoke with SACEUR this morning. He held III Corps in reserve until the Weser River counterattack. They are relatively unscathed. Also, XI Corps is assembling now on the east bank of the Rhine. They incurred losses coming across the Atlantic, but all units are intact.'

'Hmmmm…' Cheney said, 'Five national guard divisions.'

'Plus three supporting brigades. Call it six plus. About 100,000 men.'

Cheney said, 'I'm not sure the public will like the National Guard being used to liberate Eastern Europe.'

'Which is why I would insist on a NATO force.'

'What do you have in mind?'

'Three and XI Corps, with a third corps of European troops. '

Cheney nodded. 'And this National Guard issue?'

'We are fighting a war. If the public wants to take that war to Eastern Europe it will feel the pain of that decision.'

Cheney nodded again. He said. 'The British are serious about this. I talked to Heseltine this morning about some of their MOD's ideas. I'd like you to speak with your counterpart over there.'

'I will.'

'I would ask you, General, one more question. Will you recommend to the president that we attack Eastern Europe?'

'It's not for me to say. I will make one recommendation though.'

'Yes?'

'We invade eastern Europe with sufficient force to get the job done. No half measures. We go. We win.'

Norwegian Sea

'Where the hell did those missiles come from?' Lauring asked.

Through his binoculars, Stewart followed the contrail from the dawn sky to the sea. 'Looks like….the coast, somewhere north of Bodo.'

Sensors reported, 'Contacts bound for Task Force 60.'

Lauring breathed. Eight surface missiles would most likely have overwhelmed *Stirling's* defenses.

For half an hour Lauring had watched the aerial dogfight unfold overhead. Gradually it had trailed west, northwest, toward the approaching Soviet fleet. The Soviets had air attacks from their carriers to the northwest with backfire raids from bases off the Kola Peninsula.

'Captain, unidentified surface contact,' Sensors reported.

'Surface contact? Where?' Stewart asked.

'Bearing, zero eight zero, course two seven zero, speed two-five-knots.'

'What the hell?' Stewart said.

'Must have been hiding in the fjords,' Sensors said.

'Must be the ship that fired those missiles,' Stewart said.

Before he got an answer Sensors reported, 'Wreckage on radar,' Sensors reported. 'Two miles east, northeast.'

Above, Lauring heard sonic booms, and then an explosion.

'Someone just got shot down,' the OOD said.

'I think it's another one of theirs,' said Stewart.

'Look out to bridge, parachute spotted, make three thousand plus yards.'

'Very well,' Lauring said. 'We'll keep the choppers in the hangar, at least while we have Migs in the air. 'Helm, make for that parachute, ten knots.'

'Ten knots, aye!'

'Identify that contact, Sensors.'

'Yes, *Captain*!' Sensors replied with a bit of annoyance.

Stewart stepped out to the bridge wing and trained his binoculars east. He couldn't see anything but the outline of the Norwegian Coast. South he couldn't see Task Force 60, but he could make out smoke plumes, the results of several Soviet missile hits. Stewart knew that the damage could have been much worse.

'Contact identified, Soviet Kashin-Class destroyer. Further contacts, Fast attack craft, Soviet Vita class.'

'They're making a play for our downed pilots,' said Stewart.

'Alright. Comm, inform task force of these new contacts.' Lauring thought for a moment. 'What's the distance to the parachute?'

'Uhhhh, about twenty-two hundred yards.'

'Ok. Chief, we'll get a Zodiac boat in the water to recover the pilot.'

'Aye, aye, Captain.'

Lauring picked up the intercom. 'XO to the bridge.'

When Stewart arrived Lauring said, 'Mr. Stewart you have the bridge. I'm heading down to the CIC.'

'Yes, sir.'

When Lauring got to the CIC the weapons officer already had firing solutions on the destroyer and attack boats. He looked at the radar screen. The two attack boats were making 35 knots almost due west. The Kashin Destroyer was turning toward *Stirling*.

'She's heading right for us,' Lauring said. 'Alright, if she was in range, she'd have fired.'

'Zodiac in the water,' the chief announced over the intercom.

'Weapons, target that destroyer. Four Harpoons. That'll leave us four for the attack boats.'

'Aye, aye, sir.'

'Fire when ready.'

'Captain,' the radar control officer said. 'Incoming missiles, from the north, northwest.'

Lauring went over to the aerial radar. It showed two dozen blips heading for the task force.

'Jesus,' he said, 'That's their third salvo. How many missiles do they have?'

The weapons officer ran through the firing procedure. When all was ready Lauring gave the order. Above deck, one of the two Harpoon quadruple launchers pivoted east. Locked onto target, a sheet of flame stabbed out from the barrel. A second later another Harpoon followed, then another and another.

The phone buzzed, Lauring picked it up. 'Captain, message from task force, they're maneuvering for the safety of the fleet.'

'Ok, thank you,' he replied.

One of those big missiles hits us, he thought, *it'll blow us right out of the water.*

'Captain?' the weapons officer pointed to the surface radar.

Lauring followed the incoming Harpoons.

'Contact countermeasures,' the radar tech reported.

The first two Harpoons merged with red blips representing Soviet SAMs and blinked off the display. Then the next two Harpoons suffered the same fate.

Lauring picked up the phone, 'Helm, come about course two-seven-five. Twenty knots.'

'Two-seven-five, twenty knots, aye, aye.'

The air radar tech said, 'More contacts, Soviet aircraft.'

Before Lauring could react the phone buzzed, it was Stewart. 'Why are we running?'

'Shut up, XO.'

Stewart hung up the phone.

Weapons reported, 'I have a firing solution.'

Sensors reported, 'Contact accelerating, twenty-five knots.'

They're coming after us, Lauring thought.

'Hmmmm,' he said in rumination. 'Hate to go dry, but…'

'Captain?' the weapons officer pressed.

Sensors spoke, 'Contacts Bravo and Charlie coming about…two-zero-zero degrees….'

'Damn, those two attack boats are trying to get between us and the downed pilot,' Lauring said. 'Weapons, new solution, targets Bravo and Charlie.'

'Aye, aye, Captain.'

Lauring thought for a moment. He looked at the radar display. Bravo and Charlie were coming about and the Kashin was closing. *Crap, you wanted to serve in the surface navy*. He picked up the phone.

'Helm, new course. Come about zero-nine-zero. Thirty knots.'

'Aye, aye, sir.'

'Firing solutions for contacts Bravo and Charlie.'

'Fire when ready.'

Two more Harpoon missiles streaked out from their quadruple launcher. Once more Lauring watched blue blips on the radar readout.'

'New contacts!' the surface radar tech said. 'Missile launch! Bravo and Charlie!'

Without a word from Lauring *Stirling's* countermeasures went to work. A pair of Sparrow missiles were launched and then another pair.'

'Hit!' Weapons reported. 'Charlie is hit!'

'Incoming contact destroyed!'

'Bravo is coming about.'

'Incoming contact destroyed!'

'Well done counter measures,' Stewart said.

Weapons reported, 'Captain, I have a firing solution on Bravo.'

'Negative. Target the Kashin.'

'Aye, aye.'

The two remaining Harpoons streaked out. This time the Kashin's countermeasures deployed but one Harpoon got through. The remaining blip merged with the red blip representing the Kashin.'

'That's a hit!' Weapons shouted.

'Helm, come about, zero-zero-zero.'

'Zero-zero-zero, aye.'

'Weapons, prepare to engage contact with guns.'

'Aye, aye, Captain. Fire control radar, target Alpha, range....'

The first volley missed by over five hundred yards wide and three hundred short.

The phone buzzed. 'Captain, this is the bridge. She's firing.'

'Roger, Captain,' weapon said. 'We have the rounds here, missing wide.'

Surface radar said, 'Contact Bravo coming back around...contacts! Incoming missiles.'

Once more *Stirling's* point defenses went to work, with the ship's SAM launchers bringing down the incoming missiles.

The Kashin fired her guns again, but once more missed badly. At the same time *Stirling's* gunnery officer slowly ranged in on the Kashin, missing by less than a hundred yards and then less than 50. After the fourth volley, the forward observer reported. 'Hit! Hit! Looks like aft on the...holy crap! Look at that explosion. We got the helicopter deck and I think..... wow! Big explosion. I think we got a fuel tank or something. That ship is burning.'

'Weapons, you have the CIC. I'm coming up to the bridge. Keep firing on the Kashin.'

Lauring got up to the bridge in time to see the forward five-inch battery land a hit just aft of the Kashin's bridge. Stewart watched through his binoculars. By then her guns were silent and her aft flight deck was awash in blazing helicopter fuel which put a thick cloud of smoke in the air which obscured the aft of the ship. With each minute, the list became more pronounced. There was an internal explosion which seemed to sheer the aft of the ship right off the rest of the hull.

'That's it,' Stewart said without taking his eyes away from the binoculars. 'She's going down.'

Two geysers of water sprouted up before the ship. Lauring picked up the phone and dialed the CIC. 'CIC, this is the Captain, cease fire.'

'How about that,' Stewart said.

'How 'bout what?'

'Captain, the Zodiac boat has got our pilot.'

'Very well.'

Stewart said, 'We sunk a ship, in an actual surface gun duel.'

Lauring shrugged. 'Prepare our own chopper to pick up survivors.'

'Aye, aye.'

The Zodiac boat returned minutes later. Lauring went down to the infirmary to greet the pilot. He was wrapped in a bathrobe, his hair was still wet, his face white and sallow. He slumped back on the cushion and sipped coffee. A half-eaten sandwich was in front of him. As Lauring entered the pilot tried to stand, Lauring motioned for him to sit.

'Thank you, sir,' he said.

'Captain John Lauring.'

He extended his hand.

The pilot took it and said, 'Lieutenant Pete Yancy, *USS Enterprise*.'

'How long were you in the water?'

'Not sure, they shot my Hornet down pretty early on.'

'I see.'

Lauring walked over to the pantry and poured himself a cup of coffee. 'May I ask what happened?'

He sat down.

Yancy took a deep breath and sighed. 'Not sure. We found the Soviet fleet and launched. They said it's a big one.'

'That's my understanding.'

'We got a strike group up and were fighting through Soviet Navy fighters, when we got jumped by a new group, I think out of Tromso. They got me,' he shook his head.

'We know Soviet air took it pretty bad, I think you guys won.'

Yancy's face brightened up, 'Really?'

Lauring sipped his coffee. 'I couldn't follow it that closely; we were a bit busy down here. But that's what it looked like. Battle kept trailing toward the Soviets, not the task force.'

Yancy reached out, grabbed the sandwich and took a bite . He nodded his head. 'You're probably right.'

The OOD popped his head into the infirmary. 'Uh, Captain, a moment please.'

'Sure.' Lauring walked into the passageway.

The OOD said, 'Captain, bad news I'm afraid. *Enterprise* went down.'

'Went down? What do you mean *Enterprise* went down?'

The OOD had tears in his eyes, 'She's lost sir. The Soviets sunk her in that last air attack.' The OOD shook his head. 'She's gone.'

'Alright, thank you lieutenant.'

Lauring walked back into the infirmary.

'Lieutenant,' began Lauring. 'There's no easy way to say this. *Enterprise* is lost. The Soviets sunk her.'

Yancy smirked. 'Yeah, sure.'

'No, Lieutenant. She's gone. I'm dead serious.'

Yancy slumped back in the chair, as if his heart was broken. Then he fell forward, his hands in his head. 'Oh my God,' he said. 'Oh God.'

The White House

The president visibly slumped back in his chair. For five seconds, General Powell wondered if the leader of the free world was having a heart attack.

He spoke deliberately. 'I do not understand how this happened.'

'Well Mr. President,' Cheney began. He never got the chance to finish. The president glowered at him.

'I know damn well, what happened, Dick,' the president said. 'What I do not understand is how.'

General Powell saw the president close his fist and squeeze it ever so slightly.

'Billions upon billions of dollars, Dick. All those budget appropriations...' Bush shook his head. 'And all that expensive technology....What have we lost in the last week Dick, three carriers now?'

'Well, Mr. President,' Powell said. 'One was British. One was a marine assault ship, and of course...

'The *Enterprise*,' finished the president.

'I should mention, Mr. President,' the secretary of defense said. 'We lost a Tico and a destroyer as well. I'm afraid I don't have a casualty list yet, sir.'

The president shook his head again. 'Must be thousands.'

Powell said, 'Certainly.'

'What did we do to the Soviets?' Bush asked.

'We shot down dozens of aircraft, both land based and naval.'

'That's it?'

'Yes.'

'So the Soviet fleet gets away.'

'No, sir,' Cheney said. 'Task Force 60 is looking for them now. They're also preparing to hit the Soviet base at Tromso.'

Bush shook his head.

'It was part of the plan, sir,' General Powell offered. 'A brigade from the 82nd Airborne is prepping for a jump.'

'Wonderful, another target,' said the president.

'And the British are getting ready as well.'

Bush furrowed his brow. 'Maybe we should call the next phase off.'

'No, sir,' Powell replied.

'I'm sorry, General?'

'No, Mr. President. Operation Arctic Storm has begun. We have engaged the Soviet Navy and are bringing it to battle. We will see it through.'

Cheney nodded his head in agreement.

'You agree too, Dick?'

'I do.'

'Despite the losses.'

'Yes, Mr. President.'

Bush shook his head. 'Very well. But gentlemen, I don' like it.' Bush thought about his time in the Pacific and shook his head. 'All those men. All those casualties. And more to come.'

'Yes, Mr. President,' said Cheney.

Scowcroft chimed in, 'Now Mr. President. We have heavy Soviet activity in the Pacific. All indications are that they're making another naval move…'

HMS Tenacious

Lovelette stood over the sonar, the display positively spiked with contacts.

For three hours *Tenacious* had remained silent three hundred feet below the surface as the Soviet fleet passed north, northeast. Long ago Lovelette had concluded the Soviets were making for NordKapp and the Barents Sea. The eastern circumference of the fleet came to within four kilometers of *Tenacious*. Weapons was working on a firing solution on three ships, two Krivak class Frigates and a Sovremenny-class destroyer.

'Firing solution, Captain,' Ensign Bobrick said.

Lovelette wasn't happy.

'I'm sorry, Captain?'

'I don't care about the bloody frigates.'

'Our best shot, Captain, and the capital ships aren't in range.'

'I know.' *Besides, we have one job*, Lovelette thought.

'Communications, deploy buoy.'

'Captain, are you sure that's wise?'

'Fleet must be informed of this contact.'

'But the Soviets.'

'Lt. Bobrick, serving aboard a submarine is not for the timid. You'll never pass your Perisher course if you don't understand that. ' Lovelette said. 'Send message: *HMS Tenacious* has spotted Soviet fleet. Seventeen contacts including two carriers, two Kirov class cruisers.'

'Buoy deployed.'

'Send the message.'

'Message sent.'

'Reel in the buoy.'

'Shall we attack?'

Lovelette rubbed his chin. 'We shall hold steady.'

'But…'

'But nothing. Right now, Ivan may have no idea we know where he is. We launch for the sake of sinking a few frigates, he'll know. Let the Americans deal with this. They love their aircraft carriers, you know.'

Norwegian Sea

'What?!' asked a startled Lauring.

He sat upright in his bunk.

'Captain to the Bridge,' the PA said again.

'Crap,' Lauring said.

He looked at the clock. It showed he'd been down for less than an hour.

'Damn it,' he said.

The Captain reached for the Nyquil on the shelf above his bunk, knocking over the picture of his wife. He didn't pick it up, but swigged the Nyquil.

Lauring stood and tried to smooth out his rumpled khakis, which he hadn't taken off in at least two days.

Stewart was waiting for him on the bridge.

'What's up?' he asked.

'We found the Soviet fleet.'

Stewart pointed to the sky just as a wave of F-14s flew above. These were followed moments later by a pair of diamond formations of four E-6 Prowlers.

'Electronic warfare jets,' Lauring said. He pointed south toward the fleet. 'And here come more Tomcats.'

A dozen F-14s also flying in diamond shaped quartets flew over *Stirling*.

'Look at that,' Stewart pointed east, where a mixed group of F-14s and F-18s were heading north east.

Lauring followed them through his binoculars.

'Tromso?' Stewart asked.

'Most likely.'

Bardufoss Airbase, Norway

'Now Admiral,' Ingham said. 'You know what happens if you move.'

Ingham branded a rubber truncheon, with which he had twice rapped the Admiral across the buttocks, creating deep purple welts.

Romanov grunted. 'I cannot even feel my fingers anymore.'

The admiral stood in his underwear with his feet spread and was leaning forward with his fingers out propping himself against the wall. So far, he had stayed there for eleven minutes without moving.

Unable to take the pain in his fingers the Admiral stood up straight. He winced in anticipation. Indeed, Ingham whacked him with the truncheon, this time across the back of the knees. The once powerful man fell to the floor and cried out in pain. He rolled around the floor trying to soothe his knees. Already hideously purple from the rubber truncheon.

'Why are you doing this, Admiral?'

'You must ask?'

'I will give you credit, Admiral,' Ingham said. 'I have seen young IRA soldiers resist far less than you have.'

'You are proud of this, torturing revolutionaries?'

For the first time, Ingham showed a bit of emotion, his eyes narrowed a bit and he said, 'Had your mother been killed by an IRA bomb I do not think you would speak so well of them.'

Romanov said nothing.

'Now, up with you Admiral. We shall try this again.'

Romanov held up his hands, 'Just wait, I…'

Ingham grabbed the admiral by the arms. 'Sorry, Admiral. We operate on my schedule not yours.'

He stood the admiral up in front of the wall and leaned him forward on his fingers.

'Why don't you talk?'

'Would you?'

Ingham smirked. 'You are not the first to ask. You know what I tell them?'

The admiral winced in pain as his weight fell upon his fingers. 'No.'

'I would not be on the wrong side.'

'You believe so?' he gasped.

'Of course.'

'Even as you torture me.'

'Admiral, I have no moral compunction doing evil to defeat evil. None whatsoever.'

The admiral grunted and almost moved. Ingham held up the truncheon.

'Admiral, I understand you have your duty. But you are now in the custody of Her Majesty's Government. You are not going back to the Soviet Union. Not ever.'

For the first time to Ingham, Romanov looked scared.

'Not ever,' Ingham shook his head. 'So far, I haven't done anything truly harmful to you. That can change.'

'I do not think you would do that.'

'You don't.'

Romanov grinned and shook his head.

Ingham grabbed Romanov and threw him to the floor. The Admiral rolled onto his back as Ingham approached, truncheon raised.

'See, I made you lose your temper.'

Ingham lowered the truncheon. 'What makes you think that?' He laughed. 'Now, get up.'

The admiral stood. Ingham knocked him to the floor again.

'Up.'

The admiral got up again. Ingham knocked him back down to the floor.

'Up.'

Now out of breath, the admiral stood once again. This time Ingham gave him the shoulder, sending him flying a few feet and skidding across the floor. The admiral winced and cried out in pain.

'I think,' he said between breaths, 'You broke my shoulder.' Romanov grabbed his left shoulder.

Ingham grabbed Romanov by his left arm and yanked him to his feet. The Admiral screamed.

'Back against the wall, old boy,' Ingham said as he walked him across the room. He spread Romanov's feet and leaned him forward against his fingers. This time Romanov gritted his teeth, grunted, and then dry heaved. He fell back to the floor. Ingham reached down for him. Romanov held up his hands. 'Wait,' he said as he wiped spittle from his chin. 'Wait.'

'Yes?'

'Can we sit and talk?'

Ingham held out a hand and helped the Admiral to his feet. The two walked over to the table and sat.

'You are sure?' Ingham asked.

'I am.'

'There is no going back. If you recant, we use drugs. I'll make you take acid.'

Romanov 'What would you like to know?'

Ingham reached inside his coat pocket and took out a small note pad and a mini-tape recorder. He flipped it open and said, 'Tell me about...' he looked at his notes, 'Your bases on the Kola Peninsula...'

HMS Tenacious

'Another explosion, Captain,' said the sonar tech.

Lovelette took the headphones from the tech and listened. He could hear splashes, and a sound almost like crumpling paper. Then he heard a loud bang, and then another. He handed the headphones back to the sonar tech.

'It sounds like the Americans are really having at Ivan,' Lovelette said.

Indeed, they could even hear some explosions without the hydrophones.

'There's another one, Captain,' the sonar tech said.

'Helm, take her up to periscope depth.'

Ensign Bobrick asked, 'Are you sure that's wise?'

'We are Royal Navy submariners. We take risks.'

'Fifty feet, Captain.'

'Let's get some photographs for the Americans.' Lovelette walked over to the periscope. As the periscope deployed he said, 'Besides, Ivan is running for his life at maximum speed. If he wanted to search for us, he couldn't hear us. Not at those speeds.'

Lovelette put his eyes to the periscope. 'My word…' he said.

'What do you see, Captain?' the Bobrick asked.

As he pressed the button on the handle, snapping photographs, Lovelette said, 'Smoke. Thick smoke. I see a burning ship…I believe that's a Kashin class destroyer…there's another one, a Krivak aflame…'

'What about the carriers, Captain?'

'Yes, and the Kirovs,' Bobrick asked.

Lovelette zoomed in but could not see through the smoke. There was an explosion, and then another.

'Many missile contrails….oh my…another explosion…I count one, two, three….seven other smoke plumes….that ship there is badly listing….oh, and there's another!' He stepped away from the periscope. 'Down periscope,' Lovelette ordered. 'Helm, take us down, 300 hundred.'

'Captain…' began the XO.

'Yes, yes I know. This kind of chaos is an excellent opportunity.'

'Yes, Captain.'

Lovelette smiled. 'For now, we wait.'

The Kremlin

Ligachev leaned back in his chair and held a cold compress to his forehead. He had been summoned from bed and wore slacks and loafers and a button down shirt with the first few buttons of his shirt to try to cool off.

'Shall I summon your doctor, Comrade Secretary?' the head of the KGB section asked.

Ligachev shook his head. 'Nyet,' he said. 'Just leave me.'

'Da, Comrade Secretary.'

'And please dim the lights.'

'Da.'

Pavel looked at the gensec in concern before he left the office. Ligachev had always been quite kind to the captain, giving his daughter a doll for her birthday and even helping his brother gain acceptance to Patrice Lumumba University. The gensec was greatly pained.

Only his desk lamp illuminated the office.

I wonder if this is how Stalin felt as the fascists advanced through Russia? he thought. *Or is what is happening even worse?*

For the third time he read the message. Not because he didn't know what it contained, but in the hopes that he could find some good news contained within. There was none. Ligachev gave out a long sigh and held his head in his hand.

Minsk and Kiev sunk, Kirov afire, Frunze adrift. Ligachev shook his head again. The message contained a list of eight other ships that had sunk, but it was the capital ships that mattered most and they were gone. *The worst day in the history of the Soviet Navy,* he thought, *and I am the gensec.* The final part of the message gave him chills.

NATO FORCES DEVELOPING ATTACK ON TROMSO.

They meant to reverse all the gains the Soviets had made in the Norwegian Sea.

Other members of the Politburo would know by the morning, and most of the octogenarians would draw the wrong conclusions, he knew.

They will want to use nuclear weapons, Ligachev thought. *Idiots. Do they think the Americans will lie back and take it?*

Outside, Pavel tried to prevent a new messenger from entering the office.

'This is urgent news from the Ministry of Defense,' the messenger insisted, 'and it must be delivered to the general secretary.'

'What is it?' Pavel asked.

'I have no idea. If I were to open this message and read....' The messenger had no need to finish.

There began a pissing match between the KGB and the MOD with each man threatening to call in superior officers that only ended when Ligachev opened the door.

'It is alright, Captain. I will take the message.'

'Sorry, Comrade Secretary.'

Ligachev took the envelope and closed the door. The MOD had urgent news from the Aleutians and none of it was good.

The White House

The men assembled around the Cabinet Room smiled and nodded their heads at word of the great naval victory in the Aleutians.

'How did they do it?' Bush, the old carrier pilot asked.

Cheney said. 'Well, Mr. President, *Midway's* battle group commander allowed the Soviet fleet to engage Adak. Once the enemy was committed, *Midway* hit them with a squadron of A-6 Intruders and one of F-18 Hornets.'

Sununu rapped the table with his knuckles.

'*Midway's* group sunk a Soviet Minks- class carrier, one of the big Kirov class cruisers, and a pair of destroyers.'

'What about the rest of the ships?' Baker asked.

'Last seen steaming back to Petropavlovsk.'

'Good,' Baker murmured.

'Sorry, Jim?' Bush asked.

'Oh nothing. Sometimes it's good to let the enemy save face. '

Bush nodded his head.

Powell looked at Baker and thought, *those ships might still kill Americans.*

'Now, I fly to Brussels tonight to confer with NATO, Mr. President. What shall I tell them about invading Eastern Europe?'

The president pursed his lips. Then he looked at Baker. 'James?'

Baker shook his head. 'It's a bad idea. Too much risk. We've already won.'

Scowcroft said. 'I agree. I think this is a situation we cannot control.'

'The Soviet specialists in State are terrified about what the Soviets will do if we invade Eastern Europe.'

'Nuclear weapons?' Bush asked.

'Yes,' replied Baker.

'Maybe…'

'Mr. President?' the vice president spoke. 'What about the people of Eastern Europe?'

'What about them?' Baker asked.

'I mean, there are hundreds of millions of people and we are in a position to liberate them.'

Scowcroft rolled his eyes. Baker said, 'With all due respect, I don't think this is the time to be discussing liberating Eastern Europe.'

Sununu said, 'Mr. President, think of your place in history.'

Baker was about to speak but Bush said, 'James, I understand your objections.' He looked to the secretary of defense. 'Dick, what do you think?'

'People at the Defense Department have suggested the same. Wolfowitz is intrigued by the idea.'

'What do *you* think?' Bush insisted.

'We are accumulating significant force in West Germany. Two plus mechanized corps are assembling.'

'The British and Germans want to go,' Quayle offered.

Bush recalled the conference at St. John's. 'They do.'

'I suspect,' Baker said, 'that the Germans and the Brits are willing to fight to the last American.'

'I don't think that's fair, Jim,' Bush said.

'Thatcher,' Scowcroft shook his head. 'Thatcher and her plans.'

'I would insist,' Baker said, 'that any potential invasion include British and German troops. I don't see why America should go this alone.'

'He's right, Dick,' Bush said. 'Inform your counterparts that any effort must include NATO troops.'

'Yes, Mr. President.'

'Mr. President,' Scowcroft asked, 'are we committing to this?'

'No, Brent,' Bush replied. 'We will keep our options open. ' Bush looked around the table. 'Is that clear, gentlemen?'

There were nods.

Powell spoke. 'Mr. President, I agree completely. Let us prepare for a move east, but only prepare. If we need to attack, we will be ready.'

PART IV

David: Prime Minister, some say it is time to end the war.

Prime Minister: Who says that, David?

David: Don't roll your eyes, Prime Minister, I...

Prime Minister: David, who says it's time to end the war? Who do you mean?

David: Well, I...

Prime Minister: You? Is that what you think?

David: Prime Minister, but with the Soviet advance seemingly halted, is it not time to at least begin negotiations?

Prime Minister: If the Soviets wish to begin negotiations they know our terms. They must withdraw from all NATO territory immediately without conditions.

David: Do you really think that is a fair place to begin negotiations?

Prime Minister: Fair! Fair?! You talk of fairness? This is a war the Soviets began.

David: Prime Minister, what if the Soviets attempted a kind of nuclear blackmail against Britain?

Prime Minister: How so, David?

David: What if they threatened to destroy the United Kingdom via nuclear attack if we do not agree to a ceasefire?

Prime Minister: David, don't be ridiculous.

David: Why is that ridiculous?

Prime Minister: Because the Soviets know that the United Kingdom possesses a first and second strike capability.

David: What if they simply destroyed a British city as a warning?

Prime Minister: Then I will destroy the Soviet Union.

David: I'm sorry, Prime Minister.

Prime Minister: I will destroy the Soviet Union.

David: You would destroy the Soviet Union?

Prime Minister: Yes, absolutely.

David: On your own?

Prime Minister: Yes, David. Why not? As we speak, four Royal Navy ballistic nuclear subs, each armed with a dozen nuclear missiles, are at sea.

David: Without even consulting President Bush?

Prime Minister: I do not need to consult the American President to defend the United Kingdom. I do not think so.

David: And to the Soviets, what do you say?

Prime Minister: I hope they are watching. And I do hope the Soviets understand. With one order I can annihilate their entire nation, and the moment I think I need to do so, I will.

CHAPTER 1

Tromso, Norway

The largest airborne assault since the Second World War did not start well. Twenty- five miles offshore, just outside Tromso Channel, *USS New Jersey* spent two hours bombarding Tromso Island. Unexpectedly her 16 inch, two-ton shells ignited a fuel dump. The ensuing conflagration filled the sky with oily, black smoke. While the island was partially obscured, that wasn't a problem for the GPS equipped American and British transports. The flames caused an updraft and a hot air current above Tromso Airbase. When the lead battalion of the 1st Brigade, 82nd Airborne Division jumped, the wind blew it off course, scattering hundreds of paratroopers over Tromso. Dozens landed in the channel where they drowned. Several platoons' worth of paratroopers did land on the base, but these were disorganized and quickly set upon by Soviet infantry who overran several impromptu positions. A group of thirty or so paratroopers formed a skirmish line at the south end of the field where they managed to occupy some buildings. Word went out for stragglers to rally there. The next battalion came down to a fully alerted Soviet base. Dozens were killed before they got to the ground.

On the heights above Tromso, the British Red Devils had better luck. Two Para Battalion landed on an open field and quickly overwhelmed the Soviet missile battery there. Three Para followed the next hour, giving the British a force of nearly a thousand men commanding the heights. The British Paras delivered what support fire they could to the Americans trapped on the airbase below, but lacking heavy weapons, there wasn't much they could do.

With the first two air drops being disastrous, the third, carrying the brigade's supplies was called off, leaving Task Force 60 scrambling for a way to relieve the embattled brigade.

10 Downing Street

Heseltine was blunt, 'Prime Minister, has it occurred to the Americans that using West German troops in Eastern Europe could be problematic?'

'Problematic?' she asked. 'How?'

'Well, Prime Minister, one wonders if the people of Eastern Europe would like Germans invading their countries once more.'

Thatcher raised an eyebrow. 'If the British Army can fight alongside the West German Army I do not see why Eastern Europeans should mind being liberated from the Soviets by them.'

Heseltine cleared his throat, 'Prime Minister, the legacy of the war…'

'Preposterous. Besides, do you believe the Americans will go it alone? Do you really?'

Heseltine said nothing.

'I must also insist, Mr. Heseltine, that a significant British force accompany the attack.'

Heseltine shuffled some papers. 'Yes, Prime Minister. I have consulted with General Inge, he believes First Armoured Division is best suited. I think that they, along with the air mobile brigade and the motorized infantry brigade should go.'

Thatcher nodded her head.

'There is the issue of equipment.'

'How so? Are our factories not producing?'

'They are, but they can only manufacture a few vehicles per day. If our forces going east are to be fully equipped, General Inge says he will have to cannibalize some units on the Weser.'

'Then do it.'

'Yes, Prime Minister.'

Major spoke, 'Prime Minister, I must be frank.'

'Go on.'

'The Commons is becoming restless.'

'Minister, we are at war. I am not interested in the agitations of a few Labour backbenchers.'

'It is more than just a few backbenchers,' replied Howe. 'As you know, Mr. Kinnock has supported the war.' Thatcher raised an eyebrow, Major ignored it. 'But he is questioning, in private, the need to continue hostilities.'

'Politics,' Thatcher dismissed him.

'Of course, Prime Minister. But I must say, privately, a few conservative MPs have expressed concerns.'

'Hmmph,' Thatcher said.

'There is also, Prime Minister, the growing issue of some of your, ahem extra-judicial imprisonments.'

'Extra judicial?' the prime minister said with great disdain. 'Those arrests were carried out under laws duly enacted by Parliament.'

'Yes,' replied Howe, 'but that does not make them popular.'

Major said, 'Prime Minister, you arrested the head of BBC's entertainment service.'

Thatcher looked askance at her would be successor, 'He aired that awful nuclear war movie…'

'*Threads.*'

'Yes, that's it. People saw it and actually committed suicide. Was I supposed to let that man scare the entire nation?'

'Well…'

'No, I thought not.'

'Prime Minister,' Major began carefully. 'No one here opposes you.' She looked toward Major and doubted that. 'But we are trying to tell you that, the days of unrestrained support for this office and the war are coming to an end.'

'I am less concerned with that than with President Bush's reluctance. Right now, the Americans are preparing as if they will agree to further the war. But I'm afraid the president will need something to push him to the decision.'

Over the North Sea

'Is the feeling returning to your fingers, Admiral?' Ingham asked.

'Yes, thank you,' Romanov replied. He rubbed his fingers, grateful for the sensation of no pain.

'I'm so glad,' Ingham said. He held his hand on his seat tray against a spot of turbulence. Ingham read over a page of notes, 'Now, I'd like to get back to something you said earlier.'

'Here?' Romanov asked. 'In this plane?'

'We have nothing better to do, Admiral.'

Romanov frowned.

'Now, Admiral. You mentioned before that you were sending missile subs into the Atlantic.'

Ingham watched the admiral closely. The color drained from his cheeks ever so slightly.

'Ah-ha. I thought so. Now, Admiral, where are those subs?'

'Do you really believe I will tell you?'

'You have already told me all about your Kola Peninsula facilities.'

Romanov returned Ingham's stare.

'Are they in your defended bastion?'

Silence.

'Under the ice pack?'

Romanov remained silent.

'Somewhere else?'

Nothing.

Ingham got up from his chair, grabbed Romanov by the collar, and slammed him up against the bathroom door.

'Let us try a new stress position, shall we?'

He grabbed Romanov by the back of the neck and forced him down. 'Touch your ankles, Admiral, and stay there.' Ingham took his rubber truncheon out of his blazer pocket and rapped the admiral across his still sore buttocks.

'Oy!' said one of the airmen aboard the plane. 'You sure you should be doing that, mate?'

Ingham turned around, 'Mind your own business,' Ingham replied. 'I am a captain in the Royal Air Force Reserve…' he looked at the airman's rank. 'Corporal.'

'Yes, sir.'

'If you do not care for this you are free to leave, Corporal. The responsibility is mine.'

'Thank you, sir.'

The corporal excused himself.

'You look ridiculous, Admiral.'

Romanov had trouble breathing bent over the way he was.

'Shall I take photographs of this as well? They can be your legacy.'

Romanov breathed harder.

'Notice the pressure on your bladder?'

The admiral nodded.

'Also, Admiral, in that position your bowel-ways are open. It's only a matter of time. Shall we add urination and defecation to the humiliations you have suffered?'

Romanov shook his head.

'Shall we end it?'

He nodded.

'Sit please, Admiral.'

Romanov sat down.

'I'm so glad you saw reason. Now, those Typhoon subs…'

Later, as the plane landed at RAF Lakenheath, Ingham went over his notes with Romanov. 'So two are in your Barents Sea bastion, and one is off the coast of Greenland, and one more is in Hudson Bay?'

'Da.'

'Hudson Bay, Admiral. The Americans will want to know about that.'

Voronezh, Hudson Bay

'How is that possible?' Captain Filipov asked.

The boat's chief engineer was blunt, 'Simple, our replacement equipment is crap.'

'But Chazov, all the filtration equipment is fresh from the factory.'

He smiled and nodded. 'Da, Captain. Fresh crap. It has broken down, kaput and never worked properly in the first place…'

'What does this mean?'

'It means we have to find some way to get some air.'

'Snorkeling?'

'If you know a better way Captain, I will hear it.'

'Damn,' Filipov said. 'Damn.'

Over the Atlantic

The C-130, though it carried important people, did not have an escort. Hundreds of aircraft brought troops and supplies across the Atlantic every day, and it was felt that an escort would be too conspicuous. Anonymity would get the plane safely across. Besides, the Soviet Air Force was now well contained.

The two most powerful men in the military sat across from one another, a stack of British and German newspapers and magazines on the chairs next to them. Cheney read the British editorials with great interest. Only the Telegraph seemed to be supporting a continuation of the war, while the Guardian, in Cheney's view, flirted with outright treason in its exhortation to stop the fighting.

Powell said, 'SACEUR says he has more than enough troops to hold his positions. He even believes he could launch a limited offensive into East Germany.'

'Why only a limited offensive?'

'To knock Soviet troops off the border, give him some breathing room.'

Cheney nodded.

'We discussed the possibility of an invasion of Czechoslovakia. He agrees with the reasoning and strategic rationale.'

'Can he do it?'

'SACEUR expressed concerns about invading a Warsaw Pact country.'

'Mmm,' Cheney said.

'We haven't fought Warsaw Pact troops, at least not large formations, and he is worried that doing so could harden their resolve against us.'

Cheney nodded.

'There is also the concern that the Soviets would go nuclear.'

'They haven't yet,' Cheney said.

'Maybe an invasion would make them desperate.'

'Do you think they will?'

Powell simply shrugged. 'All theoretical. For now we have to deal with what we know.'

'Alright.'

'For starters, Mr. Secretary, how many NATO troops will be going?'

'The British are definite, as are the Germans. I spoke with my French counterpart, he is setting difficult conditions, but I do not think they will miss out.'

'I would say we want one division each, supplemented by one reinforced brigade each. Also the Canadian Light Armored Division.'

Cheney nodded.

'Combined with our two American corps.'

'So three corps?'

'Yes. That's too much for SACEUR to handle. I'll want to appoint a separate commander.'

'Anybody in mind?'

'Yes. We have a man down in CENTCOM with nothing to do and it must be killing him…'

MacDill AFB, Florida

The haggard staff in the CENTCOM control room simply went about their business, pretending not to notice the raging man pacing down the central bank of computer consoles.

'How the hell can you not have the Iraqi force estimates?! You got everything else, but not the Iraqi estimates!' He raged until exhausted and then stomped back to his office. The control room, manned by men who were more miserable than their chief, remained silent. A few grumbled. One took out a legal pad and went back to work on his letter of resignation.

Back in the office, CENTCOM'S commander sat at his desk and growled like a bear. 'A one million man army the Iraqis have, and my G-2 doesn't have any information on them this morning.'

General Norman Schwarzkopf returned to his G-2's morning report and read it with disinterest. For nearly a month now the reports said the same thing. The Syrians were conducting maneuvers. The Iranians standing pat. The Egyptians had mobilized their Second Army to keep an eye on the Soviet's Libyan allies. The Israeli Army remained quiet but their air force was on full alert. Partly to deter the Arabs, but also as a message to the Soviets: we are ready for you. He threw the report across his desk in frustration.

*Biggest damn war since Hitler and I'm stuck in Florida...*he pounded the desk.

When hostilities began, Schwarzkopf hadn't worried. Instead, he'd assumed, not unreasonably, that the war would spread to the Middle East. He had anticipated being handed command of XVII Airborne Corps, but it had been broken up, the 82nd and 101st being held as strategic reserve, while the 24th Mech had been delegated to Europe. Much to Schwarzkopf's irritation the 24th hadn't yet been committed to battle. He shook his head at the fate of his old unit.

What are they doing? Schwarzkopf asked himself.

His phone rang.

'Norm, how are you doing?' Chairman Powell asked.

'Lousy,' Schwarzkopf replied.

'I imagine so. Listen. I want you to come up to the Pentagon today...'

CHAPTER 2

Liverpool

Wearing jeans, a Queen T-shirt, trainers and carrying nothing but a wallet, Clarke felt like each step would take him into the air. He had to admit it felt good to get out of his military kit. He looked forward to being home, a few pints, and Jenny.

When he hopped off the train into Lime Street Station he was confronted by a gaggle of twenty protestors. They shouted and hoisted makeshift signs in the air. FREE SCARGILL! One read. A few protestors had paper bags over their heads. Standing before the lot were a half dozen policemen, all armed with FN rifles. A wiry, white haired sergeant calmly said through a loudspeaker, 'This is an unlawful gathering and must disperse at once….This is…'

'Bastard!' a protestor shouted.

'Warmonger!' another added.

The sergeant continued unabated, 'Disruption of British Rail during a time of war is a punishable offense…'

'We ain't disrupting anything!" shouted a man wearing a blue National Union of Mineworkers T-shirt. 'Free Scargill!'

Clarke watched the scene as he walked all the way across the station to a newsman kiosk.

'Can I help you, lad ?' the man behind the counter asked.

'Fags, mate. Chesterfield.'

'Ere yer go.'

The newsman reached under the counter and threw a pack of cigarettes to Clarke. 'Two quid, mate.'

'Two quid?' Clarke asked. 'You serious?'

'Sorry, mate. Wartime inflation. Hard to get ciggies into the UK with the Soviets sinking ships.'

Clarke put two pound coins on the counter and walked over to the MerseyLine rail terminal. As he bought a ticket for the blue line, Clarke smiled to himself. He had hopped the turnstile innumerable times before enlisting. On the train Clarke stood and held on to a pole. He watched people going to work, working class folks mostly and a few mid-manager types with expanding waistlines. Clarke noticed the papers people were reading, all had front-page headlines about the action in the Norwegian Sea. Below the splashy headline another article asked, *How Much Longer?*

Good question, Clarke said to himself.

He saw a couple of old pensioners, clad in tweed jackets and hats. They were pointing at the map inset on the Norwegian Sea article. 'Why I remember those convoy runs,' one said.

'Bloody cold it was,' said another.

'I was there in 1940 when Jerry kicked us right out.'

The other said. 'What's Maggie doing?'

'She's going to get us all killed.'

Clarke finally had enough war talk and he turned away and watched Liverpool roll by. The streets looked the same as always but subdued somehow. There were fewer cars in the street, moving or parked, and the pavements looked sparse. Lots more police were out and he noticed, as they went past a fire station that the bay doors were open and no engines were inside.

After a quick ride, Clarke got off at his stop and walked toward Garston.

He headed down to his old flat and passed another empty firehouse. People he passed seemed to be moving along quickly.

Clarke came up to the corner his old place was on. Across the street was his old haunt, the Mariner's Arms on St. Mary's Road. He smiled. Why not? He walked inside and sat at his old barstool. No one else was in yet. A bartender came out, Clarke didn't recognize him. He reached into his pocket and put a fiver on the bar.

'Pint o' New Castle,' he said.

'Alright.'

The bartender took the fiver and poured a New Castle from the tap.

Clarke took a long pull from the pint and asked, 'Where's Terry?'

'Called up, mate.'

'Who'r you?'

'I'm 'is cousin. Any other questions?'

'Yeah, what is wrong with everyone around here?'

'What do you mean? You been away or something or you just daft?'

'I been away. Army.'

'Oh!' the bartender said. 'Then you don't know.'

'Know what?'

'Whole city's on a war footing. People who don't need to be here advised to leave. Hospitals emptied out and such.'

'For what?'

The bartender looked up, 'For what? He asks. In case Maggie starts a bloody nuclear war.'

'Ohhhhh. Is that why the fire houses are empty?'

'Yep. Bring the fire engines back in to fight the fire in case we go bollocks up.'

Clarke downed his New Castle.

'Care for another?'

'Yeah, why not?'

Clarke knocked back another before saying. 'I best get on. See ya later, mate.'

The bartender nodded. 'Later, mate. Take one of these.'

He slid a paper bag across the bar.

'What the hell is this for?'

'In case of nuclear attack.'

'What the hell is a paper bag supposed to do?'

'I don't know. But if the bizzies see you without one they can cite you, five quid, mate.'

Clarke stuffed the bag in his back pocket.

He went down the street to his old apartment block and up a couple flights of stairs. He knocked on the door to his old flat. Sharon opened.

'Hey!' Clarke said.

Sharon looked disgusted.

'What the bloody hell are you doing here?'

'I'm home on leave.'

'I threw you out….have you been drinking?'

'What's it matter?'

'So. You have leave, come home to see me, but stop off for a few pints first?'

'What's it matter?'

'I can't believe you just showed up here.'

'Can I at least come in?'

'No.'

'It's my place too.'

'I threw you out, and you ain't paid no rent since you've been gone.'

'Some bloody welcome home.'

'You ain't home,' she said. 'And I haven't heard from you since you left. Don't think I forgot about our fight.'

Clarke held up his hands, 'All I said was…'

'That I'm getting fat.'

Clarke looked Sharon over, she hadn't lost any weight.

'That was it!' Sharon shouted. 'And don't think I don't know about you and Jenny over at the Snooker parlor.'

'I…'

Before he could finish, Sharon slammed the door.

'Oh Bollocks!' Clarke said.

He was about to turn and leave when the door opened. He smiled, 'Sharon I know…'

'Speakin' of getting fat. Why don't you go over to the snooker parlor now? Jenny's there.'

She laughed and slammed the door in Clarke's face.

Voronezh, Hudson Bay

Filipov looked at his chief engineer and considered his options. Finally he asked. 'Really, you cannot fix the filtration system?'

Chazov shook his head.

'So if we stay down here we suffocate?'

'Da,' said Chazov, 'and soon.'

You recommend snorkeling?'

'Da.'

Filipov thought for a moment. 'We can snorkel every 24 hours.'

Chazov nodded.

Filipov looked over at the boat's doctor who also nodded his head. 'That will be sufficient. More than sufficient in fact.'

The zampolit stood in the corner. Filipov looked over at him and said, 'And we can still fulfill our mission.'

The zampolit nodded approvingly.

Filipov thought of returning to base because of something as simple as malfunctioning filtration equipment.

'Very well then. Prepare to come to snorkeling depth.'

Liverpool

Clarke walked into his old snooker hall and looked around. He recognized most of the old-timers from before the war, and they certainly recognized him. Clarke could tell because as soon as they realized who he was, they started laughing.

'Ay up lads! Clarke is back!' A middle-aged man in a granddad cap chortled.

Sitting next to him, another middle-aged man; this one wearing a long beard and white sweater shouted, 'Ay! I suppose 'es come to see his handy work!' The two laughed together.

Clarke couldn't have felt more uncomfortable if he'd jumped out of a chopper into an LZ bracketed by Soviet MG fire. So he walked across the hall to the bar, giving the men the finger as he went. The two men sipped their bitter between guffaws.

In the back, at one of the tables, a young man with a mullet haircut, black leather jacket and a Def Leppard T-shirt shouted. 'Owner's been after you, there, Clarke!'

When he got to the cashier Clarke said, 'After me? For what?' The young man and the two middle-aged men all laughed together. He looked around but didn't see Jim, or his daughter. So Clarke reached over the bar, grabbed a glass and poured himself a pint of bitter.

'Ay, you know Big Jim don't like people doin' that?' the young man said.

'Ah, shut up knobhead,' Clarke replied. He emptied the glass halfway.

Wonder if Jenny's here? He thought. Clarke finished his pint. He was about to reach across the bar for another when he heard a great crash coming from the kitchen. Clarke looked over to see Jenny, a tray of fresh beer glasses broken at her feet. His eyes wondered up and settled on the rather large bulge at her waistline.

'Ahhhhh fuck!' he shouted.

'Fuck!?' She shouted back, 'Is that all you have to say?! Fuck?! That's bloody well how we're in this mess, isn't it?'

'What do you mean we?'

It was at that point that out of the kitchen, came Big Jim, Jenny's father.

'Jenny, what did I bleedin' tell ya 'bout all the cursing? I...' He looked up and saw Clarke.

Without hesitation he reached over to the wall and took down a snooker cue.

One of the two middle-aged men said, 'I'd run if I were you, lad.'

'Yeah, 'es been talking 'bout this moment for weeks!'

Big Jim raised the snooker cue and started toward Clarke. He tossed his bitter glass and ran for the door.

'Dad no!' Was the last thing Clarke heard before the cue impacted upon his head.

Voronezh, Hudson Bay

'Sensors?' Filipov asked.

'Passive contact, bearing zero-three-degrees, seven-zero nautical miles, course zero-nine-zero.'

'That same Halifax Class frigate.'

'Da.'

Filipov shook his head. Day in and out that frigate had conducted the same back and forth patrol of Hudson Bay, never veering, never changing. Sometimes it stopped a few miles from shore. The submariner in Filipov wanted to put a fish into her. He ignored the idea, of course.

'Very well. Helm. Come to snorkeling depth.'

Hudson Bay

As he had every morning for more than a decade Paul took his skiff out of Ivujivik, rounded the cape and headed out into Hudson bay. The skiff bounced in the light chop as it ran headlong into oncoming waves. Paul took a bottle of Wild Turkey out of his pocket and drank. He savored the whisky and headed out of the pilothouse onto the skiff's deck. From there he cast fishing nets into the water. It wasn't the season, and he could get into great trouble with the authorities, but with a war on, he figured they had more important things to worry about. Besides, Paul figured sooner or later the idiot superpowers would nuke themselves into oblivion, and that meant refugees coming north. They'd need food, and by then dried Arctic Char would seem pretty tasty. There was a fortune to be made.

After the nets were in the water there was little for Paul to do but wait and watch. If one was vigilant even in open water, you could spot a seal or even a polar bear. He sat on the bow of the boat with a .30 caliber rifle. Sure enough, after a few hours of waiting he spied a ripple in the water, perhaps a hundred, a hundred and twenty yards forward. He could see it, a brown head bobbing up and down in the water. He took aim and fired.

Paul was sure he landed a hit, but the head was still there. So he fired again, and again. Finally the head was gone. He grabbed a pair of binoculars and scanned the water, but couldn't see his target.

Oh well, he thought. He sipped some more whisky

Liverpool

Clarke walked into his old Liverpool haunt, a real slaughter house of a pub that catered to drunks, heroin addicts and the odd destitute pensioner or vet.

'Clarkey!' the bartender (an emaciated man in a filthy lumberjack shirt) said, 'When did you get 'ere?'

'Hopped a train, Danny.'

'I'm honored, mate,' Danny said.

'Don't be honored, mate,' Clarke replied sarcastically. 'You're the only folks who'll 'ave me.'

'What happened to your 'ead?' Danny asked as he poured a pint of New Castle for his long lost patron.

Clarke rubbed the back of his head, which showed a deep welt and crusted blood in two places.

'Angry father.'

Danny slapped the bar and laughed. 'Another one, eh!'

Clarke gulped down half his New Castle and grumbled. 'I ain't exactly having a good leave.' He finished off the New Castle.

'Let me pour you another.'

Clarke pushed his glass to Danny.

'Got kicked out of me place last night too.'

'Girl threw you out, ay?' Danny said. He pushed a full glass back to Clarke who sipped.

'Yeah she did,' Clarke said. 'I slept on a bleedin' park bench last night.'

'Least the weather's good, right?' Danny laughed.

Clarke glared at him.

'Don't you have no place you can stay?'

'Used to 'ave a girl here. You know Tricia? Used to come 'ere all the time.'

'Sure, used to trade beer and coke with her for blow jobs.'

'Yeah, that's the one. Well I goes to her place. Her roommate is there, says she's been in jail since last week?'

'Public decency blokes finally nab her slurping a dealer in an ally?'

'Na. Roommate said she'd been locked up protesting the war.'

'Protesting. I never heard her say anything that was about that.'

'I know, right? If it weren't about drugs she wasn't interested. Even had some nice pills I got from the army for her. Real pain killers here,' he tapped his pocket.

'So why was she protesting?'

'Her roommate said the local NUM was paying her ten quid a day to march.'

Danny nodded his head knowingly. 'Girls like that will do anything for a quick quid.'

'Ay.'

'What about the roommate?'

Clarke stared up from his pint matter-of-factly. 'Mate, if you'd seen 'er, you wouldn't have to ask.'

'Too fat?'

'I don't care about fat gals, Tricia you know.'

Danny nodded.

'But you should 'ave seen this porker. Big bloody bags under her eyes, track marks up and down her arms,' Clarke shuddered.

'Not even a slurp?'

Clarke shook his head.

The door opened. In walked a seedy looking man. His clothes were nice enough, trousers and a button down, but they looked dirty. A long bit of hair fell in front of his face and the rest looked like it had been slicked back with Grecian. He sat gregariously on the stool next to Clarke and nodded to him, 'Ay you.'

Clarke looked at him but said nothing.

'Ay Danny!'" the man said. 'Give me a gin would ya?'

'Sure, Reg.'

Danny poured a gin and gave it to the man.

'Who's this miserable bugger ?' Reg asked.

Clarke looked sideways at Reg.

Danny said. 'Me old mate.'

'Aint seen you around before, mate,' Reg said.

'He's in the army. Home on leave.'

'Oh yeah?'

'Yeah, 'es SAS.'

Clarke looked up at Danny.

'SAS!' Reg shouted. He slapped Clarke on the back, who looked over at him in irritation.

'My friend here, 'es a bit down on his luck.'

'Really?'

Clarke finished his pint. Danny poured another. 'Here, pal, 'ave one on me.' He looked over at Reg. 'Comes home, gets kicked out by his bird, then gets bashed over the 'ead by the dad of his other girl.'

'Is that right, mate?'

Clarke mumbled.

'Well that ain't right, mate, not at all.' Reg gave Clarke a hearty slap on the back. 'Pints are on me.'

Clarke perked up. 'That's nice of you, mate.'

'Fact, you need a place to stay?'

'I do, actually.' Clarke polished off his pint.

Reg pointed to the empty glass. 'Danny, me boy.'

'Look mate. I got a place you can stay at least tonight, you want it?'

'Aw, don't be reluctant,' Danny said as he pushed another pint toward Clarke. 'Reggie here always takes care of his new friends.'

'I do, I do,' Reg said. 'Especially our men in uniform.'

Clarke, himself from Liverpool's seedier side replied, 'Yeah, mate? And what do you want?'

Reg slapped Clarke on the back again. 'Don't you worry about that now. Let's go to this place I 'ave. Right? Even got a girl there.'

Clarke perked right up.

Voronezh, Hudson Bay

Chazov looked rather severe.

'Are you sure?' Filipov asked.

'Yes.' Chazov said. 'I have tried three new snorkels, each one simply leaks water down into the boat.'

'How can this be?' Filipov asked in disbelief.

'Comrade Captain, I am afraid the engineers didn't design the snorkel and its rigging in anticipation of it getting shot off by Canadian fishermen.'

'We can't,' the boat's zampolit said.

Filipov said, 'Da. We cannot surface. It violates orders and is against every missile boat protocol I learned.'

'We must not surface.'

Chazov stabbed a finger at the zampolit. 'You would stay down here and suffocate?'

'To fulfill our internationalist duty, yes.'

'It is good of you to volunteer the crew for that,' Chazov said.

The zampolit looked at Filipov. 'You are not actually listening to this man?'

Filipov did not speak. Instead, he thought.

'What you are saying is against party discipline and a reportable offense.'

Chazov said, 'What difference does it make? We're all going to die down here. Aren't we, Captain?'

Filipov shook his head. 'I don't know.'

The White House
General Powell began the briefing with Operation Arctic Storm .'The situation in Tromso is precarious. Two American battalions, badly hurt, are holding to part of the airbase there. One British battalion holds the high ground above.'

'Ok,' Bush said.

'Now, Task Force 60 is in contact with forces on the ground in Tromso. They're holding, but are short of medical supplies and ammunition. I got off the phone with TF 60 before I came here. They tried an aerial resupply, but the C-130 was driven to a high altitude by Soviet Triple-A fire. The troops on the ground got some of the supplies. Task Force 60 is looking into running supplies into Tromso via a surface vessel, but the Admiral doesn't like it.'

Bush got irate, 'He doesn't like it?'

'No sir. It's a narrow channel and he's concerned about Soviet artillery.'

Bush slapped the table in anger. 'You tell him I don't care. You tell him that.'

'Yes, sir,' Powell replied.

'I don't want our troops sitting in Tromso counting their bullets. You tell him to get there and get them resupplied. That's an order.'

'Yes, sir.'

'Why did this operation go so badly?'

Powell said, 'Conditions at the time of the assault, weather, high winds.'

Bush nodded.

'We appear to have an intelligence failure.'

'How so?'

'First, we felt Tromso was lightly garrisoned, it was not. We believe there are at least two Spetznaz and two infantry battalions there. Second, we underestimated Soviet resolve to hold Tromso. They have committed significant aerial resources.'

'Don't we have air superiority?'

'We do, but it is requiring a major effort to maintain it.'

Cheney spoke, 'Mr. President, I'd like to point out, that while we have not yet taken Tromso, the first goal of the attack has been accomplished, the base is denied to the Soviets.'

'Mr. President,' Sununu interjected, 'you have an almost unbroken string of successes. I think it would look bad at this point.'

Cheney winced. Powell ignored Sununu but admitted to himself that he had a point, at least if perceived victory was as important as victory itself. 'Now, as to the situation in Europe. Mr. President, General Schwarzkopf is on the ground. His headquarters is established and operational plans are continuing apace.'

'When can you start…what do you call this thing?'

'Operation Eastern Forward,' Powell said. 'Next week.' Vice President Quayle nodded his head approvingly. Powell cleared his throat.

Scowcroft and Baker exchanged glances. Baker spoke. 'Ahem. Mr. President, before we undertake Operation Eastern Forward I think we should at least attempt to open a dialogue with the Soviets.'

'Through back channels, Mr. President,' Scowcroft said.

'We haven't yet, not substantially.'

'Mmm,' Bush said.

Quayle said, 'Mr. President, I think that might be premature.'

'Now hold on Dan,' Bush said. 'Dick, what do you think?'

Cheney thought for a moment, 'So long as it doesn't interfere with planning for Eastern Forward or Arctic Storm.'

'General Powell?'

'Churchill said jaw-jaw is better than war-war.'

'Mmmm,' Bush seemed to agree.

Powell pursed his lips in thought. 'Let me talk to Admiral Crowe.'

'Admiral Crowe?' Quayle said.

'Yes. He has contacts in the Soviet Union. In their military in fact.'

'Ok.' Bush said. 'Open up the diplomatic back channel. In the meantime, preparations for an attack into Eastern Europe will continue.'

USS Stirling

Stewart checked the sight on his M-16 rifle. 'This is pretty Goddamn unbelievable,' he said loud enough for the men on the helo landing-pad to hear.

Lauring looked over at his XO and glared, not that he could see him in the moonless night.

'I mean, what are we, a taxi service?'

This time Lauring spoke, 'Why don't you shut up?'

The marines walking up the gangway looked over at the bickering naval officers. Above them the chief of the boat said, 'Over to the hangar, fellas, right over there,' he pointed.

Sixty marines, almost the entire detachment aboard the *USS Nimitz* filed aboard.

Seeing that the loading was moving apace, Lauring went to the bridge. For this mission he needed a helmet. It was an old style version, the one the army and marines had used from WW II to Vietnam, and he wore it awkwardly atop his head. He looked down on the gangway. Sailors from *Nimitz* were hauling boxes of ammunition aboard. Lauring could hear the chief yelling at them.

'You ain't storing no ammo in this hangar. Perkins! Take these guys down to the magazine! On the double!'

On the decks, *Stirling's* own sailors were setting up the ships array of .30, .50 and M-60 machine guns, cleaning barrels, loading strings of bullets, and generally grumbling.

'We never trained for nothing like this,' one rating complained.

His companion replied 'What next, bayonets?'

Lauring admitted they were right.

When the marines and ammo were loaded aboard, the boat from the *Nimitz* cast off.

Stewart walked onto the bridge. 'All ready...Captain.'

Lauring turned to the bridge wing. 'Mr. Odegaard, we're ready.'

The Norwegian tugboat skipper walked onto the bridge. He wore a flannel shirt and corduroy pants. He was old and weathered looking in the red light cast by the bridge's combat illumination. Fleet had found him in one of the fishing villages in the fjords around Tromso. When asked for his services, he agreed without hesitation.

'Mr. Odegaard, the helm is yours.'

'Thank you, Captain.'

Under his breath Stewart said, 'Why us?'

Lauring knew why. With its compliment of Harpoons exhausted, *Stirling* was the most expendable ship.

Odegaard said. 'Helm, come about to course seven-zero. With your permission, Captain?'

Lauring nodded.

'Take her into Tromso Channel.'

Liverpool

Clarke stood behind Reg, who pounded on the door. 'Open up the bloody door or I'll 'ave my man 'ere bust it in, you hear?!'

After more furious knocking, the door opened a crack. Clarke saw a grizzled woman's face.

'Now,' Reg began. 'You 'ave my sixty quid?'

'I 'aven't got it.'

'Fine then,' Reg turned around, 'Tony?'

Clarke menacingly stepped forward. 'Ok! Ok!' the woman shouted. She threw a wad of notes out the door. Reg bent over and picked them up.

The woman slammed the door shut. Reg laughed. Clarke approached the job with great trepidation, until after the first collection, when Reg flipped through the pound notes and gave him a fiver. He had done so at each flat they'd visited.

They walked out of the run down tenement building.

'What are you?' Clarke asked, 'Some kind of bookie?'

'Naah, mate. You got it all wrong, see?' I own this building.'

'You do?'

'I do. I'm collecting me rent. This money 'ere in me pocket is me due and proper.'

'Oh. Well that's alright then.'

'Hey, what about that place you said you had for me?'

'Relax, my friend. We're 'eading there now.'

'OK, I bet.'

They proceeded down the street.

'Give me another fiver,' Clarke said.

'What the 'ell for?'

Clarke pointed ahead 'So I don't tell those two bobbies up there what we're doing.'

'Ah! Go ahead. Look at 'em. Wearing helmets and carrying rifles. They got bigger things to worry about than me.'

'Like what?'

'Well look. You see them closed shops. You see people out 'ere?'

'It's late.'

'And people are scared.'

'Of what?'

They came to another apartment. Reg unlocked the door and held it open for Clarke. Like the last one this tenement building was orderly but rundown, a layer of grit seemed to be on everything. 'Place I 'ave for you is right down this way. Come on.' They walked down a long corridor. 'And the bobbies are lookin' out for NUM.'

'NUM? What for?'

'They been vandalizing. Illegal protests. Local Communists too. Bobbies keep an eye out for 'em, they do.' They came to the last door.

Reg pounded on the door. 'Open up!'

'I aint got your money!' A young female voice said.

'Just open up, you don't need it!'

'Really?' The door opened a crack. A young female peeked through. She had short brown hair, heavy mascara around brown eyes. Clarke made a quick assessment and decided that he would.

'Just take care of me man 'ere, ok? Reg shoved the door open and pushed Clarke through. 'Do that, and the rent is taken care of this week. Right?'

'OK,' she said.

Reg looked at Clarke. 'I'll pick you up tomorrow,' he said. He pointed to the girl and ordered, 'you, get to work!'

Hudson Bay

Paul picked himself up off the bottom of his boat. He looked down at the empty bottle of whisky on the floor, 'I got to lay off,' he said for the thousandth time.

He looked out on the bay and saw a shapeless mass in the distance. It was one hell of a seal.

Maybe I should drink more, he thought. As Paul's vision came back, the mass took on shape and then he realized the distance. He rubbed his eyes again sure he was seeing things.

No, I need to lay off he thought. *There is no way that's a sub. It's a dead seal.*

Paul sat down on the floor of the boat and closed his eyes. He reached for his cooler and took out a bottle of water and poured it over his face. He sat there for several minutes, cursing his bourgeoning alcoholism and waiting for his vision to clear. When he was ready he sat back up again and looked at the shape.

Nope, still a sub. He rubbed his eyes and this time grabbed his binoculars. He pointed them at the shape.

'Holy shit,' he said.

Paul reached for his radio. 'Any Canadian Forces unit. Any Canadian Forces unit. Please respond.'

The Pentagon

General Powell rose to welcome his predecessor into his office.

'Admiral Crowe, thank you so much for coming.'

The two men shook hands. Powell invited the admiral to sit.

After exchanging pleasantries and inquiries about family, they turned to the war.

'How would you rate our handling of the war, Admiral?'

Crowe shook his head. 'If these rumors I'm hearing are true, General, I don't like it.'

'Why?'

'We've already stopped the Soviets. Why push on? Why more bloodshed?'

'Well,' replied Powell, 'Thatcher and the more hawkish people here at the Pentagon seem to have won over the president. They say now is their chance to destroy the Soviet Union and make sure we never have to fight again.'

'Who? Wolfowitz.'

'Yes,' said Powell, 'with some of the old hawks from the Reagan administration.'

'I bet I know who. Pearle? Abrams?'

'Your sources are good, Admiral.'

Crowe smiled now. 'I still know people here.'

'Of course, Admiral. I have been grateful, that you have not used those sources in your press interviews.'

'I will only go so far,' replied Crowe. 'Is the president upset that I have been critical of the war?'

'No, Admiral,' Powell replied. 'You have never come up in the NSC meetings. In fact, I think Scowcroft agrees with you. Baker leans your way.'

'And what say you, General?'

'I say we have a historic event and we should execute it properly.'

Crowe smiled once more. 'Very diplomatic, General. Almost political.'

'I'm no politician.'

Crowe leaned forward. 'Let me tell you something, General. Let me tell you something about presidents, because you may be one someday.'

'I doubt it.'

Crowe smirked at that. 'I watch your press conferences, General. All presidents, the great ones anyway, need one thing. A big war. Bush certainly has his. Remember that.'

Crowe shook his head.

Powell interjected, 'Admiral, I've asked you here because I have a mission for you.'

'Oh?'

'Yes, and I told the president you could see it through.'

'I suppose you want me to try to contact my friend General Akhromayev?'

'I do.'

'Telephone links are all down.'

'We'd like to send you to Switzerland.'

'I see,' Crowe nodded. 'And, assuming contact can be made with Akhromayev, what shall I tell him?'

'Baker will have instructions. But essentially, tell him we are willing to talk if they are.'

Crowe nodded again. 'With Wolfowitz and his crowd in the Pentagon, are you so sure about that?'

HRCS Iroquois

Captain Desaix grumbled to himself. For weeks he had read with envy of the great naval battles being waged in the Atlantic and cursed his luck. Two of the Royal Canadian Navy's other Iroquois Class Frigate were on transatlantic convoy duty, one had even sunk a Soviet sub. Not HRCS Iroquois though. Desaix had wondered who he had pissed off to draw the Hudson Bay patrol. And now this.

'Captain, that sealer won't stop calling us,' the OOD said.

'Did you contact the RCMP?' Desaix asked. *You weasel*, he didn't add.

'Yes, Captain, but they say they're too busy to send a boat out.'

'Very well,' Desaix replied. *Try to get transferred off my ship, you....*

Sensors interrupted, 'Captain! Contact. Bearing six-zero degrees. Distance fourteen nautical miles.'

'You're kidding,' Desaix said.

'Come see for yourself, Captain.'

Desaix walked over to the radar readout and looked.

'Well, something is over there. Helm, set course for that contact. Twenty knots.'

'Aye, aye, Captain.'

Ten minutes later the OOD reported, 'Uh, Captain. I have a contact. It's definitely a conning tower.'

'Give me those glasses,' Desaix said.

As Desaix scanned the bay, the OOD said, 'See Captain, a conning tower, about ten degrees.'

'I don't....holy cow, there it is. That's a hammer and sickle painted there...' Desaix grabbed the PA mic. 'This is the captain. Battle stations. All hands, battle stations.'

Desaix cursed himself. It took the crew almost a minute to get to battle stations. The squadron commander would kill him for that...unless. 'Number one battery, target forward, estimate two thousand three hundred meters....'

'Number one battery....target acquired.'

'Fire when ready.'

Tromso, Norway

Odegaarde would have liked to take *Stirling* through the southern channel, which would have led the ship to the airbase without having to pass by Soviet positions on Tromso Island. However, earlier in the war, a bridge over the channel had been knocked out by the Soviet Air Force, blocking the channel with debris and shattered pylons. He was forced to take them through the northern channel. The night was cloudy and without a moon, Lauring tried to take comfort in that. Still, as Stewart had remarked, 'You'd have to be blind not to see us.' Indeed, they sailed through a mile wide channel, with great mountain slopes looking down upon them. If Soviet observers on the mountains above didn't spot them, the troops inside Tromso would, long before *Stirling* got to the besieged paratroopers.

After several miles, the channel narrowed before opening up into a big fjord. Odegaarde ordered helm to steer *Stirling* to port, taking her south into the fjord. Tromso lay ahead. Even from five miles away, they could see gun flashes and fires.

'Hold her steady at ten knots,' Odegaarde said.

As they approached, a pair of American A-6s came in over the fjord and bombed a Soviet position on the island. They saw the flash and a few seconds later heard the explosion. Tracers and missile contrails followed.

Stirling drew closer to Tromso, coming parallel to the island and passing a few of the small villages before Tromso proper. The crew could see and hear gunfire now, and light artillery as the Soviets hammered the paratroopers trapped on the airfield.

After several minutes Odegaarde said, 'Captain, we are within 200 meters.'

Lauring sipped his cough syrup. 'Thank you, Mr. Odegaarde,' Lauring replied. 'Signal the paratroopers. We're here. Prepare to receive boats.'

'Aye, aye.'

Lauring walked out onto the wing, 'Mr. Stewart. Load the boats, launch when ready.'

'Aye, aye, Captain,' was Stewart's disgruntled reply.

Marines filled out of the hangar and got into *Stirling's* four Zodiac boats, seven at a time, one spot was reserved for a sailor to act as pilot. Each man had a crate of ammo in his lap as well. Lauring winced as the firing around the base picked up, but relaxed when he saw it wasn't directed at the zodiac boats. The boats soon disappeared into the night. A Few minutes later Lauring could see them coming back. The sailors below secured the boats. Crewmen aboard began lowering small cargo nets full of ammo. Other sailors casually pointed machine guns toward the shore.

From the deck, Stewart shouted to the bridge, 'How many loads we delivering, Captain?'

'As many as we can. Cast off lines when ready.'

Minutes later the quartet of boats sped back toward Tromso. As he waited Lauring took a big swig of Nyquil.

Odegaarde said, 'You know, Captain, I can get you some actual alcohol if you like.'

Lauring shook his head. 'Against navy regs.'

'But cough syrup is not?'

There were jet engines above. Another A-6 came over the island and hit a target, to Lauring's eye somewhere between the 82nd and the Brit paratroopers. There was a loud secondary explosion, and then a massive flash which illumined the whole area.

'Shit,' Lauring said as the ship was bathed in light.

'The Soviets will spot us,' Odegaarde said. 'I can see your boats returning.'

Lauring watched for several painful seconds, willing the boats to come back to the *Stirling*. He breathed again when they arrived. The fire on Tromso died down, returning the ship to darkness.

'Take in the boats?' Stewart asked.

'Negative.'

'Captain?'

'While we can, we will deliver ammo to the men on Tromso.'

'Aye, aye,' Stewart said. The XO mumbled something under his breath.

'Get it going, XO.'

'Aye, aye…Sir!'

Another batch of cargo nets were lowered down to the boats. After securing the ammo crates, they cast off and made for shore again.

A search light came on from shore and started making its way toward Stirling. Stewart, standing next to the .50 caliber machine gunner, pointed and said, 'Kill that light.'

The sailor manning the gun said, 'Aye, aye, sir,' pulled back the firing pin and let loose a burst.

'Hold it!' Lauring shouted, but the sailor couldn't hear him as he squeezed off two more bursts. The last knocked out the light, but by then other search lights were on and coming out of the water. Muzzle flashes popped up ashore as well.

'Ah, to hell with it,' Lauring said. 'All guns open fire!' He shouted, 'All guns, open fire!'

The ship's machine gunners fired, sending streams of tracers toward the shore. Soviet bullets kicked up geysers of water and bounced off *Stirling's* hull. Lauring buckled his helmet strap.

'Mr. Odegaard, you can head below if you want.'

In the red combat lights, Odegaard looked over at Lauring. 'Captain, don't you ever suggest such a thing to me again.'

'Ok, Mr. Odegaard.'

Then Lauring heard shells coming in. Instinctively he ducked and waited for an explosion. The shells slammed into the water and kicked up a great geyser, washing over the fore of the ship. Lauring stood back and saw no damage. Another volley came in and landed fifty meters or so from the bow.

'Captain?!' Stewart shouted.

'I am not leaving any sailors behind, Mr. Stewart!'

Lauring watched his men bring the shore under fire, following their tracers across the water to a line of trees and beside that a line of houses. A third volley of mortars came in, but fell behind *Stirling*, sending water cascading across the ship.

The zodiacs raced back to Stirling. Lauring was about to shout something when one of the bridge's Plexiglas windows shattered. Everyone ducked. A line of bullets slammed into the bridge, then another.

Lauring knelt beneath the shattered window, peered over the lip and shouted down to the deck, 'Get those men out of the water!'

Another mortar volley came in, this time they missed wide of the bow.

Odegaarde looked over at Lauring and said, 'You are lucky the Soviets can't shoot.'

Several bullets slammed into the bridge.

Lauring shook his head. 'Those shells can't do anything to us.'

When the sailors were aboard, they reached down for the boats, Stewart said, 'All aboard, Captain!'

'Mr. Odegaarde, get us out of here. Comm, Signal Tromso we are leaving.'

As the ship got underway Odegaarde ordered helm to come about hard.

'Mr. Stewart!' Lauring shouted, 'Get those guns to the starboard side!'

'Aye, aye, Captain!' Stewart shouted.

A volley of shells came in, this time they were heavier and louder. Four geysers went into the air, straddling, Lauring noted, *Stirling's* previous position. The mortars fired too, but once again missed wide. Soviet machine guns followed the ship and peppered her with fire. By the time Stewart got the machine gunners to the starboard side, another volley of heavy artillery came in, bursting above the water a hundred yards before Stirling.

'Mr. Odegaarde, any reason why we can't increase speed?'

He shook his head. 'No navigational hazards, Captain.'

Another volley of mortar shells came in, this time they splashed in a line to *Stirling's* port.

'Helm, take her up to 20 knots,' Lauring ordered.

'Twenty knots, aye.'

They accelerated past the edge of the airfield and around the point. Artillery chased *Stirling* but the mortar and machine gun fire stopped. A volley of fours shells splashed down well forward of *Stirling.* Lauring stopped worrying about the arty. He stepped out onto the wing.

'How are things down there, Mr. Stewart?'

Sailors grabbed their machine guns and pointed them toward the shore. 'No casualties, Captain, except the paint job.'

Finally feeling at ease, Lauring said, 'and the window up here.'

Lauring looked back toward Tromso.

'Radio to bridge,' the intercom chirped.

Lauring picked up the mic. 'Go ahead.'

'Task Force says well done. Prepare to receive more marines.'

Liverpool

Clarke and Reg walked down Mather Avenue arm in arm.

'Where the 'ell we 'edded, Clarkey?' Reg said.

'Never mind that,' Clarke said, he started singing again, 'And its nooooo waaaay neeverrrrr.'

They stumbled along past Old Saints Church as Reg joined in. When they finished the chorus Clarke said, 'Let's pick it up again, right?'

'Right!" Reg replied enthusiastically.

Clarke began anew, 'Arrrrrrrrre you gonna take me home tonight!'

'That's a good one, mate!'

'Ahhhhhhhh right beside that red fire light!'

By the time they had finished *Fat Bottomed Girls* and sung *Keep Yourself Alive*, they were opposite the cemetery.

'Well, this is me, mate,' Clarke said.

'Bleedin' Allerton Cemetery?'

'That's right.'

'What the 'ell for?'

'I gotta head back to me base this morning. Wanted to see someone important to me first like.'

'Ohhhhh,' Reg said jovially. 'I see.'

Clarke said, 'Reg, you're me mate. When I get back, you need me again? I'll need work.'

Reg slapped Clarke on the shoulder, 'Clarkey, when you get back, you look me up. We'll work together.'

Clarke smiled.

'An go out on the piss!'

'You know we will lad!'

'You're a top bloke, Clarkey.' The two men hugged. Clarke went down the street. 'Ay!' Reg said. 'It's after dark. How are you going to get into the cemetery?'

Clarke turned around and said, 'Reg, I'm bloody SAS, remember?'

'Nice one mate!' he shouted back. As Reg walked the other way down the street, he picked up the singing, this time *Radio Ga Ga*.

Clarke hopped the fence and went into the cemetery. He knew exactly where he was headed.

Anthony Clarke
b. 27 August, 1919
d. 18 January, 1985
British Army
Western Desert, Italy, France, Korea, Malay States

Clarke looked down upon his grandfather's gravestone.

'Well, Granddad. Here I am, at war, just like you. Been on one campaign, headin' back to me unit now. Goin' back in the soup, as you used to say.'

Clarke didn't utter the words I love you, after all, Granddad never had, though he showed that he did a hundred ways each and every day, right down to the time, when Clarke was 14. A Bobby harassed him on the street and tried to take him in. Granddad had confronted the man, beat him to a pulp and got him fired. So Clarke reached into his pocket and took out a small bottle of Jameson's, Gramp's favorite. He opened it and poured it into the ground before the grave. Then he stood at attention and sapped off a crisp salute.

He hopped the cemetery gate and walked toward the train station.

'You there!' someone shouted. 'Halt!'

Clarke turned around to see a Bobby hustling toward him, hand on his truncheon.

'Just what the bloody hell do you think you're doing?'

Clarke puffed out his chest and said, 'I was payin' me respects.'

'At one in the morning?' replied the incredulous Bobby.

'What difference it make what time? Still payin' respects.'

'Bollocks,' the Bobby replied.

'Bollocks!" replied Clarke. 'Fuck off, pig.'

'I'll tell you what I think. I think you're one of those agitators planting white flags on soldier's grave stones again, that's what I think.'

'Agitator?!' Clarke said, his blood starting to boil. 'I'm British Army! I'm bleedin' SAS, you got that, mate?' Clarke pointed his finger at the Bobby and poked him in the chest.

The Bobby drew his truncheon. 'That's it, mate. You're going in.' He grabbed Clarke's wrist. Clarke jerked it away.

'Get fucked!' he shouted.

The Bobby swung his truncheon at Clarke, who easily ducked. Crouching now, Clarke swung at the Bobby, aiming for his chin but catching his nose. The massive blow sent the Bobby's nasal bones flying into his brain.

Tromso, Norway

Stewart said, 'Captain, I have no idea what I am looking at.'

'What do you see, XO?'

'Dead ahead, three hundred, three fifty yards.' He pointed.

Lauring put his binoculars to his eyes. 'I see it. Looks like a lump.'

'Right in our path. Send up a flare?'

Lauring thought. 'Reveal our position...' He thought some more.

'Helm, all stop.'

'All stop, aye.'

Lauring picked up the intercom mic. 'Captain Gregg to the bridge. Captain Gregg to the bridge.'

Lauring waited. Captain Gregg arrived. He was six-four and towered over Lauring. 'What can I do for you, skipper?'

Lauring pointed out and described the unknown object ahead.

'I see it,' Gregg said as he peered through Lauring's binoculars.

'Make anything out of it?'

'I don't like it, that's for sure, skipper.'

'Can one of your sharpshooters hit it?'

'Absolutely.' He indicated the intercom mic. 'May I?'

'Please.'

'Specialist Martinez to the bow, with his weapon. On the double.'

'If you don't mind, skipper, I'd like to go down there.'

'Of course, Captain.'

'This won't take but a minute.'

Lauring couldn't see anything in the dark except shapes. He saw a man with a rifle stand on the bow and take aim. There was a flash and then an explosion illuminating the fjord.

'Those are barrels,' Lauring said. 'What'd they fill them up with, gas?'

Another shot and another explosion. Then another and another. When he was finished, the marine sharpshooter stood and was sent back to the holding area in the hangar. Before he got there, flares went up from the shoreline.

'Mr. Odegaard?' Lauring said. 'Take us in.'

'Helm, fifteen knots.'

Lauring heard artillery coming from Tromso. A line of geysers spouted up in the water a hundred yards forward. There were gun flashes from the shore, Lauring could actually hear bullets slapping into the water around the ship. He scanned the shore, two hundred yards away, he estimated. Then the bridge Plexiglas shattered, the entire bridge-crew hit the deck as bullets slammed into the bulkhead.

'Anyone hit?!' Lauring shouted.

No one spoke.

The bridge crew cautiously stood.

'Get us there, Mr. Odegaard.'

Another line of flares raced through the sky near *Stirling* as more small arms fire hit the ship. Machine gun crews on the port side returned fire, aiming for the pinpricks of light ashore.

'Captain,' it was Gregg. 'Let me deploy my men on the port side. With all due respect…'

'Yeah, I know, you're better shots than my guys. Do it!'

The bridge crew hit the deck as Soviet machine gun fire slammed into the bulkhead.

Gregg went down to the hangar and deployed his men in a line along *Stirling's* port side. Several marine-manned .30 and .50 caliber machine guns opened fire on the shoreline.

'We are getting close, Captain,' said Odegaard.

Weapons said, 'Captain, let's fire the five-inch guns on the shore.'

'Our HE shells aren't going to do much good.'

Weapons shrugged, 'Might keep their heads down.'

'Ok, go ahead,' said Lauring. He picked up the phone, 'Chief, get those zodiac boats ready on the starboard side.'

'Aye, aye, sir.'

'And send someone to get the marines left in the hangar.'

The forward and aft five-inch guns fired. Moments later, the five-inch shells made impressive explosions on the shoreline.

'Mr. Odegaard...'

Lauring was cut off by a volley of mortar shells that splashed into the water a few yards short of *Stirling*.

'Mr. Odegaard, get us as close as you can to the shore line.'

The five-inch guns fired again.

'Helm, five knots,' Odegaard said. He looked at Lauring. 'We can get close, but we shall go in slow.'

There was the sound of mortar shells coming in and then an explosion as one of the rounds impacted upon *Stirling's* bow. Lauring peered forward.

'I don't think that did anything.'

The five-inch guns fired.

'Captain, this is as close as I dare,' said Odegaard.

The phone buzzed. It was the chief. 'Captain, I have the boats loaded.'

'Wait one, chief.'

Lauring looked at the shoreline. The fire had died down some. Another volley of mortar shells came in overhead, this time they impacted well forward of *Stirling*.

'How far?' Lauring asked. 'I make it about a hundred and fifty yards.'

'About that.'

'All right, Mr. Odegaard.' He spoke into the receiver. 'Chief, launch the boats. Tell the sailors aboard to move quickly.'

'Aye, aye, sir.'

'And send someone over to Captain Greg and tell him to get his men ready.'

'Aye, aye.'

When both waves of marines were safely ashore Lauring said, 'Alright Mr. Odegaard, take us back out of here.'

'Helm back ten knots.'

They took some desultory fire from the shore, but the mortars stopped. With the marines already landed, it seemed the Soviet troops at Tromso decided firing on *Stirling* was a waste of time. Odegaard took the ship up to 20 knots once they cleared Tromso Island. Lauring breathed a little easier. He took a bottle of Nyquil. Odegaard saw him and Lauring absent-mindedly offered him the bottle.

'Thank you, no,' the Norwegian said.

Lauring laughed at himself and took another swig.

The White House

'Are you sure, Prime Minister?' Bush asked.

Mulroney was adamant, 'Mr. President, I have photographs of the Soviet sub right here on my desk.'

'I see.'

'I will have copies sent your embassy here.'

'Please, Prime Minister.'

Bush felt a headache coming on, a bad one.

'A ballistic nuclear submarine in Hudson Bay,' Bush said. 'I'm sorry we drew this trouble into your waters, Prime Minister.'

'Nonsense, Mr. President. We are in this war too.'

'Do you think they were targeting Canada as well?'

'Our intelligence people are asking the Soviet crew that question right now. I assure you they will get the answer. If you will forgive me, Mr. President, I have an emergency Cabinet meeting to prepare for, and consultations with the opposition.'

'Of course, goodbye Prime Minister.'

'Thank you.'

Bush hung up the receiver. He had already asked for and received from Cheney a Defense Department file on a Soviet Typhoon Class missile boat. The president went over the estimate and felt a sensation of dread. Twenty ICBMs each with an estimated ten nuclear warheads within. *A nuclear missile boat in Hudson Bay, oh my God*...he thought.

CHAPTER 3

Geneva

The trip to Switzerland had been long. As the Soviet Air Force could not guarantee a safe flight outside of the Soviet Union, Marshal Akhromeyev had traveled by special train across Romania. The Romanian officials had been downright hostile, and advised Akhromeyev and his party to keep their identity secret, lest they be set upon by angry Romanians. Akhromeyev wasn't surprised. The regime of Nicolae Ceausescu had been difficult in the best of times. Now it was getting outright hostile. Akhromeyev's personal baggage had even been searched by Romanian customs officials. He understood that the situation was even worse in Poland.

Hungary was not much better. Here NATO aircraft were actually in the skies bombing strategic infrastructure. Akhromeyev's party had switched to automobiles as most of the railheads across the country had been hit at least once. The Hungarian Army was arrayed along the Southwestern border where the self- proclaimed Croatian Republic battled the pro-Soviet and Serbian dominated Yugoslavian government. Several Hungarian divisions manned the eastern border with Slovenia, whose independence was being guaranteed by a pair of Italian mechanized divisions. On the Hungarian-Austrian border a Swiss government helicopter had taken him to Geneva.

It was in the aftermath of this arduous trip (that was hard on an old man like Akhromeyev), that the retired marshal sat down across the table from the retired American admiral. 'You look tired, my friend.'

Akhromeyev gave his colleague a weary smile and then explained his trip to him.

After the two exchanged pleasantries and asked after one another's families, Akhromeyev asked, 'Can I assume, by your presence here, that common sense is prevailing in your government?'

'Sergei, I am here at the request of the president. But the idea was General Powell's.'

'I like that man.'

'So do I. I think he will be president one day.'

'I wish it were him rather than Bush.'

'Sergei, your government has greatly angered him.'

'How?'

'With this Alaskan adventure. I know for a fact that he was inclined to wind down the war.'

'And then Comrade Ligachev decided to attack Alaska.'

'Yes,' replied Crowe. 'That gave the hawks in the administration the ammunition they needed. There are people in the administration who want to destroy the Soviet Union and think this is their chance.'

'Over Alaska?'

'I don't think the Politburo understood the gravity of what attacking Alaska meant.'

'How so?'

'To you it's just another invasion. How many times has Russia been invaded?'

'Too many times to count.'

'That is sovereign American territory. A state no less. You did something that no one has ever done before. And it has scared them.'

'Is that your message?'

'No, Sergei. My message is that the president is filled with resolve and is acting upon it. You have to talk some sense into Ligachev.'

'He retired me.'

'You must find a way to deliver the message, my friend.'

'Do you think we will let you destroy the Soviet Union? Do you think we will not use nuclear weapons to defend Russia?'

Crowe noted his use of Russia rather than the Soviet Union. 'I know you will. But the hawks in Washington don't think you have the guts.'

'They are wrong.'

'I know that, Sergei.'

'You have to talk to the responsible elements in your government. You must make sure the cowboys do not hold the president's ear.'

Crowe thought of the emerging personalities in the administration, (Quayle's new assertiveness, Kristol, Wolfowitz) and frowned.

'Tell them, Sergei,' Crowe said. 'The president is still wavering. He won't forever. And when he decides to attack, he will see it through. There will be momentum for only one decision. Victory.'

'Do not be so confident, my friend.'

'I see no reason why I shouldn't be. We've taken your best blow and survived. You won't be able to hit us that hard again.'

Akhromeyev grunted. Crowe was right, he knew.

'You get weaker, while we grow stronger.'

Akhromeyev nodded.

'Tell the Politburo to end the war, Sergei. That is my message to you. Tell them to end the war while we still can.'

London

The prime minister walked into the Cabinet Room and slammed her handbag down onto the table. The assembled cabinet knew they were in trouble. The chairman brushed his blonde hair out of his face and braced for the onslaught.

'Right now, gentlemen,' there was a hint of disgust the way she said the word *gentlemen*, 'I should be preparing a speech thanking the navy for its work in the Norwegian Sea. Instead I am here.'

Thatcher reached into her handbag and took out a folder marked: TOP SECRET: Not to leave Number 10. She threw it onto the table, and it slid across the lacquer and settled roughly in the middle of the assembled men. No one dared reach out for it.

'You gentlemen are fortunate.'

No one spoke for several seconds. Finally, the War Cabinet's chair, (driest of a wet lot in the PM's estimation) tried to speak. 'How so, Prime Minister?' Michael Heseltine asked.

'How so?' Thatcher said icily. 'You are fortunate, in that I am not taking your ill-conceived plan of attack to the chief of staff.'

Heseltine, who would have liked nothing better than to resign, or be fired, spoke again. 'Ill-conceived Prime Minister? In what way?'

'You propose to simply push through East Germany. A blunt assault Mr. Heseltine. What you propose is almost Soviet.'

'Yes, Prime Minister.'

'Do you think our manpower reserves are limitless? We have already called up the Territorials, each week a few hundred recruits are processed. But we simply lack the resources your plan requires, Mr. Heseltine.'

'I see, Prime Minster. Then what do you propose?"

'I am no military strategist.'

Which isn't stopping you, Heseltine didn't say.

'But have you gentlemen noticed that Czechoslovakia borders not only in East Germany, but Hungary and Poland as well?'

The White House

'Gentlemen, this will be our last meeting in relation to Operation Eastern Storm,' said the president. 'Now is the time for a decision.'

He looked at the secretary of state, 'Jim?'

Baker nodded his head slightly.

'Brent?'

'I still think it's unnecessary,' said the national security advisor.

'Ok, Brent. Jim, what made you change your mind?'

'Simple, Mr. President, this business with the sub in Hudson Bay. For me, this is about protecting the United States.'

'General Powell?' Bush asked.

'We have sufficient force, Mr. President. We can push the Soviets back. We have sufficient allied help. This is not an American effort, it is a NATO effort. Even the French.'

Bush thought, *If you knew what I know about Mitterand..* 'Dick?'

'I'd like to second what Jim said. Eastern Storm will protect America. To that end, since we are all here, I'd like to discuss another operation I've had some people working on. As you all know, since the Soviet attack on Alaska…

Munich

Though the Soviets had not been able to fight their way into Munich, the city had seen plenty of devastation via air roads, artillery strikes, and nihilistic chemical attacks delivered by dumb fired Scud Missiles. Many blocks had been burnt out by the attacks. Rubble had also been pushed aside by city snow plows pressed into service. Polizei stood on every corner, and Bundeswehr reservists manned several roadblocks. Schwarzkopf marveled at the sheer evil of it all.

His Humvee took him to VII Corps Operational Headquarters outside the city, a farm house outside of which were paired a half dozen American and German APCs. SACEUR waited besides one of the APCS. The two generals saluted and shook hands.

'It's good to have you here, General.'

'Thank you, sir,' Schwarzkopf said.

SACEUR invited Schwarzkopf to sit on a folding chair.

'I assume General Powell has briefed you.'

'Yes.'

'Now, we're creating an entire army around you. Eleventh National Guard Corps plus First Cav, 5th and 24th Mechanized.'

Schwarzkopf whistled at the assembled combat power.

'You'll have British 1st Armored, refurbished, and the Canadian Light Armored Division. One French Armored and One Infantry Division. Two German divisions; 12th Panzer and 2nd Mechanized.'

'I see.'

'For political reasons you'll have a French deputy commander, General Belanger.'

'OK.'

'He can be troublesome.'

'He is French.

SACEUR laughed. 'Norm, you have no idea. But he fought his corps well at the Battle of the Weser.'

'Good to know.'

'Also, I think his personality will be a good contrast to yours.'

Stormin' Norman laughed.

'You'll have all the air I can give you. A-10s, British and German Tornado squadrons, and a half dozen French squadrons. Mirages, Jaguars…'

'Who's commanding the regular corps?'

'I'm taking Fred Franks away from VII Corps. You know him?'

'I do. Why Franks?'

'I want a man who's fought the Soviets. General Belanger will hold operational command over his corps. Rupert Smith, 1st UK Armored will command his Commonwealth Corps.'

Schwarzkopf nodded his head. 'Now, I've thought about how we're going to go into East Germany…'

SACEUR held up his hand, 'Stop right there.'

'Why?'

'We're not invading East Germany.'

'We're not?'

'No,' SACEUR said. 'Here's the plan…'

Tromso, Norway

The sound of gunfire came from Tromso but it was mostly American and British. With the marine reinforcements ferried in by *Stirling* they had taken the airstrip, allowing a battalion of the 82nd Airborne to be flown in.

Once the paratroopers arrived, the Soviet commander realized the battle for the airstrip was over and retreated into the town.

From the fore, Lauring and Mr. Odegaard followed a C-130 as it came in for a landing.

Mr. Odegaard said, 'I would like to thank you for what you are doing for my country.'

Lauring took a swig of Nyquil and shrugged. 'You steered us in.'

'I don't mean the action here. And I don't even mean you. I mean, America.'

Lauring looked at the Norwegian. 'You're welcome,' he dead panned. 'It's my job, my profession. I have nothing else. My wife doesn't even talk to me.'

'Really?'

'She says I'm a drunk.'

Odegaarde motioned to the Nyquil.

'And I am, I suppose.'

'Do not suppose.'

'You really don't approve of me, do you, Mr. Odegaarde?'

'I do not.'

Lauring looked down at the bow of the ship as it plowed a wake in the frigid fjord water. 'Well, there's nothing more I can do here,' he said.

'Sorry?'

'Nothing more.'

Without another word, Lauring jumped over the rail and into the water below.

The White House

President Bush made his nightly phone call to 10 Downing Street from the Oval Office. As he waited for Thatcher to come on the line, he ran the conversation he'd just had with Helmut Kohl through his head. Bush was surprised at the man's continued belligerence. When the prime minister was on the line, Bush began, 'Is it too late to call, Maggie?'

'No, not at all. Barely midnight here.'

'Good to know.'

'Really, George, you mustn't worry about waking me.'

'Sorry, Maggie.'

The two leaders discussed the current situation for several minutes, and then went over the invasion preparations. Bush informed the prime minister about Cheney's plans to expand the war even further.

'The Pacific, then?' Thatcher asked.

'Yes Maggie.'

'I'm sorry, George, we won't be able to help.'

'I know.'

'If your people think a move in the Pacific is best, then you have my support.'

'Thank you, Maggie.'

Finally, Thatcher asked, 'Have you spoken with Chancellor Kohl today?'

'I have. He remained committed to Operation Eastern Storm.'

'Good, as am I.'

'I know, Maggie,' Bush replied.

There was silence.

'Something wrong, Mr. President?'

'Well, some of the papers over here are wondering why we're still fighting, what with the Soviets out of West Germany now.'

'Yes George, here as well. The usual suspects, the *Guardian*, the *Times* and the like.' Bush still remained silent. 'Honestly George, you must learn to pay these people no heed.'

'I know, Maggie. But I wonder, is this invasion really necessary?'

'Whatever do you mean, George?'

'I mean, the papers are right. NATO has succeeded. We've repelled the Soviets and saved Western Europe.'

'I think you are right to be cautious George.'

'These are obviously preparations that the Soviets are making for a nuclear attack.'

'Therefore, we must make our own then.'

'I also have qualms about the French involvement.'

'Not unreasonable given what Mr. Mitterrand attempted.'

'One of their generals is Schwarzkopf's deputy.'

'It is a risk. But given the need of French involvement a political necessity, George.'

Bush paused for a moment. 'Sooner or later, we'll have to tell Kohl about what Mitterrand tried to do.'

'But not now.'

'I don't know Maggie, given all these factors...'

'Yes?'

'Is this invasion really wise? Is it necessary?'

On the other end of the line, there was an irritated pause. Then Thatcher said, 'Now George, this is no time to go wobbly...'

To be continued in *World War 1990: Operation Eastern Storm*

Made in the USA
San Bernardino,
CA